Mwila Agatha Zaza

THE ENGLISH SPEAKERS

DATURA

DATURA BOOKS
An imprint of Watkins Media Ltd

Unit 11, Shepperton House
89-93 Shepperton Road
London N1 3DF
UK

daturabooks.com

A Datura Books paperback original, 2026

Edited by Ella Chappell
Cover by Sarah O Flaherty
Set in Meridien

ISBN 9781917415262
Ebook ISBN 9781917415279

Printed and bound in the United Kingdom by CPI Group (UK) Ltd, Croydon CR0 4YY

The manufacturer's authorised representative in the EU for product safety is eucomply OÜ – Pärnu mnt 139b-14, 11317 Tallinn, Estonia, hello@eucompliancepartner.com; www.eucompliancepartner.com

1

MIX
Paper | Supporting responsible forestry
FSC® C013604

Chapter 1

Charlie

Everything he owned was gone.

Charles Yeats stood in the cold consumed by the knowledge that he'd been robbed of his life's belongings.

In front of him a row of brown brick buildings burned, fed by the terrace's age, unmet regulations and decades of flammable Styrofoam ceilings and vinyl floors installed by home DIYers and self-taught house flippers.

Charlie stood outside on his street with a hangover already creeping in, his body heavy and his mind in a haze. Emergency services in red and yellow arrived with their sirens blaring – too late to save his home. Fire officers drenched the street and its inhabitants with water. As the fire evaded their efforts to quash it, they evacuated a neighbouring street, herding more terrified people from their homes. Children screamed, adults wept, and a halo of red, orange and yellow flames lit up the sky as smoke poured from the inferno.

He was rigid with astonishment watching as garden sheds and an outdoor sauna were engulfed in flames and bicycles crushed in the melee. An explosion in a garage made a sound so deafening that it made even him, a seasoned policeman, hurl himself to the ground in fear.

Just before dawn, Charlie realised the full extent of the fire's destruction as the hoses were turned off and the skeletal remains of a row of houses stood, naked and charred.

The other survivors tried to engage him in pointless speculation and blame. *I told you so* and *She should have been evicted years ago,* they repeated over and over again. Fingers were jabbed against shoulders, police and responders were sworn at and the newly homeless were so irate that they hadn't stopped to say a word of thanks to their rescuers.

It was at the cusp of winter becoming spring and that night it had been warm enough that his back door had been briefly propped open as James smoked in the garden. This was what Friday nights were to them: James Grey, Aija Kivinen and a handful of others, American, Canadian and English, relaxing in his terraced house from which, if you stood on the balcony on the second floor, you could see the sea.

"First floor," one of his guests had reminded him, when he'd first described his view to her. But all of them here knew when they meant first, ground or second, flat or apartment, terrace or town house, or when the word escaped and *rivitalo* was used instead. They swung between English and Finnish in their daily lives when they needed or wanted to – but here, among friends, every word was in English.

Charlie's end-terrace had been cosy, with large and firm yet comfortable sofas that begged to be sat in. Staring at the ruins now, he remembered the hours earlier, how

James, who came every time Charlie invited him, had leaned back in an armchair with his legs crossed and feet beneath the coffee table. Susanna was almost asleep as she talked of her need to see family in Dublin. Brad had popped in and out of the back door to smoke. Aija, who also attended every one of his open nights, had led a game of charades which ended with six people descending hopelessly into laughter.

As always, at least four different tastes in music had vied to be played on Charlie's state-of-the-art speakers in a room in which an eighty-five-inch television dominated. One of his guests had brought a box of cheap wine from Tallinn. They'd complained as they'd depleted the box and talked about how prices there were rising and how long it would be before it was no longer economical to buy alcohol at the city's quay.

Charlie had brushed his hair before they came, smiling at the way he'd recently had it cut to above the nape of his neck. His high-neck shirt hid the slight loosening of skin around his neck and his jeans sagged but not, in his own mind, horrifically – they made him proud of how much weight he'd lost. He was fifty-four, but, he told himself, he was looking better than he had in twenty years.

At some point, a knock on the door announced the arrival of takeaway Nepalese food, which was consumed around the coffee table and cleared away by the guests, who stacked the dishwasher to show their appreciation for his hospitality. Aija was the last out of the kitchen, her light brown skin perfectly matching her thirty-two years, looking neither younger nor older than she actually was. Her hair, as it often was, was covered in an assortment of pins that kept her long, thin, black spirals of hair in place.

Charlie was the oldest of the group and Aija the youngest. James and the others speckled somewhere within the twenty years in between. Despite his age most items in his house were newly bought in the previous two years. Even his clothes had been recently purchased. It was hard to tell he had lived here for so many years, the sofa and cushions were still firm and unmarked and the carpet plush.

His home had long ago been sensibly selected. Rastila, the suburb in which he lived, was a reasonable trip to both work and the city centre. It was a place people came to when they decided square metreage meant more than proximity to night life and cafés. His two children had been nearly teens when they'd moved here and had spent their time exploring the nearby forest and small rocky windswept beaches.

When the evening was over, he'd watched from the door as James, who'd been the last to leave, began his walk to the metro station along Rastila's well-lit streets in a haze of cigarette smoke.

And then it went wrong, he thought.

He'd been left alone in a pleasant near silence of suburbia. Somewhere an engine ran briefly, music played and was quickly smothered, and the shout of a merry drunk rang through the night air.

He'd thrown himself on his sofa smiling at his recollection of the evenings. He was tired and merry and briefly considered picking out one of the uncounted books that lined one of his walls. It was a small luxury of being single, again – he had no one's permission to allow his living room to be covered in books. He'd finally drifted off on his sofa, knowing Saturday would bring a long bike trip along a forest path followed by coffee in a café somewhere along the seafront, or that he could be called into work.

Now, he stood beside the smouldering embers. Beside him, a police officer explained that it seemed a neighbour who Charlie knew to be a perennial drinker had built a fire in her sixties-constructed building whose chimney had long been out of service. Her reasons would never be known – she was her first and only victim. Her action had sent a blaze racing across her living room – engulfing her – fuelled by garbage and the detritus of a decade of alcoholism-induced hoarding.

Charlie had been woken by a peculiar, angry crackling, followed by an intense chemical odour – not a smell that he would have recognised as smoke. He'd still been heavy with sleep and alcohol and had struggled to get to his feet. In the time it took him to cover the short distance from his sofa, through the corridor and to the front door, his home had turned into an inferno.

It seemed the now-deceased drinker hadn't kept her smoke alarms operating. However, in quick succession, those in his house and his other neighbours' sensors detected the smoke and their sirens began to beep frantically in succession before they too were engulfed in flames.

"Oletko kunnossa?" A police constable recognised him in the chaos and stopped beside him. His blue-and-white police uniform crisscrossed with reflectors was designed to keep him warm even in the light snow that during the night had started to fall.

"Jep," he replied as if he was actually all right. Firefighters now trawled through the buildings to ensure

the fire was completely extinguished. Charlie knew that the scene was now their jurisdiction. There was nothing left for him to watch and there was nothing he could do or could have done.

He felt old and useless.

Aija and James appeared, dressed and apparently ready for a crime scene. Charlie doubted that the assignment belonged to either of them. James didn't work weekends thanks to a new contract to work part time and Aija was Charlie's adjunct – *Vanhempi rikosylikonstaapeli* Kivinen. He knew she was supposed to be off today and that was why she'd been able to spend the previous evening so freely drinking. Brad had been asking her silly questions such as why detective constables never got their own TV series – the honour always went to *Rikoskomisario* like Charlie and James. Brad had mistranslated her rank by conflating constable and sergeant. She'd staggered out of his house to the taxi, believing that she had the weekend off to lie in bed and do nothing but recover. Aija, even at this time of morning, was in low heels that raised her to almost match his own height. A large puffer jacket covered her from neck to knees and a leather satchel was slung across her shoulders.

He smiled to himself when he saw them. They must have felt like hell but neither looked like it.

He patted his hip pocket and remembered that his phone had been on the table beside him and was now probably nothing more than a melted slab of plastic and metal.

He knew no one would officially declare the cause for a while, it would take specialists who spend their lives studying what ignites a fire and what keeps it burning to finally pronounce what had happened. His neighbours were all certain of the guilt of *that anti-social bitch, that bloody drunk at number three, that filthy woman,* until they were herded away to safety. Charlie resisted, saying he was fine, and he'd leave soon. The police officer looked harassed and tired and probably didn't have it in him to battle with a *rikoskomisario*.

Charlie realised he was cold but said nothing about it. It was March, though winter had eased, without a jacket or the heat of the fire Charlie became aware of his physical condition – he was shivering. He stuffed his hands in his pockets and wondered what he should do next. Thankfully he'd fallen asleep in his clothes, but the socks on his feet were damp and cold.

James sauntered towards him, stopped a constable and muttered something to him. In minutes a weather-appropriate police jacket appeared. Charlie put it on, and James said, in English, "You looked about to freeze to death," in a strong accent which identified his origins as somewhere other than Finland.

"You should have called." James's face was turned towards the fire as he spoke. It hadn't occurred to Charlie to call James or anyone else – what would he ask for? Would he ask for a shoulder to lean on as he mourned the reduction of his life to ashes? No doubt when he returned to work there would be a few friendly pats on the back, like when someone loses a parent or survives a crash, he'd accept a few drinks on James's account, but right now, when his house was burning, would he call him?

"No phone," replied Charlie, revelling in the warmth of the jacket. "What are you doing here anyway? Aren't you a part timer?"

"Word got 'round. Can't believe I was here just a few–" he glanced at his watch– "some hours ago," he corrected himself. "You're welcome to stay with me," he offered, sounding even less convincing than when saying Charlie should have called.

Charlie had never even been to James's house, but James had always been comfortable in his. The thought of going back with James, not as a guest for a few drinks and a meal, but because he was now an object of pity, did not appeal to him.

"Doesn't look like you'll be sleeping here for a while." James was joking, but his expression was solemn, and his eyes were fixed on the carcass of Charlie's house.

"I'll go to a hotel," he insisted. "I'm sure the insurance is going to pick it up, why not enjoy myself? Besides, I'm not going to be very good company," he continued honestly. "It's not every morning I wake to an inferno. Everything I own's gone."

"What about…?" James seemed to have either forgotten her name or opted not to say it.

"Nah, there was nothing left of hers here." He'd long ago disposed of the things his wife had left behind.

"Aija seems to be sorting everything out for you." James began backing away.

They both started when a woman shrieked. They turned towards the sound. One of his neighbours was wailing, one whose children he'd watched grow from toddlers to teenagers, who always nodded in greeting as they passed him. Her husband was holding her, trying to calm her. His efforts seemed useless, their sons stood beside them, hands in pockets.

He turned back to find James watching him, as if he knew that was the final straw. His children, now adults, were probably comfortable in their beds, his daughter in a suburb hours away and his son in the heat of Australia. There was no one to huddle beside, no one's hand to hold. All he had besides the worn jeans and T-shirt he'd fallen asleep in that night – everything: books, laptop, clothes, scraps of paper with hastily written notes upon them – had either been burned to cinders or drowned in the deluge created by the fire engines.

He nodded at James and a smile flickered on his friend's face.

As they drove back to James's house, he found he couldn't speak. His life had to start again. He reminded himself that this was, once again, a temporary glitch in what seemed to be an unending effort to move past his marriage.

They arrived a short drive later. After a moment standing rigid at the door, he looked around upon James's behest. As he climbed the stairs he looked at the framed photos that lined the wall. Among them was a large, framed print of James, his twin sister and their parents taken years ago – he could see the youth in their unlined faces. James's hair had been a tall, thick mass of curls, and all four of them looked as if something had amused them.

He'd glanced into the third bedroom, which was being used as an office. Its door was slightly ajar and it was easy to identify it as such with pages of paper and a printer. He could see pictures stuck to a noticeboard and reminder notes that he could not decipher from his vantage point. There were a few A4 notepads beside a closed laptop and many, many pens that filled several cups on the table.

The guest room which was to be his was pleasantly bland. It was devoid of personality as if it were an afterthought – as if no one was ever meant to use it. In the middle stood a bed with a grey counterpane and a blue throw. One large print on deep blue walls and the odour of cleaning detergents in the air.

Once in bed, Charlie sighed, closing his eyes for a moment. A sense of safety descended on him like a warm, comfortable blanket as he lay there.

This had been a glitch – no – the universe, coincidence, the laws of large numbers even, were pointing him in the direction of his new life, he told himself.

Maybe his next house could be more contemporary, he thought as he looked at the gleaming bathroom. His children had their own lives, even if Rachel returned, it wasn't as if they could continue from where they'd left off. He shrugged as he often did when he thought of her, it was a physical act of forcing himself to disregard that surge of emotion he sometimes felt even though it had been two years since she'd left.

He was humming to himself as he, in a pair of too-tight tracksuit bottoms and T-shirt, walked with his head held high and a firmness in his step back down to where James sat writing at the kitchen peninsula.

Charlie entered quietly to the sound of the scratching pen. Only when he cleared his throat did James look up, close the notebook, take a deep breath, rub his face with hands and continue as if he hadn't been been writing as he always seemed to be.

Something began bubbling within him as the kettle began to boil.

This, he reassured himself, was the new start he'd longed for. Like a swift and powerful strike of a scalpel, the fire had sliced through his life, cutting it neatly into old and new. In the last year, he had hesitated and vacillated, he'd disgorged his house of the tangible remnants of his marriage but still he'd spent fifteen years with Rachel in that house, and something had lingered in the air stopping him from moving on. But now this was it. His new life.

"Anything else I can get you?" asked James.

"Nah," Charlie replied, "I'm fine."

James

Somewhere along the way he'd become a cliché, James thought, as he closed his front door and carefully wiped his feet on the mat. He exhaled with… what was it, disappointment? He recognised that he was that single man in his mid-forties, given to long periods of solitude, immersing himself in books and occasionally grumbling about the state of modern music – which may have seemed sexy in literature and TV cosy mysteries but in reality was tedious.

Charlie had arrived with him and gone straight into the downstairs bathroom.

"I'd better look for something for you to wear," James had said, though, he thought as he took off his white shirt and trousers, the chances of him finding something among his own clothes for a man much larger than him was unlikely.

If the fire had been his case he'd have arrived prepared to spend a long period outdoors in the often inclement March weather, but this time he'd simply thrown on his regulation outdoor jacket over the clothes he'd fallen asleep in. In the time he'd stood there it had snowed, drizzled and stopped and despite there still being snow on the ground, the hem of his black trousers was damp.

He wasn't sure what he'd gone there to do. Commiserate with him maybe? See what was happening himself? He'd been glad when he found Aija there, he didn't feel like a gawker standing around marvelling at what was quite a spectacular fire. By the time he'd arrived the sky above the terrace of houses had been iridescent, as if dawn had broken but only for them. He'd savoured the raging of the flames as his clothes became warm to the touch and his face felt as if it too was on fire.

Wasn't it strange about friendship, he'd asked himself while looking at Charlie in his socks staring at the fire, that, when an event of such immensity happened, he had no idea what his response, as a friend, was supposed to be?

James took out a hardcover notebook from his laptop bag. It was always from the same Japanese retail brand, lined, its paper off-white. He held his pen in the other hand, and then realising he was standing in the corridor, walked towards the kitchen counter, almost unaware of his surroundings. When he arrived at the kitchen counter, he put the notebook down and began to write. Only when he'd finished perhaps ten minutes later did James emerge, look around and decide he was bored.

It was times like this when he regretted having cut his working hours. He had long hours with nothing to do but write or wander around the city. As a part time police detective inspector he was rarely called out at night. His newfound affluence meant it would have been ridiculous to continue going to work each morning and arriving home exhausted each evening. He regretted it because scenes like this morning excited him. He tapped his fingers along the counter considering the possibilities – who was responsible: a jealous ex, a greedy con, a drunken youth?

When he'd bought the house a year ago, he'd underestimated how vast a three-bedroom home would seem to a single man, who until then had lived in studios and single-bedroom flats. From his upper floor he'd look down at the next-door neighbour's children playing in the melting snow. Their house was the mirror image of his yet it held five people plus their pets.

A short walk away from majestic nineteenth-century homes, his was a cream-coloured nineteen-fifties-style building in a coveted neighbourhood. Its original features had been retained, large windows, banisters made of wood and iron, and parquet flooring.

Each week he received email offers that promised him a small profit if he sold. But he knew he'd be unlikely to afford anything else of this grandeur in this neighbourhood. Besides, he liked to think it wasn't impossible that someone would move in with him someday and perhaps the garden would be used for something other than smoking cigarettes and contemplating life.

If his house burned down too he wouldn't miss it, he thought, frowning.

He'd had guests here. His sister came in and out of the house as if the large garden had announced that her two boys were welcome to visit him at almost no notice. At the behest of his editor he'd held a few dinner parties at which he'd met a few writers but mostly people who were involved in the sale of books.

At the first of these gettogethers, Saana, who he hadn't been sure how she'd made it to the guest list, had made it obvious she wanted to be invited again. Her hand had lingered on his shoulder after she'd managed to gently re-order his seating plan to ensure that she was beside him. She'd found excuses to touch his hair and his thigh, such as, "I wish I had curly hair!" He'd invited her back to each party, but he could sense her growing impatience at his reluctance to invite her somewhere alone or to ask her to stay afterwards.

They spoke in Finnish, though his was hesitant and vocabulary limited, because he found her funnier and more interesting in her own language.

She didn't particularly care about what he'd written – which suited him because he didn't either. It was the result of years of writing, filling notebook after notebook with mostly incomprehensible and illegible scribbling. When he'd finally directed his mind towards a plot and written it down, the public had lapped it up. His second book was to be released in the next few months.

It was time, he decided, to do something. He found her beauty bland and uninspiring, nothing about her hinted that she could be someone he could love. It was, however, either her or being alone.

He smiled at his assessment of her, turning a page in his notebook and staring at a blank page. She wasn't dull. He was being mean – she was good conversation; she'd spent years as an aid worker in East Africa, she could as easily discuss world politics as she could the best manicure she'd ever had – in a corrugated iron-roofed salon without running water in a slum in Nairobi– and she never confused Zambia with Namibia or asked if it was near South Africa.

In the kitchen he picked up his mobile and looked up Saana's number. The dial icon flickered, daring him to *call Saana*.

With the mobile in one hand, he opened the notebook again and reached for a pen. He swore at himself and put it away without writing anything more.

Dinner? he resorted to a text after a few moments.

Sure! came the reply in an instant.

I'd love to. Her next message came after he hadn't replied for a few minutes. He'd immediately regretted having asked her.

What time? she continued. He still didn't reply. He slumped back. He knew that with very little effort she would satisfy the longing that sometimes grew so intense it kept him up at night. He wouldn't have to be witty, or to shower her with gifts. In fact, the sex could be pathetic and uninspired, and he was sure she'd pretend it had been wonderful and come back for more.

His fingers hovered over the phone, unsure what to do to rescind his invitation.

He was already doing it, telling himself he didn't want to exploit her desperation and her admiration. He was making excuses. *Might have to go to work, will let you know.*

Then he scrolled up to her profile and tapped *block*. His phone asked him if he was sure he wanted to block Saana and all communication with her and he tapped *yes*. When the mobile confirmed that she had indeed been barred from his life, he returned to his notebook. He was writing when Charlie cleared his throat. James smiled at the much-too-tight outfit and asked. "Anything else I can get you?"

Charlie looked incredibly cheerful for a man who'd just lost his home, thought James, as his friend replied, "Nah, I'm fine," and smiled.

Aija

When she'd got home, the first thing Aija did was to take off her top, underwear and jeans and throw them into the washing machine. She stood naked in front of the machine as it began and only when several minutes had counted down did she walk away from it. It wasn't that she didn't trust it not to start, it was that she had nothing else to do.

After a shower she'd checked her phone for a message or missed call and only read an abrupt, unadorned goodnight from Matti. She'd checked the messages from her mother and from a colleague and answered both with an overused emoji of a yawning yellow face. She slid into bed with her phone and begun scrolling through Instagram. The app promised her the best way to fix box braids, revealed what every African woman supposedly did before bed and showed her myriad videos of babies taking their first steps.

A book that she'd been reading sat on her bedside table with a piece of tissue stuffed between its pages to mark the spot where she'd abandoned it weeks ago. She reached for it but stopped and instead stared at the ceiling of the flat she and Matti had bought; he had spent less than a week in it before he'd returned to Singapore. It was newly renovated, nestled in a post-war building in the style that was coveted among middle-income professionals, not as expensive as the old areas of Helsinki such as Punavuori or Munkkiniemi, and each building individually unique unlike the newly built condos in Verkkosaari.

A night like this had been unusual – almost exciting. She'd had a fair amount to drink at Charlie's house, a place that she loved to visit on evenings such as the one they'd had. Then after what seemed a very short spell at home, she'd heard from dispatch that Charlie's house was on fire and she'd returned to the scene of her enjoyment to find it burning down. Watching the fire progress she'd imagined what it must feel like, not just for Charlie, but for his neighbours too, to watch everything turn to ash. She'd arrived home just after dawn. She'd poured another glass of wine and then after sitting beside it without drinking, she'd poured it away and tried to get some sleep in the daylight.

Where would she go to pass the time between work and the brief, relentlessly cheerful calls from her husband? She thought as she tossed about in her bed. Where was the armchair that she could sink into, where would friends and acquaintances congregate? She hadn't grown up and gone to school in Helsinki, the few friends she stayed in contact with from her childhood lived lives that seemed strange to her in small towns not far from where they had been raised.

Aija pressed her fingers over her eyes as hot tears welled up. She recalled Charlie's face as he watched his house burning. She couldn't imagine what it must have felt like – or perhaps she could? Her family was far away and her husband in another country; she'd never thought about why Charlie had invited her to his house to begin with. She wasn't really like his friends. She wasn't foreign. They all had some tale of how they came to be living just short of the Artic Circle. Maybe he'd recognised her solitude before she herself had.

After a few hours of fitful, unhappy sleep she rose, dressed and put on a clean spring jacket and considered going to one of the cafés near her flat.

She thought of sending her mother a message, but she suspected it would bring a long, dull conversation about the travails of her large extended family. Charlie was probably getting some much-needed sleep and as for James, as good a friend as he was, she didn't know if he would accept an invitation to breakfast with her.

There her list of possible companions ended. She absentmindedly flipped through her scribbled notes on the case she'd been removed from. A gang of teenage thugs had been terrorising an organic food hub of small businesses in Sörnäinen, and the public, like hounds, had been baying for a response. Had it been that she'd asked too many boring questions compared to her colleagues? As usual, she had been too deliberate, too slow.

"It's hard enough to survive financially, let alone having to wait for you to find these hooligans who attack our business almost every week," one owner had said.

Inconsequential, she'd scribbled when Hart had told her to hand her notes to Tolya, who held the same rank as her.

Superintendent Hart hadn't even bothered with a proper explanation, just a brisk, "Tolya will get it done in half the time and with twice the style." Days later he had appeared at her desk and asked her if she could look through the report because she was "so good at that sort of thing".

This had been a new low. After two years she was supposed to be moving up. Tolya hadn't done anything she couldn't have done – perhaps he did it faster, yes, but… She let her thoughts wander. Her mother's irritated voice came to her: "Pull up your socks!"

She wrote slowly, trying to formulate a plan. After a few painful moments all it said was:

Get noticed.
How?
Solve something.

Chapter 2

Charlie

Charlie surveyed what lay before him: it was a body, but he'd never seen one like this. Over the years he'd become familiar with fresh blood spatter still dripping down walls, bodies stiff with rigor mortis and corpses that had begun to fester after weeks hidden behind locked doors.

He wished the rain would stop, but it didn't. Though the drizzle was light, it was persistent and it was churning the soil into a dark mud and making their work harder.

The glow of phones and bright lights mounted above their heads illuminated the scene. Lying in a newly excavated grave, layers of black plastic bags had been split to reveal a body. To Charlie the person appeared at first to have lain down to sleep, rolled to one side, arms folded in front of them. The soil that surrounded the body was dark, black and rich in the not-quite dark of the summer night. The forest surrounded them, hiding them from the rest of the world. There was a small army of police officers of varying specialties on site. Many of them had been woken from their beds having long left the office, the day ahead was going to be tough. Charlie hoped he'd have enough time to recuperate with a few hours' sleep before returning to the station to continue the investigation.

"It's definitely a woman," said Camilla, the pathologist, seeming almost gleeful. She was clad in the white plastic jumpsuit that covered her usual jeans and sweater. Its plastic also kept her dry, the rain that had started several days earlier had settled into a light, seemingly ceaseless patter. He'd heard her humming as she'd looked over blackened shrivelled remains. "I can confirm her sex at least, though everything has to be verified. I think she was young, early twenties perhaps, or in her late teens."

Charlie watched her get to her feet. He noticed that she did this with effort, pushing off her knee with the palm of her hand. She had just turned fifty, he knew this because she'd held a party at her house. At least twenty people including Hart had celebrated with drinks and loud music. Every time she brushed against him as she walked past he'd felt a boiling of desire that had driven him to leave early.

He saw her reasonably often. He'd never paid her any attention when he had Rachel. Camilla had an active life, sometimes mentioning a new, trendy drinks place or a Tinder date. He knew she didn't notice the strain he had to suppress when she told him about the men she met. Why couldn't he ask her out?

And what would you say? he thought, *never mind my missing wife, come back with me to the spare bedroom I'm sleeping in.*

He didn't particularly want her, he'd realised, he just wanted someone. But how could he do that with Rachel in the way?

Like Camilla, his wife Rachel had been an attractive woman. Slender right until he saw her last, he couldn't imagine that she'd changed in the time since.

"Her neck was broken. Here, look," Camilla said and pointed to the back of the girl's neck. When he asked her when, she shrugged, and replied, "Fifteen – maybe more – years previously."

"Was she raped, assaulted?" He had to ask. Even after all these years he hated the wait for that answer. If she'd been killed, couldn't she have died without the pain, a brutal but swift and painless end?

"I don't know yet," Camilla paused. "Her clothes were torn, so there must have been some violence, but–" here her excitement seemed to dull– "we have to wait for an expert, I don't usually deal with bodies this old."

Charlie had never seen such a corpse before. He'd never been called to a crime that, it appeared, had been committed perhaps decades earlier. He'd seen many images, in training, in consultation with other departments. Such cases were few and far between, no matter how frequently they seemed to feature on TV. His entire professional life had been in Finland, one of the safest countries in the world. The whole country saw just about a hundred murders a year. He could spend months on end without being assigned to a murder case, though there were sufficient suicides, manslaughter cases and attempted murders to go around.

Charlie, when he'd first seen the body, had pressed his eyes shut and opened them again. Long black hair splayed in waves away from her face, which was newly split across – smashed – by the shovel of a wilderness enthusiast who'd found her body while trying to dig an outdoor toilet. The area was still remote, but when the body was buried here his campsite would have been even more distant from the ever-encroaching housing developments.

"Look," Camilla said, leading Charlie around the scene. "It could be that someone hit her several times." She pointed at the broken bones, especially the fingers – which were not just broken but shattered.

Aija walked towards him, pushing her phone in her pocket and glancing around as she came. "We're trying to secure the area, fifteen years too late."

She seemed sprightly though it was three o'clock in the morning on an early summer's night. "We have absolutely nothing in the vicinity that hints at being related to the deceased. Just some junk from over the years, broken walking equipment, shoes. The area isn't that popular with casual walkers – there are no cafés or camping facilities. The nearest road was only recently tarred." She looked away from the body.

When they had arrived together and Aija had seen the body, for a moment she'd become rigid. Charlie was glad his people saw so few cases like this that many of the younger officers would have felt shaken, ill even, at the sight of the victim, not yet being inured to such violence.

He'd stood ready to reassure Aija, but she'd taken a deep breath and carried on without his help.

Camilla, despite saying that the specialist was on his way, was still examining the body.

"She might have even been alive when she was put in the bag – this mud is just making everything so hard." Camilla again raised her head, but this time she was frowning. "I hope," she sighed, "she was already dead when he buried her in this hole." Then she seemed angry. Her words came out clipped, she sighed heavily and looked around at the bleak forest in which she again rested on her haunches beside a newly excavated body. "She appears to be black, er, African."

Charlie, for an instant, imagined the terror of finding himself in a black plastic bag, suffocating and certain death was near. "How do you know? Her hair's..."

"Extensions. You can see it still sewn in here." Camilla pointed at the barely visible wefts at the end of the victim's hair.

"*Ihmiskauppako?*" her assistant suggested just as Camilla made her observation.

Both Camilla and Charlie glared at her

"I only suggested human trafficking," the assistant started in defence, "because there were very few black people here then, and in those days, hair extensions were far more expensive than they are now." She stood rigid in defiance. "My mother was a hairdresser."

"Still, let's not assume it's trafficking or sex work – let's keep an open mind," Charlie spoke directly at the assistant.

"Might be something to talk to your rather cute housemate about," Camilla grinned at Charlie.

"Now who's being racist?" muttered the assistant. "Not all black people are African, and–"

"I was just joking," Camilla hissed as Aija passed them. "He would have been here twenty years ago, he would be able to tell you more about what kind of–" she fumbled for words – "immigrants were here then."

Two years earlier when Charlie had seen he was to have a new colleague called James Grey, he assumed he would be of English stock: American, English, Australian – he'd come across a few in the service, being one himself. Instead, he found himself with someone who glared at anyone who suggested he was anything other than an African from a country that Charlie had had to look up.

Still smarting from her suggestion that James was cute, Charlie looked around, sweating beneath his police-issued raincoat. He'd opted to keep it on to stay dry rather than to take it off and slowly get wet as some of the officers had done. To make things worse his evening's trip to the gym had left him tired and his arms sore.

Some officers clad in plastic trawled through the immediate surroundings. Charlie knew that the years would have cleaned the forest of any evidence that would have been left behind. Rain, snow, illegal dumping, trail walkers and campers abandoning crisp packets, bleeding, crying, spitting, vomiting…

He thought hard. The murderer could have been anyone, perhaps someone who just found the place by accident and realised a body could be hidden here. So he said nothing and watched the constables continuing their plodding through the trees and shrubs.

We're not going to find who did this. Despair washed over him. He'd never left a significant case unsolved. In twenty years, he'd never arrived at a crime scene and immediately felt lost. He couldn't understand why he felt overwhelmed, perhaps the age of the body just made it seem so much harder to know where to start.

Detective work was mostly middling, strange as it may seem to most people, a case like this was unusual, there would be interest from the press and migrants and human rights associations who would demand answers.

If he failed he'd never again regain his standing.

This feeling, a growing inner pressure, had been intensifying over the last few weeks. It had been two months since he'd moved in with James. Perhaps it was watching James's star rise. James could afford to work part time; everyone was talking about his literary career and it was rumoured that certain people higher up were bent on keeping him in the force – not just for the publicity but because he was a good policeman. He had a new book about to be released simultaneously in English and Finnish. James even had a publicist, who treated Charlie with an almost comical eagerness to please now that she knew they shared a house, inviting him to special events and buying him drinks.

The woods were at the immediate end of the Helsinki precinct. Had her body been found a few hundred metres away, it wouldn't even be his case. It wouldn't have been him woken in the middle of the night by a cheerful dispatcher's voice.

"There's no rush, we know that at least. I'm going home, we'll pick it up in the morning," Charlie told the other officers. As soon as he finished his sentence, he knew that his words sounded callous.

Aija had appeared behind him and smiled fleetingly. She was in her usual trousers and floral shirt. Charlie knew that she understood what he meant – that nothing would be solved by them standing there thinking about the warm beds and hot cups of tea that could be found at home. There was no urgency. The killer had at least fifteen years on them, a few more hours while he caught some sleep would hardly make a difference.

"Right, I'm off, anything else that I can ponder over my breakfast?" he asked Camilla.

She smiled once again. "It will have to be validated, but I can tell you that she died a maximum of twenty years ago."

With a triumphant expression, she held out a set of tweezers clasping the remnants of a white piece of paper, a ticket perforated in one corner to show that it had been used.

It was now Charlie's turn to squint. "*The Passion. Grand Opening!*" He read out the date. "That's that club on Kolmas Linja in Kallio, I remember it opening. Was that twenty years ago?"

"No idea, I would have been twelve," called Aija from behind them.

He'd already have been well into his thirties with one child already aged eight and the other five.

"Young'un," chuckled Camilla.

He began to feel some excitement. In just those last few minutes they'd made a new discovery.

"That could narrow it down at least. She was either from around here or was visiting for this outing," said Aija.

"The clothes and the ticket aren't necessarily hers. All it really tells us is that her body had to be accessible to the killer after the grand opening," Charlie replied in annoyance. The ticket may have only just narrowed down their search but it had also thrown up more questions. "She could have been..."

"We have one possible match so far, Lucinda Barnaby. Last seen January that year." Aija was looking at a glowing tablet.

"Lucinda Barnaby, where from?"

"American, it says."

Craning her neck to see, Camilla added, "What did she look like?"

To Charlie, the photo showed a girl, not fully a woman – despite the age given in her details. A girl who'd disappeared leaving behind a family who, if they were correct, only now decades later would know what happened to her. He liked to think he no longer loved Rachel, but he knew what it meant to wait like they did, to not know, to resort to prayer and bargaining with God he'd never believed in.

Her face was bare and her hair a mass of afro ringlets in the photo. He imagined her mother telling her off for covering her beautiful hair with straight shop-bought tresses. He was sure her mother would have replayed moments like those countlessly over the years because all that remained were memories.

She's never coming back. He shrugged and turned to Aija.

"For now let's get some sleep. In the morning we'll see if anyone else fits the description."

Aija stretched, raising her arms above her head. He wondered if she too thought it was futile. Films and TV shows made it seem so easy; find a body, find a killer – and maybe find a woman to love along the way. He guided his thoughts back to the case in front of him.

Aija retreated and went to inform the rest of the team of the plan.

Later that morning he and Aija would begin the investigation proper. They would dig through the years to uncover who killed this young woman and buried her body in the forest. Her family and her friends would finally know – he wanted them to know.

But first, he thought, bed.

Chapter 3

Aija

"How's the flat share going?" Charlie's office door was open and both Aija and their detective superintendent Lovisa Hart stood within the frame.

"The insurance is almost sorted out – I'll have my own place again soon," Charlie explained.

"Mmm." Hart nodded thoughtfully, suggesting she hadn't particularly heard him. "Anything interesting – no detailed outline of his next book lying around?"

Charlie's office was little more than a cubicle that he and James had found themselves sharing due to part of the building requiring renovation – it would be months until he'd have his own space again – something he'd earned as a detective inspector. Aija, as a detective sergeant, still shared the open-plan area with the others of her level.

The smile Aija gave Charlie and Hart was devoid of that heaviness she was growing accustomed to after sleeping badly after the two or three glasses of wine she'd taken to having before bed. Instead, that morning she felt fresh, ridiculously so, and energised and, although she was slightly ashamed to admit to herself, she liked it.

"You wish," he replied, and Hart replied with an exaggerated sigh of disappointment.

Hart was a fan of James's books and their superior officer; she kept their office in check with a mix of what Aija saw as emotional and professional manipulation. Aija found it hard to decide if she liked Hart or not. She fluctuated from being a friend, having a drink in a pub with them, and being a leader – an often forceful one. She told them about herself in little snippets of conversation such as having been terrified when she first walked into the office and seeing so many people expecting her to be in charge. She'd once told Aija, quietly, that when she'd met James, she'd realised that she was growing older and past a point in her life when a man like him would look at her. Aija was sure Hart had said that knowing that Aija would never dare repeat it.

"I want to know what happens to the creepy female senior detective." Hart rubbed her hands together as if excited. "He's left me sort of hanging."

"Why are you so sure it is you?" asked Charlie, though to Aija it was obvious that the character was largely drawn from Superintendent Hart.

"Well, who else could it be?"

"She's blonde and athletic?" Charlie raised his eyebrows.

"I was once blonde and athletic," Hart replied, straightening her posture and pushing her shoulders back. Her hair was now a deep brown, and while she was not nearly overweight she was slightly larger than the image of her in dress uniform taken several years earlier that was tucked in a corner of her office.

"But she's mean and nasty – why would you want to be her?" asked Charlie.

"And she shares Merimies's racist sentiments – in the book," added Aija speaking of the protagonist. "Like, she agrees when he says he doesn't want to spend his time on crimes against immigrants."

"But he says *'However, with your beauty, it could be worth the time and effort to impress you'*," quoted Hart.

"Then he nudged her attacker off a cliff," added Charlie, "and called it justice."

"Well, at least we know Merimies isn't James," said Hart, "James's hygiene is impeccable."

"Anteeks," a constable excused herself with a few sheets of paper in hand. *"Allekirjoittakaa tähän,"* she nodded to Hart and pointed at the bottom section of a form with a pen.

The conversation continued in English as she departed. The officer probably understood them perfectly but knew that this clique did not include her. It wasn't just that this group spoke English without effort or hesitation, it was the fact that somehow they'd gravitated to the status of outsiders. Hart, though the team leader, was more likely to have a casual conversation with them than anyone else. She was a Swedish-speaking Finn, with a twenty-year marriage to an Irishman which, though dissolved, required her to travel to Ireland when she wanted to see her children and grandchildren.

Still, no one could dare accuse her of favouring James, Charlie or even Aija; Charlie's career had stalled though it wasn't his fault, and Aija knew that she'd earned her own position due to a diversity drive. However, it was generally known that if James stayed with the police he would become someone. He was one of *those people,* as Aija put it. He was efficient, intelligent and was always counted as black in the statistics, Hart had added.

Hart could be brutal when discussing how race and sex could hurt or help their careers. When Aija had first arrived she'd told Hart that she was originally from Angola. Hart had replied, "Really, because it says here you're from Mikkeli."

"Well…" Aija had leapt to her own defence.

"Do you speak Portuguese or any other African language? Always useful," demanded Hart as Aija had stuttered something about her origins.

"No, but…"

"Then you're Savonian." Hart had leaned back in her chair, adding, "What's the use of saying you're from Angola if you don't know anything about it?"

Hart had dismissed something that mattered to her so quickly and abruptly. Her Angolan heritage got her invitations to parties, free tastes of foods from food trucks and at festivals. But according to Hart, she was as much from Savo as Paavo Kännelmäki, a fellow sergeant with dark blond hair and quick-to-burn mottled white skin.

Right now standing beside her she was nothing like that, she was friendly, jocular – a colleague rather than a superior officer.

"There've been quite a few conversations upstairs," Hart continued. "The general consensus is that a famous crime-writing cop is good publicity for us – even if his principal character is doing stuff that would get him fired and jailed in an instant – especially if I was his boss."

"Maybe that's why he makes you share his sentiments?" said Aija.

Hart glared at her.

"In the book," Aija clarified. "I've got stuff to do." Aija fled to her desk knowing that she'd probably crossed one of Hart's many lines. Hart continued talking to Charlie.

On her desk was a thermal mug of warm berry juice made from the concentrate that her grandmother made every autumn from the berries in the forests that surrounded Aija's childhood home. This warm deep purple liquid, her grandmother had told her, had made many mornings bearable after one of those many nights when alcohol stood in for human company.

Now elderly, this woman's sudden and occasional revelations would shake Aija when spoken in her heavy Savo accent. Stories of brief infidelities and illicit euphoria told with impenitent nostalgia by a woman who'd raised five children while her husband had worked hundreds of miles away in a Swedish forest, coming home only every few months.

"A bit like you?" She'd brushed a hand through her thinning hair that she still coloured blonde, before adding, "Except you don't have children."

She was supposed to be enjoying her husband working far away – that's what many women had told her. She had the chance to be single and married simultaneously. Her husband was a continent away making money that was biting chunks from their mortgage and in a few years they'd be mortgage free, and then they'd probably buy a new flat, a new mortgage – until...

"We're still young," Matti had said. They would reap the rewards of his work abroad; they would be affluent.

"It's not like we're poor now," she'd replied. He was an engineer with excellent prospects that were unmarred by the current global crises.

"Everyone will always need fuel," he'd defended his choice of career, "unless we want to move back to prehistoric times."

But his latest suggestion had been for her to give up her job and move to Singapore as an expat wife. Even then most of his time would be spent travelling to remote sites in Asia – she "could sit by the pool..." he suggested, playfully lifting his eyebrows during their video chat.

"And get a tan?" she'd asked, her sarcasm obvious.

So they continued into their third year apart. Her job didn't allow her the flexibility to relocate that his did. Police officers couldn't pick up their portfolios and enter foreign police services.

How she ended up being supervised by Charlie was well known. She hadn't earned her position like most of the others at her level of seniority. They needed an adjunct for Charlie, who though he had been able to keep his job, had become almost a pariah. The cloud that had descended on his personal life and career meant some staff didn't want to be associated with him to a point that even his former sergeant had applied for a transfer.

Having an underperforming diversity hire as his adjunct was a message to Charlie that despite him still being valued for being one of their best detectives, keeping him had not been by consensus. There had been many dissenters, people who felt the force should distance themselves as far from him as it could, while others felt that the force should stand by their people – he was not guilty of a crime and should not be punished for it.

For a short while Aija had been angry, annoyed that her inability to flourish as a police officer on her own had been noticed. There were other black officers, many of whom had achieved promotions and won accolades due to their own efforts. There was a tiny number of black female detectives, and she was meant to bolster that number. But the management was careful not to forcefully promote those who were capable of achieving promotions on their own – or so she'd heard. Before her promotion she had just been told she had to try harder – her investigative skills were weak, her former superintendent informed her.

"You can't see the small details," he said. "On the Aalto case, for example, it was bloody obvious that they were involved in a scam, they had a massive house – so you got that. But you went over their house twice and still missed critical documents which took the next constable less than ten minutes to find."

"They were hidden..." she began.

"Taped beneath the table, Aija," he said. "Who doesn't look beneath a table?"

"Look, Aija," he continued. He'd tapped his coffee mug. "If we hadn't found the files, we would have probably have convicted Aalto, but it would have been bloody hard. You had the bank accounts, you had the paper trail – but the man was sitting in the same room as you so nervous that he was pouring with sweat. You should have sensed that he was scared, that he was sure any minute you were going to look under the table beside him."

She hadn't responded.

"When you see these good detectives–" he'd nodded at the glass partition– "working late into the night, they are doing the equivalent of looking under tables, they are going over every possible scenario: why did the suspect run to Espoo, not Vantaa? Why did the woman take one child and not the other? And–" here he pointed at her– "why would anyone cover a ten thousand euro dining table with a cheap plastic table cloth?"

He'd abruptly got to his feet.

"Anyway, you're being promoted," he said in a tone that implied he wasn't happy with the idea. "I'd prefer for you to stay and learn a little more, but you can learn a lot from Charlie – if he stays." Her superintendent then handed her a sheet of paper and made it clear she was dismissed.

And that was it. She found herself working with Charlie at the main Helsinki police station.

Soon she'd realised she liked not being on the bottom rung, that it was pleasant to meet friends from school knowing she appeared to have achieved something as well – and being a detective had some sort of glamour and mystique.

She and Charlie had developed a friendship, she liked to think. It was normal for police officers to socialise with each other. Who else could penetrate the world they lived in? Who else had spent their morning warning a skinhead biker that his bike would be impounded and he'd lose his licence, while her backup kept an eye out for knives and guns? Who else had a colleague who was on sick leave for having been battered by a group of teenagers who'd threated to rape and kill her? And who else after that carried on despite avoiding the recommended counselling that the wellbeing managers said they must need?

She would have given Charlie a place to stay if it wouldn't have set tongues wagging. Especially since his appearance had improved so dramatically over the last year and a half. He'd lost weight and his clothes were much better quality and as stylish as one would want a fifty-something year-old man to be.

And, she'd thought when she'd been contemplating inviting him, what would she and Charlie talk about hour after hour in the evenings, would she wait outside the door as he showered, waiting her turn? What about the intimate sounds – the grunts, the flatulence, discreet burps, the flush of the toilet in the middle of the night, the sounds she associated most with her family, and Matti?

James came in, his long and lanky frame covered in black, his regulation rain jacket open and ID tags swaying around his neck. He nodded hello and asked with surprise, "Tea?"

"No, blueberry juice. Hot," she replied, smiling.

"Sounds awful," he said with a wink. "What you people think up."

He smiled and sauntered to the cubicle he shared with Charlie.

In the early days, before she would have considered James a friend, he'd fleetingly and under the influence said to her, "My father went to Angola, but he killed people there." Then he'd turned to Charlie, and they'd launched into discussion on cricket fixtures and the best place to watch a world cup of some sort.

It was only then that she'd read into her father's country's history – for she'd never truly considered it her own. She imagined an older version of James, perhaps now balding, his eyebrows a mix of grey and blond, would have gone to Angola and killed, raped and pillaged in the name of preserving their perceived superiority of the white race. She'd read voraciusly about how the South African government had sent young South African men of all races to uphold the ideals of Apartheid and to wrest control of neighbouring countries from the perceived threat of independent black governments. She learnt more about her father's history in these few weeks than ever before in her life.

James's father would have served there during his national service. Someone James's age might even have childhood memories of Apartheid and of what his father did.

She hadn't known what to do with James for few days while contemplating her newfound knowledge of him. At the time she was still trying to make up her mind about how many of his idiosyncrasies she was willing to put up with in order to be friends. She wasn't sure she liked the James she knew, of boiled milk tea and cricket, who could be found crouched over a notebook, writing – his pen scratching over the paper. There was also the James who would be silent at a question, or who could simply stop talking in the middle of a conversation.

Having to put her mind at ease she consulted Charlie as they were having filter coffee the way they both liked it – the mild, light roast that they'd both grown up with. They were on a break after a morning spent at their desks reading heaps of printed-out paper related to a crime they were investigating.

"So, you're judging him based on what you think his dad may have done – you don't even know what he meant by it?" Charlie asked her gently, though when she heard him say it, it sounded ridiculous. "Have you thought of asking him?" he asked with a smile forming as he spoke.

"Well, yeah…" She wouldn't know where to start.

"I suggest," said Charlie, "that before you do, you get your countries right – that's Namibia you're talking about. It was part of South Africa."

She clapped her hand over her mouth and swore through her fingers.

Charlie chuckled.

"You mean I've been down internet rabbit holes about bush wars and mercenaries and things and– I'm so embarrassed," she babbled with her hand still covering her mouth. Charlie's laughter grew louder. "Hart would have loved this. This is so typical of me." This is what Rostadt had meant.

"Thank heavens you didn't say anything." Charlie was still chuckling. "He'd probably never speak to you again."

"But seriously…" She'd flexed her fingers and rolled them into fists. *What if this was a suspect's background I was looking up?*

"We all make mistakes," Charlie wiped away a tear. "I know you're thinking what if it was a case."

Charlie had empathy. She considered it was one of his greatest traits.

After a moment in which Charlie recovered and sipped his coffee, he said, "So, are you going to ask what he meant?"

"No." She was looking at James's statement in a new light. How he'd quickly turned away and stayed away from her for the remaining hours of the evening. "It wasn't something he meant to say."

"Good." Charlie nodded. "It's best to respect a friend's secrets."

"Yeah." Aija slowly took a deep breath. "I guess you're right."

Chapter 4

Charlie

The police station was already alive when Charlie arrived. He found the usual hum of activity. His colleagues walked around with official identification hanging around their necks, leaned over desks, got on with their tasks or stood in corners talking in low voices, nursing cooling cups of coffee.

The sun had already been up for hours, if hiding behind dense grey clouds counted as being up. It was warm enough to be deemed summer in a city in which twenty-five degrees qualified as *helle* or a heatwave. But the relentless rain was ruining summer, the time of year all Finns looked forward to after winters that lasted half the year.

Many Finns took long summer holidays and the cafés already had customers outdoors enjoying breakfast and drinking coffee on slivers of covered terraces. It lent the city an air of sophistication, as if it were normally a city of leisure – a continental European city – people reading books and slowly sipping wine during the day.

Inside, he made his way to his department where nothing had changed because a twenty-year-old body had been found. His colleagues were still predominantly men, three of whom were standing by the coffee maker discussing something that seemed to be of immense importance judging from the intensity of their expressions. That was one of the problems with this place, he thought, everything was of immense importance – murder, rape, football, the latest episode of Finland's best bakers. In between conversations, they arrested drug dealers and seized their produce, they harassed wife beaters and prodded desperate parents to return kidnapped children according to the terms of the divorce settlement. They listened to desperate shopkeepers whose underpaid staff constantly pilfered their goods and let loose vegan activists with a warning. It was worth it because they knew that sometimes they might arrest a man for attempting to slice an ex-girlfriend's throat, and he'd leave jail two years later having been through a decent prison system and an almost zero per cent chance that he'd offend again.

Charlie knew that on most days, he'd be home in the early evening. It's what those at his level earned after years of doing the hard work, he earned the commendations and status that allowed him to live a lot like normal people. But when these cases appeared and it was his job to solve them, then he knew many long evenings would be spent here at the station. He put his bento lunchbox in the fridge, ensuring he had snacks and meals for the day. He poured himself a mild black coffee from the coffee maker and drank it without sugar.

Their office was in a large colourless building constructed when it must have seemed futuristic. Though it was perfunctorily cared for from the outside, over time it started to look dull and uninspiring. Some rooms such as the tech department were contemporary, gleaming white, but the rest of them were plain spaces filled with people and computers – very little of which was personalised. Here and there were some discreet photos of loved ones, postcards from friends and Post-it notes listing groceries. It gave the impression that those who worked here could at a moment's notice be replaced and their work would continue uninterrupted – Charlie had learnt that this was true. Little cubicles served as offices for senior officers, but in keeping with the Finnish perspectives on equality, none of them were truly private.

James was at his desk in their shared office. In front of him were two empty cups which earlier on had held tea and crumbs as evidence of the few biscuits he usually referred to as breakfast. Ridiculously efficient. That's what James had been called. He'd also been called far unkinder things – snob for one. This morning his electric blond hair was neatly brushed into his usual Tintin coif. He wore a brilliant white buttoned shirt and black jeans.

He looked calm and well rested as usual. When Charlie had returned home after returning from the crime scene, he had heard a stirring from James's room. He might have just returned from a run or he could have been leaving for one, depending on his schedule for the day. Sometimes they talked when their free time overlapped, other times they didn't. But their silences were a pleasant continuation of the relationship they'd had for the last two years. It hadn't been ruined by sharing a home.

Their cohabitation had fallen in place with little effort. When they both happened to be home, James read but occasionally joined him in front of the TV for quiz shows and cosy mystery series. The house was quiet and clean and both men liked that. Occasionally he overheard James speaking to his parents or sister with his mobile's microphone on. They were loud, surprisingly so considering James's generally quiet demeanour, but when they spoke their accents intensified and made it impossible for him to discern what they were saying.

They didn't travel to work or go shopping together, but somehow they managed to always have what they needed in the fridge and pantry. They hadn't had guests yet – not even Aija, Brad or the others from their regular drinks group. That group now convened at someone else's house and both Charlie and James found excuses not to go. Dolly, James's twin sister, had passed through several times, but Charlie had not been home to meet her and her twin boys. He'd arrived once to find James wiping away traces of chocolate from the sofa and cleaning blood from the spikes of a cactus that stood in a corner of the living room.

"Once James stopped screaming," he explained, "they wanted to go home right away."

Charlie had opened and shut his mouth without speaking, momentarily at a loss. Why would James refer to himself in the third person? Then it came to him. "She named one of her twins after you?"

"Both of them actually, James and Alexander. Said it was a sign of affection." James had chuckled as he replied.

"I thought the two of you didn't get along that well?" he said, though he couldn't really recall what gave him that impression.

"We do and we don't," he replied and then declared, "*voila!*" with dramatic flourish and had walked away from the plant.

Seeing James on his side of their shared cubicle, on his phone scrolling through something that from Charlie's vantage point looked nothing like police work, Charlie realised that he could be of help on last night's case, and not, as the assistant had suggested, because he was also black. James was a gifted detective with a knack for analysis, for picking things apart. Both he and James were detective inspectors. Both of them had achieved the rank relatively young, but over a decade apart. He and James had traded expertise on several cases. In the world of mystery novels that were peppered with wise detectives who had sidekicks who inevitably had a swathe of knowledge of obscure facts immediately at hand, James was that person. James would fit nicely in such a book, an initial education in a dull-sounding field followed by a police qualification, and either voluntarily celibate or incredibly unlucky with women.

Charlie also had Aija, who in the last two years with them had failed to differentiate herself in any way. She could be described with words such as competent, reliable and... he searched for a third adjective, and eventually settled on uninspiring. Her sole gift seemed to be that in those two years she'd proved herself incapable of losing anything – not a file, not a note. She knew where he was supposed to be and his schedule and she always knew James's whereabouts as well.

She would make a perfect secretary – except that such positions no longer existed.

He was glad no one could read his mind.

The back wall of their cubicle was covered in files and paper, despite much of their work being done on computer. It was the legacy of a system that had endured for decades, recording cases or events of note that took place under its watch.

"Your hair's going the other way?" Charlie nodded at James to mean hello.

James looked up at him, his face seeking an explanation. Aija, who'd just entered the room, chuckled.

Charlie drew an outline of James's hair above his own head, the coif was still sleek but swirled in the opposite direction. James smiled, they knew each other well, long enough to have gone through short hair and long hair, and haircuts and beer-fuelled discussions about thinning hair.

"He thought he'd be daringly different today," Aija said and placed a sheaf of paper on his desk.

He noticed Aija had gone home; her clothes had changed and she'd brushed her teeth, but the smell of the woods still clung to her and her tightly coiled afro curls were still pulled back in the exact manner they'd been hours earlier. It seemed to him as if she hadn't bathed.

Charlie knew that for detectives, appearances were important. Both the detective inspector and detective sergeant were up to scratch from a distance, but when one looked up close, James spent too much on his clothes and Aija not enough. James was too neat, fastidious, and Aija was not neat enough. James's labels were made from high-quality durable fabrics that fit well but they hinted at conceit or else that his work was an overriding priority in his life. He'd seen Aija on her nights out – she dressed well – hinting that her clothes money went to party dresses and heels, while for work she trawled through the cheapest items. Her jeans were always just a hint too tight and her tops too gaudy, the kind with floral splodges in blues and yellows.

Charlie had thought of taking Aija aside and giving her advice. He'd wanted to tell her to take a cue from Superintendent Hart, who'd just swept through the room like a storm in black trousers and heels that were just high enough to be considered powerful, but low enough to be taken as practical. But he wouldn't do that now, it was too easy to be misconstrued as having a dubious interest. It was bad enough that two of them had been at James's book launch a few weeks ago and that there had been other officers to see them standing together.

James leaned back in his seat and asked, "I hear you were out last night? A twenty-year-old corpse sounds exciting. I've never dealt with such an old case." Charlie could see in his eager grin that he was curious and that he would have leapt upon it if given the chance.

"Me neither," he replied honestly.

Aija was standing with a file in her hands, with the half smile of someone who'd momentarily drifted into space, perhaps killing time while he and James caught up.

"How's your insurance going?" Aija asked after he and James hadn't spoken for a moment.

Charlie snorted in response and James asked, "That bad?"

"A guy I knew took over a year to get compensation, turned out that someone had misspelled his name," continued Aija.

"Aija, you're not cheering me up. Tell me what you've uncovered in my four-hour respite." He glanced at his watch.

"Lucinda Barnaby, an American, matches the description of the body in the woods. She'd just finished university, she was doing well, everyone says she was happy and healthy. She had a part time job as an assistant in an advertising firm. Before she disappeared, she told her sister that she was going out and was never seen again. Parents reported her missing just under two days later. Last time she'd been to a dentist, she was eight, so we don't have significant dental records. We're waiting for a DNA confirmation." Aija flipped the page of her notepad over as if to signal that was all. She leaned against the desk looking at Charlie and waiting for instruction.

He'd wondered about the deceased's family. This was the kind of case that ended up on filler shows on cable channels with families haunted by loss, but not quite able to give up, talking about how wonderful their daughter was.

"We have a lot of paperwork on her case from back then," began Charlie.

Lovisa Hart pushed open the door and stood with her hand resting against it. She seemed excited, like a girl who'd found her older siblings playing a game that she wanted to be a part of.

"Can I join?" she asked cheerfully, though she was the superintendent and of course could if she wanted. Her lipstick today was brighter than usual, her hair down to her shoulders. Charlie nodded and she entered.

"As I was saying, we have a lot of paperwork," said Charlie, "simply because there was a hell of a lot to record. There were masses of interviews, but no one interviewed came up with anything of any interest or any use. There were no leads to follow and no persons of interest."

"Oh." Hart seemed disappointed. "I was hoping for a bit more, like maybe a witness that saw everything and we forgot to chase it up. Then we'd look like absolute stars if we solved it now." She tugged the file towards herself saying, "May I?" which again she could, of course. She glanced through the pages silently and quickly. "Looks like the family gave up, no one to prod us to keep on looking." She shook her head as she read.

Hart was almost impossible to read. He was sure that she, like the rest of them, was hiding some emotion. He wasn't sure which he felt the strongest: anger or sadness. It wasn't right that a young woman – no, any person, young or old, male or female – should be stuffed in a plastic bag and buried. He squeezed his fists to contain the feeling of loss – yes, that's what it was – an overwhelming sense of loss as if he could feel what her family must have felt.

"Between ourselves," she picked out a page and scanned both sides of it, "the chief at the time was determined to be seen as giving her, as a minority, all the attention a white woman would have received – I've been told. He threw everything he had at the case. It was more about public perception than him actually caring. He wanted a big win to mend his image in minority communities – something about a misplaced comment regarding Polish women."

Hart sighed and pondered the view from the window. "Don't make too much noise about it. Send out a press release asking for more info, give it a couple of weeks and if nothing happens, shelve it." She opened the door to leave, but paused, adding, "Although it would be nice to solve it, you know, to give the bastard what's due to him."

With that she exited in a manner that suggested she didn't expect a response.

"Choose one – to solve or not to solve," said Charlie. James and Aija responded with furrowed brows. They probably had the same thought he did – if not even their supervisor was interested in making a real effort to solve the case then they were off the hook.

He latched his fingers together. Even her family had given up. Their file had shown not a single enquiry had been made in eighteen years – perhaps they'd grown tired of the police having nothing new to add.

"I don't care if we have a twenty-year-old body, a compromised site, too much filing and a family that hasn't held us accountable," he said, rapping his fingertips against his desk. "We have to find this killer."

James and Aija both smiled.

"Right, Aija," he began, "we have to confirm how she died – find out how far the autopsy people are and when we can expect a confirmed ID. Then we need a list of absolutely everybody we know was linked to her and we have to find out where they are now and how to contact them – starting with family and friends."

Aija was briskly taking notes but she offered nothing, so he continued a process he'd learnt from years on the force. "If any investigating officers are still around we'll have to talk to them. The Passion club. We know it's closed but what else can we find out, were any records kept – maybe in an archive? Let's look at their press, rumours and maybe any regular patrons. We need context, what would her life have been like at the time for a young, affluent, educated migrant?" He was about to say something light, about his life at the time being about children and that The Passion had been something he'd only known in the news, when he realised James, who should have been enthralled, prompting Charlie with ideas and offering to take up tasks that weren't his remit, had quietly walked away.

Aija

She'd been working since morning without stopping. So when Charlie told her to stop for the day, she was glad. It was one of those days their schedules aligned – hers, Charlie's and James's, and they could have drinks after work. Even Hart had decided to join them.

Hart had gone to the Ladies. James had arrived while she was gone and was at the bar ordering himself a drink. Aija sat alone with Charlie, trying not to talk about the case. "Have you guys been boozing it up with cricket fests and football?" she asked. James and Charlie had been living together for over two months now, which was longer than Charlie had anticipated.

"Not really, a lot of relaxing and looking at house ads. I'm still spending much of my free time shopping or planning to shop," he replied.

They had managed to find a covered table outdoors to accommodate James's smoking which also let them bask in the relative warmth. Aija was wearing a raincoat despite being shielded by an umbrella.

It was still raining but the long days brought some aspect of summer. Being a police officer meant little change; every public interior space was dense with people trying to enjoy their time off. The beaches and parks were abandoned, more people were indoors with alcohol, which meant there were more threats and fights, knives and abuse.

Aija had moved on to saying something about taking a weekend off on her own, but cut herself off and instead said to Charlie, "Hello, who's this?"

As he walked back towards them, James had stopped and nodded at a woman who had approached him. She was slender and long, with waves of thick blonde hair cascading to her shoulders. She was the kind one assumed from a distance was beautiful and only when she came closer could Aija see that she wasn't. Something about her made Aija look for imperfections – her nose was too narrow, almost pinched, and her eyes a bit too small. Her skin colour matched James's only it was layered with a substantial amount of foundation and blush.

The woman was standing close to James, very close, they spoke for a moment and then Hart joined and they stepped apart as she stood between them. They were too far for Aija to hear what passed between them but the woman broke out in a broad smile while Hart spoke. The trio headed to where Aija was sitting beside Charlie.

"This is Eva. A new detective inspector," announced Hart, as the woman arrived. "And if any of you showed up for debriefing you'd know." She spoke in Finnish, though before she'd gone to the toilet the three of them had been chatting in English. To Aija this meant she wasn't someone Hart was inviting to be friends with them.

"*Moi!* Has Lovisa corralled you into hanging out with us?" asked Charlie in Finnish while the three of them took off their rain jackets. "She's off duty, you don't have to do what she says."

Eva's smile was confident. "Hi," she stretched out her hand and shook both Charlie and Aija's hands, Aija's first.

"I can only stay for one. But I'm really glad to meet you," Eva said in English.

Everyone at the office knew that they spoke to each other in English and to no one else, unless it was absolutely required. If a witness needed a translator, or they were discussing something with foreigner police, as with most Finnish workplaces, most could switch easily into English. It had evolved that way over the last two years. Early on Charlie had told Aija he was not a free English conversation class for everyone to practise with. But they'd gravitated into speaking English together, mostly around James whose spoken Finnish was problematic–after thirty years in the country he still battled with the nuances of the language. When they were together socialising or simply without their colleagues at work they always spoke in English and naturally James had written his novel in English.

No wonder they didn't have anyone else at the station they could call friends. When Aija had arrived Charlie had been solitary. He'd avoided socialising and drove home straight after work. Aija wondered how much of it had been because of how he'd been treated by the other officers and management because of what happened with his wife and then him finding himself alone.

Eva sat down on one of the long sides to the table between Aija and James, the three of them in a row parallel to Charlie. Hart alone had a short side of the table; directly opposite her, beside James, was an empty space.

"Oh, that's what that was about, the coffee and cake this morning," Aija replied in Finnish, recalling a memo she'd ignored about welcoming someone or other. "I've been hellishly busy today."

"I thought you were a friend of James's, *eikös niin*?" asked Charlie, and Aija saw the hint of a suppressed smile. She'd been thinking the same as him, the woman had been standing with her breasts thrust at James.

James was looking across the ground and lit a cigarette, seemingly oblivious to the conversation. She felt a flutter of satisfaction. There was a confidence about Eva that she didn't like.

"I'm more of a stalker," she responded brightly in Finnish as if she'd understood that they were not going to speak to her in English. "I read his book when it first came out, and when I heard he was actually a policeman, I got a bit ahead of myself and contacted him. I've bumped into him a few times before and now it's cool. We're working together."

James took a long drag on his cigarette and contemplated the glowing embers.

Aija hoped her study of them was discreet. Could this be a code for having had sex? She liked to look for clues about James's love life. There had been rumours about James's sexuality. When someone never left hints, offered any evidence of a relationship – people speculated and filled in the blanks themselves. Was he gay, straight, asexual or even sexless? It all depended on who you believed. She herself had not seen him display any real interest in a woman, or a man, in the two years she'd known him.

The character in his books, Merimies, was boldly promiscuous and physically and emotionally cruel to the women in his life. She couldn't imagine James being like that. She hated to say it but sometimes she felt he used her as a buffer to the rest of the world. Because she was beside him it would take a brave, or brazen, woman to come between them. At his book release she'd felt like a secret girlfriend, the one who knew more about him than any of the other women who tried to insert herself into his life.

Even the other woman – she had to struggle to recall her name – Saana. Saana had tried to intimate that she and James had a thing. But during their only night out together, James had stopped a waiter and handed Aija a drink while Saana had to get her own from the tray.

This woman, she could see, was hopeful. Aija smirked and covered her face with her hands.

"I've just finished his new book and I want to schedule a chat about it," she said. "And he's been avoiding me, even though I've told him my review would be kind." She gave what she seemed to think was a coy smile at James who flicked ash off his cigarette and missed the ashtray. "Maybe I'll have to do it at the office canteen since I can't get any time from him otherwise."

"What did you think of his latest then?" asked Hart.

"Brilliant. Nothing short of it." Eva beamed at James.

Hart nodded, perhaps satisfied because she'd said it too – that she loved the book. "Let's celebrate your joining the team. I'll get you a drink." Hart turned to Aija and Charlie. "Eva has quite a starry career, fast track all the way," explained Hart, looking at Aija as if saying *listen to this*. "Four languages – Swedish, English and Somali. Can you imagine – Somali?" Charlie and Aija nodded at the novelty of a white officer speaking Somali.

Aija smiled with her mouth full of wine. A knot formed in her stomach when she recalled the few Portuguese lessons she'd tried and then given up.

"Are you with anyone? Kids?" Aija asked.

Eva shook her head and gave a most fleeting glance at James. Aija again felt a jolt of jealousy.

"And now I can say I might be sharing an office with a literary superstar. I'll have free drinks for life," Eva said smiling widely.

James smiled at this – as if he was about to laugh. "Eva asked Hart if she could share an office with us. I explained that it would be a bit tight."

Charlie added with a suppressed smile, "You're right. That would get a bit crowded. They're cubicles, not real offices."

Eva leaned forward but this time towards Charlie. "I've also heard that you have a twenty-year-old cold case. Something to do with trafficking?"

Charlie raised an eyebrow but didn't ask where she'd heard this, instead he said, "I do. But we've been hacking away at it all day. The last thing I want to do is talk about it over drinks."

Eva hesitated and then Aija realised she knew she was being shut out.

Oh no, Aija thought. They'd become a clique, hadn't they? They were a little gang that kept everyone else out. She was reminded of the little gang in the IT department. They used jargon intentionally to keep everyone else out – bootstrapping and black hats. They swooped by her desk to show her a new and still obscure dating app, assuring her it would be the next big thing and when she reminded them that she was married, they dropped cheap sexual innuendo encrypted in techno-speak – suggesting deep diving into her software or having some horizontal end-to-end testing to do that evening.

"You don't want to share an office with them – James might make you tea," she said, trying to at least seem friendly.

"And Hart will be 'stopping to chat', as she calls it," added Charlie.

They all laughed. But still, in Eva's presence, not a word of English had passed between them and Aija felt a sense of relief that she still had James and Charlie to herself.

Charlie

Eva stayed for the rest of her cider and then left, saying she had to go home. They learnt that she had been living and working in Vaasa, a historical town five hours to the north-west of Helsinki, but had wanted to move to a larger city, a tougher city.

Charlie watched her as she spoke, aware of the way the muscles of her shoulders worked beneath the light fabric of her top, the way the outline of her nipples was visible. He sipped and pretended to listen as he thought about how long it had been since he'd been with a woman and just what he'd do if he could, just could, find his way into Eva's bed.

It had been over two years since Rachel had vanished. How much time had passed was now meaningless because he knew that even if she returned at this moment, they couldn't simply resume where they left off. His sexual desire had become so intense that some nights he had dreams so explicit that when he awoke he scanned his bedroom in embarrassment, afraid that he'd find someone in the room judging him, having seen into his dreams.

In the months after Rachel had left, his weight had started to decline, perhaps because she was not there to share meals and wine with in the evenings or for splendid English Sunday dinners. She'd never seemed to mind the bulk that accumulated as they'd grown older together. She'd always been trim, a woman who enjoyed walking and ate fruit and vegetables with gusto. Then he'd realised that losing weight wasn't as impossible as he'd always thought. He realised that the habits of his past could be jettisoned and that since he had been forced to start anew, he might as well tackle his weight.

Now with the goal of turning his life around, the weight had come off pound by slow pound. Health magazines had filled his shelves before they were turned to ash. To the surprise of those around him he'd begun to decline second cups of sugary tea, had switched to delicately sipping his wine and choosing higher-end beer after work rather than drinking fast and cheap pints for hours at a stretch.

Charlie knew that the weight he'd carried had held him back, not just physically but in the way most of his colleagues had perceived him – good at his job but fat, slow, slovenly, eating his way into a grave. It was sheer luck that he hadn't had a heart attack or developed diabetes. But then Rachel vanished.

He felt younger now as if the pounds had taken years off with them. He was no longer Charlie, the son of an English plumber from the outskirts of London who grew up in the tiny town of Loviisa. He was now a detective inspector in the Helsinki police, a runner of half marathons, a man who'd travelled, read great literature and could discuss history and philosophy. At James's book launch he'd surprised himself when he'd talked with ease with a professor and editor about the evolution of Finnish literature and where someone like James, a writer in English, stood.

Charlie considered James now with his packet of cigarettes beside the crisps. A foul habit for a young man – or rather a man younger than him – to have. This was something he could think now, but in the first months of their friendship, Charlie still used to spoon mayonnaise from a jar into his mouth. James's inertia around women, even with his success, irritated him. A pretty woman had expressed interest in him, but he did nothing. James could have asked Eva if he could walk her to her car or promised to talk to her about his book. Instead he was eating crisps from an open bag on a table and occasionally stopping to delicately lick the flavouring from his fingers. Many officers chose to have relationships with each other, if this was what was stopping James from acting, some of these worked and some were spectacular in their failure – shouting and screaming in front of colleagues, crying in the toilets and, once, a slap in the meeting room.

Aija chuckled, bringing Charlie back to the conversation. "So, you won't be sharing an office then?" she said to James who replied with silence.

"Oh, for god's sake, don't you at least think she's sexy?" demanded Hart.

"She's a colleague," Charlie defended James. "It would be uncomfortable at best."

"Unless it worked," suggested Hart. "I suppose this way we get to keep him to ourselves."

James looked in his crisp packet, found them empty and took what remained of Aija's.

Charlie knew the others gravitated around him: James probably from empathy and a certain pragmatism – they shared a language, an office and now a house. Hart because she had no one else, Aija who'd met him after Rachel left, when he'd been launched into a new life regardless of if he wanted one or not.

But somehow James was the most interesting. He'd arrived at Pasila station with an occluded history and an irritating habit of writing in notebooks. He'd worked in Espoo and Vantaa, both part of greater Helsinki, but no one from there offered any insight into this strange man. He could be funny, witty and then fall silent or wander away in the middle of a conversation. He could be attentive and then other times you wondered if he'd heard you at all.

He knew James went to dinners with writers and editors, that he saw his twin sister usually at her instigation – but after more than thirty years in Finland there were no other visible friends. After two years of companionship and working together, he'd be hard pressed to identify a single secret, any intimacy that the man would have shared with him in trust. He'd never mentioned a first girlfriend – or boyfriend – a broken heart or a sexual longing or ambition.

Even the books had come as a surprise, no one had known he was working on them. The first had been published the previous year. At an occasion when he met two of James's former colleagues from Espoo they'd said they were shocked at how he'd completely omitted them from his novel – the novel that was filled with thinly veiled caricatures of people with whom he'd worked in Helsinki – Hart, Charlie, the guy in IT who'd been caught smoking in the men's toilets twice. Not a single one of his former colleagues could be recognised among its principal or minor characters. It suggested to Charlie that James had already written them out of his life.

This was what was stopping him from asking James about Lucinda. When James had left the room earlier that day it had suggested to Charlie that James didn't want to talk. He didn't know, however, if James didn't want to talk about Lucinda or about his youth in Helsinki twenty years ago. He was also confused as to what this meant. James could give him context. Lucinda was one of a tiny population of what could have been called "expats". Her father had been a professor. Like James she'd have learnt Finnish in school. James didn't talk about the past – not that far back. Even in the shared office today, when he'd returned, he made no mention of the club – The Passion. He said nothing about other people, immigrant or other, that he'd known at the time. There could be an overlap, James could know someone who saw or did something that could lead to a break in the case.

Charlie had dared not ask but sitting here, James seemed back to his normal self.

"Wouldn't it be awful," asked Hart, as Charlie returned to their conversation, "to have James wandering around the office doe-eyed and in love?"

"Doe eyes wouldn't look good on me," James replied, in his deadpan humour. "Besides, you're the one who's always telling me that marriage is a bad idea."

"But what's wrong with her?" asked Hart, drinking down at least half of her cider. Charlie knew that Hart had learnt to handle James as well. She too knew that James, if pushed, would withdraw into himself. He could tell because she deflected the conversation. "Anyway, never mind, I feel like a wine instead. Get me one, James."

James fished his wallet from his jacket, swung in his seat and stood, exposing himself to the rain.

"How come that was so easy?" asked Charlie. "We're not at work."

This time he received no answer, James was past the point at which he wanted to communicate.

Aija called to James as he started towards the bar. "Talking to you is like wringing a dry sock, nothing comes out of it."

"Why would you wring a dry sock?" he asked as he walked away. "Anyone else for another?"

Chapter 5

Charlie

Charlie had spent the previous day tracking down former officers. Half of them claimed they couldn't remember any details other than what was on the files.

"I remember my feet hurt a lot," said an older detective called Mäkinen. "We had to write down every single thing. The superintendent was on us every afternoon reminding us. We have to make sure everything is above board. *No one should be able to say we didn't do our best – no one,* he kept saying. We interviewed all the men we could imagine knew her, every single male university student on her radar, the men at her company, in her family, her family's friends," he explained. "We took every possible route from her house asking bus and taxi drivers, taking logs and crosschecking them."

"What about the club The Passion?" asked Charlie.

"I didn't go there myself, but I'm pretty sure someone did. We went to pubs, restaurants and clubs," replied Mäkinen. "You have to remember that we were only informed after close to two days – and it was a weekend.

A place like The Passion would have been heaving with people, not everyone had CCTV like these days and we would have had no reason to believe she went there."

This seemed to be the story among the police.

We did everything we could.

No one can accuse us of not trying.

We worked day and night.

Today he had more files to go through. There were written statements taken from door-to-door canvassing and every conceivable potential witness. The files told the same story. One after another of monotonous responses: I don't know her; I haven't seen her since we graduated; who?

Two men had been arrested and released. Their responses had been consistent. Yes, they knew her but hadn't seen her since Friday at work.

As Mäkinen said, in the mid-2000s there simply wasn't as much CCTV footage.

At lunch he'd shut his computer and chewed his packed lunch without tasting a thing. Aija had been trying to generate a list of employees at The Passion, but when speaking to a former manager earlier that morning, he'd sheepishly informed them that a lot of them would not have been on an official register as employees.

"Please don't tell me you were paying them under the table," Charlie'd said as both he and Aija listened to the manager's nasal drawl on the speaker phone.

The manager chuckled. "I suppose I shouldn't tell you that I wouldn't remember ninety-nine per cent of them?"

"OK," Charlie replied. "Please send me the list of who you do have." He could hear the disappointment in his own voice.

After that let down, he felt a jolt of excitement when Aija sailed into his office, her face triumphant.

"I've been in contact with Lucinda's sister. I wanted to arrange to see her, to inform her about finding the body. But she guessed. She said there was no other reason a detective should call her." Aija leaned against the door, her eyes bright and her countenance that of someone who was very pleased with herself. "Then about five minutes later she called me and said she'd like to clarify her original statement. She says there are some details she may have omitted."

Charlie bolted upright in his chair. "She's about half an hour away," explained Aija. He'd been planning to talk to James that morning. He hadn't wanted to broach the subject at home. "Seen James?"

He too felt energised that morning. He felt optimistic, he'd smiled in satisfaction at his slowly expanding wardrobe, admired himself in the mirror and whistled as he walked downstairs. Despite the financial implications of replacing everything, even when insurance money was imminent, he felt his life falling back into place.

"No, he's out at Oodi dealing with the crazy librarians. I told him it was his fault for going there so often. Now he's stuck with them," she replied. Oodi was Helsinki's flagship library in the city centre beside the historic train station. It was an enormous wave of wood and glass that drew the eye to it regardless of one's taste or preferences. It had become a must-see for tourists who walked through it oohing and aahing as they focused cameras on its ceiling.

James had been there one afternoon. He'd described an altercation that began when a pair of librarians had started arguing in public. They were a married couple and also worked together. A few security officers had arrived to settle the matter and the husband had flashed a handgun at them in the presence of about fifty people. Absolute chaos had ensued with people running for safety and screaming in fear. When James had flashed his police identification, the man had quickly dropped the gun. Uniformed constables had arrived in minutes. However, the gun meant it was not just a matter of public nuisance and as the first detective inspector on the scene, it was his case.

He had since found himself wedged in an ongoing battle between the two that involved the library calling the station and asking directly for his intervention several times.

"Apparently, they've been causing a scene at peak hours again – scaring tourists. Hart reckons a good talking-to will get them to stop. You know community engagement – being nice to people… He didn't look very happy about it," Aija continued. She usually knew where he was, James's adjunct's position had been vacant more often than it had been filled over the past year, and Aija had ended up providing continuity.

Charlie paused, rising to leave. He glanced out the window and sighed as, despite the warmth, it was raining outside. He picked up his rain jacket. "OK, let's see what this woman has to say. What about her parents?"

"Retired and moved abroad, they don't want to talk to us. They say we disappointed them. But the sister says she'll talk to them and see if she can change their minds."

The drive seemed longer than he'd anticipated. He checked his watch every five minutes hoping that Lucinda's sister wouldn't have enough time to change her mind. This could be it – a possible new version of events could be exactly what was needed to solve what otherwise looked like a crime destined to be forever unsolved, at least by him.

Maddie, Lucinda's sister, had dark brown hair extensions and thick eyebrows and the resemblance between her and the woman in the photo of Lucinda on file was strong. Their resemblance gave Lucinda's image life, if Lucinda had lived she would have looked like this. He and Aija entered her house after she'd answered their knock with a smile and the deep breath of someone who'd been waiting, anticipating the worst.

"You're the woman I spoke to?" Maddie seemed surprised at seeing Aija.

"Yes, Detective Constable Kivinen," Aija replied, and he could tell Aija had to resist the urge to sound more challenging, as in *What were you expecting?*

"If you don't mind, my husband Markku will be with us. He's a lawyer, but he's just here as my husband." She waved away their credentials as if she fully trusted that they were who they claimed to be. The house was a standard suburban house from the late nineties. From the outside it was in perfect condition, recently refaced – a growing trend following many popular home décor and renovation shows. They entered a small rectangular entry room with space for visitors' shoes, which they kept on as they were here for work. In Finland the prevailing tradition was to take off one's shoes at the door, and she was in a pair of fabric-soled indoor shoes.

She led them through a short and narrow corridor, the walls were beige and held generic acrylic paintings, the kind from a décor chain store, the polished wood floorboards emphasised the sound of their footfall as they followed her. They passed a wall where he paused to look at a picture of her at her graduation, a framed certificate beside it. It showed she'd graduated, many years later, from the same university her sister was attending when she vanished.

The room was large with a matching settee and armchair set and more stunning but mass-produced paintings on the walls. Maddie introduced Charlie and Aija to her husband who, with a wave, signified that they should sit down on the large grey sofas that encircled a coffee table in a large kitchen diner. Family photos adorned the fridge, were blown up on the walls and were propped up on shelves. Girls in pink ballet regalia, in swimming costumes as babies. *Happy birthday, Lucinda,* a huge crescent of rainbow-coloured letters stood in a halo above Maddie with a toddler in her arms. Charlie remembered that only the day before, Maddie would have found out the fate of a sister lost twenty years earlier. She was obviously tense, flexing and unflexing her fingers and looking around the room as if it were her first time in it.

"How did she die?" Maddie asked before she'd sat down. "My imagination has been running wild. I've been imagining all sorts of scenarios. Please tell me it was quick and that she didn't feel anything."

For a moment too long Charlie was silent. "We're still waiting for details from the coroner's office," he replied, but no murder was ever quick enough or painless enough.

She stretched her fingers and flexed her jaw as if preparing to give a speech. "It's nagged me over the years, but I think I realised a while ago that it didn't make a difference. I think we, my parents and I, decided a long time ago that she was dead. The possibilities – if we imagined she was still alive – were too horrific. Her being dead was easier to deal with. This is, I suppose, better than having spent the last twenty years as a sex slave..."

"Maddie... *älä.*" *Don't,* her husband took her hand and with the other one she covered her eyes, took a deep, asthmatic breath and exhaled with her lips pursed.

"I've imagined every possible permutation of missing," she framed the word with air quotes. "I've imagined her running away to live with an Arab prince, living in a monastery in Tibet... any place and any reason she'd have for her choosing not to come back to us, hoping that wherever she was, she was happy."

"I think you should tell them and get it over with," her husband said quietly. He glanced at the two of them, his suspicion discernible in his eyes. Then he turned back to his wife and squeezed her hand as if to say *go on*.

She nodded, took another quieter deep breath. She told them about being young, fourteen, when the police came knocking, saying that Lucinda hadn't been seen in days by her friends. The friends hadn't noticed at first, assuming she was busy with her own life as they were with their own. The policeman that had come had been large, energetic, enthusiastic and seemed to have already decided that her father, brother and any other cohort of black men were in some way responsible and their women were hiding their secrets. His disappointment at their verifiable alibis had been palpable; her brother had been in Paris completing long shifts as a medical student, her father had so many witnesses to the various events he'd been at that there was no way he could have travelled all the way to where his daughter was last seen.

"Funny thing, he treated my mother and I as if there was no way a woman could have been responsible for her disappearance, or even that we could have known anything of significance." She continued after a long pause, "We were barely asked anything apart from where we'd seen her last and if she was seeing someone. Maybe if he had pushed us I would have... anyway." She exhaled. "My original statement was that I didn't know where Lucinda had gone."

Charlie nodded. He had a copy of the document in a brown paper folder on his lap. He was thirsty and the air in the room was close and had grown even more stifling even in the short space of time they'd been in it. Sunlight had broken through the clouds and lapped the windowsills, warming the room; it would continue its journey through the thin curtains and turn the room into an oven. Charlie wished himself elsewhere – not listening to a woman whose memories would be inaccurate, influenced by two decades of TV, imagination and grief. A fan stood in the corner, and he wished it could turn itself on.

"I told the police that the last time we'd talked to each other she'd been completely normal and that nothing unusual had happened," Maddie continued.

Her husband leaned forward and wove his fingers together as if ready for the police officers' responses.

"She'd been excited – expectant. She'd told me she had a boyfriend. He worked in an office somewhere in the city. She said he was introducing her to the right people, that he was connected, his dad was in business – that sort of thing. She had changed quite a bit over those last few months, she'd turned into a real lady. Mum and Dad were pleased, she'd always been a tomboy, always climbing up and down things. She loved being outdoors. Then she started shopping for nice clothes," Maddie shifted in her seat and turned her eyes to the ceiling, "she even started dressing up even if she was just going to work."

From the corner of his eye, Charlie saw Aija adjust her position in the chair. He could see a trickle of sweat forming along her hairline and running down the side of her face.

"Mum used to say, whoever he was, he had to be from a good family, how else could he turn her into a lady? Dad just said she was a late bloomer. I remember we had a family wedding, and everyone just admired her and her clothes, like it wasn't the same person who'd come to another wedding in a pair of jeans and floral shirt."

"And you had no idea who he was?" Charlie asked gently. "Was she deliberately hiding him?"

Maddie looked at her husband, who looked to the floor. "Yes. You see–" She looked embarrassed for a moment, then continued, still avoiding eye contact. "Our parents didn't like us to go out with boys," she paused, "of other races."

Charlie was caught by surprise, Maddie was fairer-skinned than Aija, still clearly of Black African origin, but to his eyes she looked like a melange of colours, or races, or whatever his police sensitivity training had told him was the correct terminology. Her husband was white, Finnish, and the pictures across the walls showed children who were a blend of the two.

"I know," Maddie said, glancing at Aija, "it sounds odd. But they hated the idea of us choosing men that would dilute our heritage." Then she looked away. "My dad couldn't walk past a mixed-race couple without sneering. It was what they wanted to know all the time. We didn't even have posters on our walls of white pop stars. Lucinda told them that she was interested in a Kenyan man, and that he could only meet them when they were sure it was serious, that it was their tradition."

Charlie ran his finger along the file on his lap. Back then, the mention of a possible boyfriend, a black man, had been made. But no one, none of her friends, had been able to verify it. Two or three young black male students at the University of Helsinki and a university of applied sciences had been questioned, but the police had found nothing, not even a description to pursue.

"She phoned that afternoon. It was a Friday and we chatted. I didn't have a mobile yet, so she called home and whoever was there answered. It just happened to be me. She said she had a great night planned. He was taking her to some dinner party, this might be the one where he would finally tell everyone that they were dating." She crossed her legs. "I think I realised then that he'd been a man she wanted rather than a relationship she already had. She told me I would obviously be a bridesmaid when she married him. I was a romantic and it sounded heavenly."

Charlie nodded, not wanting to interrupt her.

"When she disappeared, I kept quiet. I didn't want her to get in trouble – which sounds strange since she was missing. But it made perfect sense to me at the time. By the time I realised she was gone, properly gone, no one was interested anymore. I was completely convinced that she was coming back – there was no reason why she shouldn't come back. There was no reason..."

With that she burst into tears.

"Thank you, Maddie," Aija said and slid forward to the edge of her seat, closing the gap between them, but not touching her. "It must be hard for you."

"To be clear," began Charlie gently, "when you say a boyfriend from an office... You mean he had a job?"

"Yes," Maddie looked up at him. "I don't think I ever told anyone that. Everyone thought he was a student like her. She liked him because when we came here she was already well into her teens, Finnish was really hard for her. This guy was English or possibly American, or, I don't know, Irish – she liked the fact that he was like us – whatever that meant. He wasn't black or Kenyan. That I know."

"Was he much older?"

When all she did was exhale heavily, he continued, "Can you tell us anything else at all? Any details that could point us in the right direction?"

Maddie looked at her husband as she spoke, "I didn't get the impression that he was much older, he did the same kind of stuff, clubbing and going to pubs. Once we were out at Itäkeskus and she pointed at some guy and said, 'Look, that's a friend of his,' and I looked over and saw a blond. Very blond, very tall – I can't remember anything special or notable about him. But again, I had no reason to remember him at the time."

The conversation came to an end soon, there was no line of questioning he could think of that could spark a concrete, useful recollection. She seemed to understand that if she'd mentioned this to the police twenty years ago it would have been useful, something that could have steered them in the right direction.

They walked back to the car after finishing their tea and saying their goodbyes.

"Young guy with a job in an office," Aija repeated Maddie's description.

"First thoughts?" He could only speculate, "He could be anywhere in the world now. I wouldn't stick around if I killed someone."

"I can't get over the fact that she couldn't tell anyone about her boyfriend because of his colour," Aija said. She shook her head as if in disgust. "But really, Maddie's testimony doesn't add much."

"Well," Charlie began, clawing for something helpful to say, "let's try to look on the positive side. We know that these people she hung out with were foreign. You might not be old enough to remember, but, once upon a time, that wasn't so common in Helsinki."

James

James tried hard not to glare at the couple. He even forced a smile onto his face which flickered and then waned.

He and a constable stood outdoors in front of Oodi, attracting glances from passers-by, with their uniform and his vest clearly identifying them as police.

It was the same as last time so far. She had accused her husband of involvement with illegal trade in antiquities and he accused her of drug smuggling. When James pointed out that their accusations were strangely similar to the plot of an episode of a popular TV series, they abandoned their claims and each accused the other of gaslighting.

They accused each other of cheating and James was forced to listen to them because each time the well-meaning staff at Helsinki's most renowned library called, they asked for him. He couldn't ignore them, the husband had been charged with illegally possessing a weapon and was waiting for a court date. He was meant to stay away from work, she too worked at Oodi and he'd followed her here.

He was a librarian and spoke in a measured baritone, almost like a character on TV. He seemed unflappable – the Finnish stereotype or rather caricature – incapable of vivid displays of emotion. He was neat, his facial hair and fingernails clipped short and his clothes casual yet perfectly laundered and ironed. He didn't have a history of violence, his colleagues didn't know he owned a gun and had been shocked when he brandished one in front of them.

She looked as if she'd started her day tidy, but in her hysterics, as the staff had called them, her clothes had come loose, and now, while the rest of them shielded themselves from the rain under the overhang of building, she remained where the rain could get her.

It was difficult to believe that the behaviour they'd described had come from her. She was composed despite her shoulders starting to show the strain.

"Again, Mrs Saunela." He sighed heavily. His boredom evident. "It really isn't in the public's best interest for you to be causing a scene at a library as well known as Oodi."

"I wasn't making a scene," she replied. "I was making a point – erm, James." This was their third meeting. She was speaking to him in English, he was sure, as some sort of power play over her husband. In English, she could speak down to her husband as if showing that James was on her side. When the couple were together, James had repeatedly steered the conversation back to Finnish and for his efforts, she corrected minor errors with his suffixes and offered suggestions with his word choices like a teacher. People like her were a constant reminder that his language skills held him back, that he would always be marked as foreign. He thought for a moment about Charlie's case, Lucinda. Twenty years ago he wouldn't have imagined he'd be a detective.

When he finally separated them, she immediately returned to English, saying, "My husband is a drug dealer, he's an abuser, and he's with an underage girl."

It was a new accusation. But he knew to always listen. Trust came slowly and sometimes painfully and when someone trusted him they often said more than they had initially.

This couple weren't saying what the problem was. Their discord was a public performance, but the real reason they hated each other didn't come out in the shouting and screaming. He couldn't understand why their conflict was only revealed here at work and according to the police files neither had made a complaint or caused a scene at home or in their private life.

"She's seventeen, can you believe?"

His interest dissolved. Unsavoury as the age discrepancy was, seventeen was not legally underage. "Who is she? Do you know?" he asked anyway.

"No," she shook her head.

"Mrs Saunela, have you considered seeing someone? A counsellor perhaps?" Hart had told him to be nice and had reminded him that the welfare of the tourists was paramount.

"For what?"

He had no idea. To help her leave him perhaps.

"He has too much money..." she declared, jutting out her chin, "and he spends it all on..." Here her veneer cracked for just a moment. Then with a deep breath, she continued in a deeper, more authoritative voice, "I moved all the way here for this. Look at him. He's a librarian and thinks he's James Bond."

James considered the large apple jam-filled doughnut he was going to pick up from the supermarket at Postitalo, which was less than a minute's walk away from Oodi.

"Where did you move here from? If I may ask."

"Ivalo," she replied. "I was happy there."

It was a couple of hundred euros a ticket enough to deter most people from flying. It was perhaps fourteen hours by road. It was far away.

"Look, I can't fix your marriage. But I can look into this drug thing."

She looked a little more cheerful.

"But please could you not take your anger out on your husband at Oodi again. The staff want you banned as well…"

"I know the tourists get frightened."

"What about at home?" he asked. "Are you safe?"

She shrugged.

The rain was getting worse and he was hungry. She was confusing. She seemed intelligent. She was a woman capable of extreme swings in emotion – she could be lying about her husband or telling the truth. She raised her hand to touch her hair and he caught a glimpse of her bare flesh between her blouse and the top of her skirt – no bruising or evidence of violence there or anywhere else.

"So if you tell the constable absolutely everything that you know, I promise I'll follow up on it." He was already backing away as she nodded. He spoke briefly to the constable and then was about to ask the husband to leave the area when James asked, "Are you OK?"

"Of course," he barked back.

That didn't surprise him.

When the Saunelas had walked away he typed his notes into the police system. These two needed watching – he suggested a complicated domestic situation and that it required an investigation.

Then he walked in the direction of Rautatientori, the central railway station, dodging the clusters of damp tourists and office workers, the mother and baby groups and construction workers, and through the doors of the supermarket where a doughnut was waiting.

James's mood brightened when he found Aija and Charlie in their office.

"How are your librarians?" asked Aija.

"Each one claims the other is either mad, on drugs, or in some sort of illicit relationship, but at least no weapons again."

"Do you think he would have used it or he was just a time waster?" asked Aija.

"Not necessarily," he bit into his second iced doughnut of the day.

"Is that lunch?" Charlie asked.

James nodded and ignored the question. "They seemed to think I'm either a friend or general complaints department. I understand her anger; she came all the way here from Ivalo for someone who turns out to be a complete fool."

"As opposed to staying in the same place for a complete fool," said Aija.

"Very funny," he answered in a voice that said it was anything but funny and continued. "Anyway, we have to keep following them up. The last thing we need is some kindergartener being trampled over. She's pretty adamant that he's some sort of evil villain and wants us to investigate but can't offer any real evidence. Anyway," he said, waving the matter away with a hand, "tell me about your adventures – far more interesting than mine." He reached forward and tugged a file from Charlie's desk without asking. Their case drew him and repelled him simultaneously. It happened at a time of his life he preferred not to think about.

"Her sister has changed her testimony," explained Aija. "It's still not very helpful."

"Now she claims Lucinda talked about running off with a guy who had an office job, that she never did date a Kenyan man. And that's all she knows," replied Charlie who made no objection to James reading the file without asking.

"So a young foreign, English-speaking man in Helsinki," James contributed an unhelpful observation. "That could be hundreds of possible suspects, especially if you consider the big tech company that employed dozens upon dozens of foreigners. And that's if you only consider those who were actually foreign, what about if they were like you, part Finnish, or had lived abroad long enough to seem foreign?" He saw Charlie lean back, showing frustration at his line of inquiry. "Did she give any physical description other than European? Fat, thin, blond?"

Charlie shook his head and ran his hand through his thick brown hair. "He had a tall blond friend."

"Maybe she meant you," offered Aija, who was now leaning against the doorjamb.

The two of them turned to look at her.

"White male, university, here in Helsinki, twenty years ago – a job?" She shrugged. "That's you to a T. And not to be unpleasant..." implying she would be, "but the first description of you I'd give is white."

"Are you allowed to say that?" asked Charlie, in jest. "I don't want to end up in another multi-, inter-, or intra-, take-your-pick, cultural training course – that's two days of my life I won't get back."

"At least you didn't get into an argument about if you are or aren't African," said James.

"That was priceless," Aija chuckled. He and Aija had needled the trainer without respite when the trainer had tried to discuss identities. It hadn't been malicious, but pure fun. Afterwards he and Aija had laughed about it like students who'd played a trick on a teacher.

Like with almost every other training they took, unless they left it with practical skills, these attempts to change their attitudes to sex, gender, or race went largely unheeded. In his opinion, no one on the force ever became less racist or more mindful as a result of having signed up for a class just to fulfil their professional training obligations. Listening to other officers, especially at social events when they'd had a few drinks each, provided him with fodder for Merimies's perspectives on the world; there were men who believed it was their right to hit a woman, female officers who believed women should return to abusers, and a good many of either sex who believed that people of other colours were different – at the least. James had his main character speak opinions held as truths he'd overheard in men's bathrooms, in corridors by female officers sipping lukewarm coffee and foreign-born IT specialists who believed Finnish citizenship was of such value that not just any would-be migrant should be allowed it.

"It's a different perspective," James explained now. "Aija's saying that, as a black woman, the first thing she'd note about me is my colour. Where I grew up, one of the first things you'd use to describe someone is their colour – James the white guy, or the guy who looks Indian – it's not an insult – it's a descriptor. And when it comes to black people – people were described as fair, dark, really, really dark, or even black. I suppose in Finland everyone was pretty much the same shade of paper white."

Charlie was watching him. "Says the platinum blond to the brunet." He pointed to his own hair. "At least I can tan."

Aija chuckled and then grew serious. "Because Lucinda was afraid of how her parents would see this boyfriend because of his race, no one knows who he could be, and, because her sister was equally afraid, the police spent their time chasing Kenyans. Oh, and of course this suited the police nicely because it pandered to their own prejudices."

Hart walked past the glass front of their cubicle, Eva in tow. Hart glanced at them and frowned while continuing to speak to Eva, who seemed thoroughly engrossed in their conversation. Hart was almost exactly as her avatar was in his novel, complex people were far more interesting to him. It was virtually impossible to discern what lay beneath her veneer. As always her clothes were perfectly fitted and not a hair was out of place, sometimes it was possible to see shadows under her eyes as if she'd had trouble sleeping but one would only see them if you watched carefully, like while she briefed them on cull policy changes or obligatory upcoming events.

Eva was the opposite. James tried not to show how little he liked her. Usually, it was that he liked a woman, but he found himself unable to move. Frozen. It hadn't always been like that, but this is how it was now. Once upon a time he'd found it easy to initiate relationships – brief relationships – but that seemed so long ago.

He hadn't considered himself promiscuous at the time. He'd have preferred to call himself free, unfettered, young with prospects and in a country where issues such as AIDS and violence were minor compared to the country he'd left. Sometimes he wandered the streets at night, just because he could. Helsinki's violence, while it existed, was mild, and when it happened, it leapt out at you unexpectedly, it wasn't the norm.

"I went through Eva's file," said Aija. "Her list of achievements was, erm, lengthy. You'd think she's eradicated crime in the western world."

James swivelled around to her and focused. "Jealous?"

She slapped the file down on his desk and said nothing.

"So, Lucinda... what else have we got?" Charlie slid forward in his chair, signalling that they should begin.

Chapter 6

James

James strode up the few steps into an apartment block that had once been a warehouse many lifetimes ago. A toneless, rhythmless noise was beating within his temples. Dehydration, hunger, he speculated, wishing he'd had more than a cup of tea before abandoning his desk to get to the incident as fast as he could.

There was always the chance that it wasn't a suicide – and that chance was what piqued his attention. However, in his years on the job, when he had been called to a suspected suicide it had always been a suicide, except where, once, it had been an amateur attempt to stage a suicide as a murder. There were far more suicides than murders in his jurisdiction. Sure, suicides offered their own complexities: the reasons why someone took their own life could be as varied and complex as the reasons why someone killed another person. But murders were, to him, far more exciting.

He arrived at the old building which had a completely refurbished exterior. Its brick walls spoke of it having been a factory at least a century old. It was prominent in its stature, a monolith that once would have taken central place on the landscape. Now, from where it stood, new construction – bland and repetitive blocks of flats – stood across the road from it on one side and a stream ran along the other.

Police tape surrounded the building and police cars blocked entry to the site. The building's surroundings were impeccably cared for, in front and on both sides, what once would have been a delivery area had been turned into a large grassy lawn.

He saw Charlie's car parked among the distinct blue-and-white service vehicles. This was supposed to be his case, in terms of official seniority neither he nor Charlie were above each other. But Charlie had many more years on the force, the other police officers deferred to his years and experience, and perhaps they liked Charlie a bit more than they did him.

The dispatcher hadn't been descriptive, James had little idea what he was going to find. Now he knew he'd find Charlie, going over the body with the forensics team, his shrinking frame replacing his former image of an ageing detective with a new energy and athleticism. James knew that somewhere during this exchange over the body, James would have to assert his position and Charlie would have to find another case to solve.

It was humid and uncomfortable and the muggy warmth made him feel queasy. It was only mid-morning, but he was sweating in the light rain jacket which he had to wear since the rain was not easing. He'd underestimated the rain like many other people across the city. Across the country a heatwave was supposedly imminent but seemed to be constantly delayed. Every forecaster had been predicting for days that by now they'd have had record-breaking temperatures. But day after day the rain persisted, never heavy, never substantial but seemingly endless. The office was now stifling, dominated by sweat-stained armpits amid the ripening smell of people working in insufficient air conditioning.

He entered the ground-floor corridor and found the door to the flat open. He saw the blood first and took a quick breath but continued. It was spattered throughout the living area of a large loft with five- or six-metre-high ceilings. The TV was shattered, showing the most blood and brain matter. James deduced that the victim would have been facing away from it when he killed himself. A neighbour had called the police, he'd been in the corridor going past the front door at the moment the shot rang. The apartments were mostly empty of their tenants, as it was an ordinary working day.

The pathologist would have already moved the body to help her work, behind her two dark-suited men stood hands in pockets seeming impervious to the sight of the flesh, blood and other body parts. Aside from them two policemen were in the room, one standing without any particular task and the other poring over the shelves of books and ornaments – they were waiting for instructions from James. A police photographer was packing away his equipment.

Someone somewhere had lost a family member that afternoon, in the body's presence he took a moment, a fleeting instant to lower his head in respect. In the cacophony around him, his mind calmed as it spoke a send-off to the dead, though he wasn't sure that there was a place where a soul would be suspended, waiting for someone to help them on their way.

The pathologist was Camilla, as usual. "Ah, you're here!" she announced as if she hadn't been expecting him. This told him Charlie had already started the investigation without him.

Charlie appeared just over her shoulder pointing at a detail of the body. "Morning, James, something to bring up your breakfast."

James stared at the body, the dead man's face coming into focus and then fading out. He felt his stomach lurch and at least had the wherewithal to race through the open door into the grassy knoll to retch, little coming out of his long-empty stomach.

When finished, he wiped his mouth off and tried to straighten, only to see the world swimming around him. He leaned against a tree trunk and slid to the ground, wiping his mouth with the last of a packet of tissues in his pocket.

He had no idea how long he sat there, incapacitated. Each time he tried to compose himself to return to the scene a wave of pain attacked his gut and rendered him immobile.

Why was Gerry lying on his living room floor dead, his brains blown out of his head?

"You all right?" came Charlie's concerned voice through the haze the morning had become. Charlie had his hands behind his back, standing like a professor in conversation. James eyed his stance, trying to imagine its significance.

"Don't know what came over me," James replied, trying to regain his composure. "Teach me to come to a suicide without breakfast." He hesitated, his stomach tight and his brain still swimming, he tried to stand and almost lost his balance, having to clutch Charlie's arm for support.

"Sorry," he coughed.

"You know the victim?"

"A little," James replied quickly, lying, "from years and years ago."

"Name is Gerald Venter. Are you sure it's him? Are you sure there isn't a conflict of interest?"

"Not particularly." He had to expand it, "I didn't even know he lived here."

"You wouldn't call yourself friends or wouldn't have a close relationship of any kind?" Charlie's concern was gone and had been replaced with an authoritative, almost interrogative, tone.

James shook his head, his tongue thick with thirst. A constable passed her head back glugging a bottle of water. He watched her drink it.

"I have to ask you again, are you sure there's no conflict of interest?"

"Why?" he asked louder, pushing back just a little more. He had work to do, he had to find out why this happened.

"Then do you know why he would have this on him?" Charlie raised a photo, showing him the back, small, neat handwriting in black marker saying something he couldn't read from his vantage point. He reached for it but Charlie snatched it back as if not wanting James to touch it. "The suicide note on the back says..." It was as if he was prevaricating, going around an unpleasant task. He read it out like a schoolboy caught in class with a filthy book and made to read it out to the class: *"I'm sorry and goodbye. I will always love you."*

He turned the photo over to reveal a picture of him, James, taken from a distance, standing outside a bakery pondering the products in the window. His shirt was blue and green from his last half marathon, the first of that spring only a few months earlier. In the image, he was a willowy figure standing with his hands in his pockets, sunglasses on – if he had seen this photo in any other context, he'd have thought it a flattering picture. He had no idea that Gerry still felt so strongly about him that he'd take a photo like that and address, what they could take as, a suicide note to him.

"Like I said," he thrust his hands in his pockets. "No conflict of interest."

"I don't think you should go back inside," insisted Charlie as James turned to do just that.

"It's my case," James drew himself up taller than Charlie. "I'll have a bit of water and I'm on it. Thanks for getting started, I'll pick it up from here."

"No." Charlie's voice rose just as Chief Superintendent Hart arrived, driven by a constable.

"Why did you call Hart?" he bristled.

"I didn't." Charlie shook his head, and James would've believed him had Hart's arrival not been so conveniently timed.

They walked towards her. "It's my case," declared James before Hart could speak.

"Only if I say so." She held up her phone, an image of the photo Charlie still held clear on it.

James spun around and then turned back to Hart. "Are you going to drink that?" He eyed a bottle of water in the crook of her arm, still with a plastic wrap around its lid indicating that it hadn't been opened. She handed it to him, and he ripped it open and drank half in swift gulps. His trembling stopped and his stomach began to calm down.

Charlie and Hart waited for him to speak.

"It's the suicide of someone I once knew. That is not personal involvement, especially when our personnel are otherwise engaged."

"Sorry, we can't afford to shortcut on this, apparently the family have a bit of money."

"Is that all that gets a case any attention these days?" demanded James.

"Watch it," warned Hart in a low angry hiss, meeting his gaze from where she reached in heels at his shoulder. He retracted his glare in lieu of an apology.

"Do you know why he's done this?"

"I told you I haven't seen him for years – well, not really." He tempered his statement, because Charlie was a good policeman and would find out that he had.

"But he's seen you really recently." Charlie waved the picture at him.

James glared at Hart hoping that she would intervene. She turned away from them both, folded her arms and was surveying the crime scene.

"This man was stalking a police officer." Charlie sounded almost gleeful. "I want to be one hundred per cent clear that all it is is a broken heart and nothing bigger."

James could feel a tension mounting in his head and the urge to smoke overtook him. He patted his pockets and felt nothing, somewhere in the rush to get here he'd left them behind. He clenched his hands into fists and insisted. "Then it's my murder, you already have Lucinda to deal with."

"Sir," said the constable he'd seen indoors, approaching Charlie, "there's something you should see."

James frowned. He could see that a decision had been made without him, she seemed to have no doubt about Charlie's authority in this case.

"Look, I have to insist on this one." Charlie spoke to Hart in a low voice. He was hiding something from him, James could tell. "James can't keep an open mind on this, someone he knows has possibly committed suicide or been killed. If nothing else this might be traumatic."

"I'm a big boy, I'll say what's traumatic," James replied, wanting the argument to end but his anger towards Charlie growing. He had to find out what had happened here, if only it was to confirm that it was a suicide. "This is my case," he insisted, fighting to keep calm.

There was a stalemate. Charlie, James and Hart all stood, him with his arms crossed, hers clasped behind her back and Charlie's in his pockets.

All he could do was scowl, like a teenager.

"Hart, we have to talk first." Charlie pointed towards the building, "James, could you just hang on a bit?"

James took a step forward, but Hart stopped him with an open palm.

"You'll have to convince me," she said to Charlie then turned to James, "You stay here."

He paused, without any intention to do as she said.

"First, is this actually a suicide?" Hart was asking as the two of them walked away.

James gave them a few moments. Only when he saw them inside through the window did he follow their tracks, not bothering to check if they had seen him. Once in Gerry's flat, he saw that they had walked in the direction of the bedroom, where an officer was giving Hart an overview of the flat.

His heart began to thud. The other officers seemed oblivious to his presence. He wandered through what was an exclusive building with every fitting pristine. Gerry's family would have ensured that he was comfortable, though he had his own income. They had been wealthy, perhaps not obscenely wealthy, but they would have had the expectation of life in renovated century-old buildings in Helsinki's Old Munkkiniemi.

Aside from Gerry's body and blood, what he could see of the flat was tidy. The furniture was mismatched and lacking a discernible style. A tufted brown sofa held court in the centre of the room, with several armchairs dotted in corners and beside a door. The floor was plain and unadorned, as were the walls. Gerry had left a small shelf of books. They were mostly bestselling genres, fast and easily digestible, thrillers, spy novels and a smattering of pornographic literature. James recalled having tried to read titles such as these at Gerry's behest, shaking his head at the smooth chests and low-slung trousers of their semi-nude cover models before laughing through the implausible plots and explaining to Gerry that no, they did nothing for him.

James stopped at the first thing that he recognised, a fridge magnet, trite and silly. A buxom woman in a gondola holding a balloon-sized glass of wine. James had bought it. The vendor had latched onto him – repeating himself, gesticulating, telling him that he was such a polite young man – that he preferred to just buy the damned thing rather than argue. It was the same one – chipped in exactly the right place. Once it had been on his fridge in the small one-roomed flat he'd rented after university. At some point it had disappeared, he'd never imagined it had found its way here – to Gerry.

"You, out," called Camilla from where she stood. Her smile was brief and obscured what was probably real anger at the prospect of him contaminating the crime scene. Still, he thought, it was unusual for Camilla to talk to him like that.

She turned back to her work picking through pieces of a dead man with precision and care. He got to the door, felt for his cigarettes again, took a final look at the room and left.

Charlie

Charlie guided Hart through the incident scene. He'd arrived here before James. He knew that James was meant to attend, but he'd been only minutes away and he wanted a peek at the case knowing that James would politely hint at him to leave and he would – he had no desire to encroach upon his friend's ambit.

Hart was looking around with the care of a professional who knew that details mattered. He wanted to hurry her along to where it *really* mattered but at the same time to seem normal and unhurried.

"Oh good, you got here," said Camilla. "You can't let James on the case."

"You'll have to give me a good reason." Hart's lips were pursed and brow furrowed.

He led Hart around the scene.

"The place is awash with fingerprints and most likely DNA," he explained. "This place had its fair share of guests apparently. I've told the team to focus on anything in less social places, where most people don't go during a gettogether – the pantry, laundry, private bathroom, walk-in wardrobe. I'm not suggesting that the killer made himself a snack, but they might have been more intimate guests."

Hart nodded, her expression one of patience.

Charlie glanced behind himself to ensure everyone, including James, was out of reach.

"It seemed like a suicide at first appearance," he explained to her, "but we're pretty sure it's not so clear cut. We're just treading around James. I'll show you Venter's bedroom first and you'll see why."

They went down a short corridor and past an open bathroom. Each room was enormous, as if the architect hadn't known what to do with all the space at their disposal.

Everything in the room seemed in its place, almost as if he'd been a visitor in his own home. But then again he recalled how he'd often slept on his own sofa when getting in the huge bed he and Rachel had owned made him feel sick and empty.

Hart pulled on her latex gloves as she looked around the room, keeping any observations she made to herself. He nodded to a notebook that was neatly laid along with other books beside Venter's bed. "That's about where the team found it. Camilla had flicked through and sounded the alarm, so to speak."

Hart picked it up, and, after a few pages, her forehead creased and she squinted at its contents.

"Has James seen this?" she asked as she carefully continued through the pages.

"No. You can see why. It's all about him."

"So, did they have some kind of relationship?" she asked, stopping at an image in which James was in the city with several books under his arm and a cigarette in his mouth. Another showed him at a café table writing in one of his usual notebooks.

They were mostly mundane photos, Charlie noted, that captured nothing of note. It worked backwards. The first pages were newer images of James, some with traces of other people that had been cut out. Some were taken in bars, at restaurants, and a few were taken from local and international websites and newspapers. Venter had glued in an article showing a commendation James once had in the paper. As time went in reverse it became interspersed with older pictures preceding James's literary career. James getting younger. The difference was that most of the older photos seemed to be on printer paper, one or two showed borders and splices of text that suggested they were most likely from social media, some were still on photo stock but there were fewer of these as it went back.

"He insists they have mutual friends, nothing else."

"They aren't in any of the photos together. This Venter's some kind of a stalker," she suggested.

"Not quite," he trailed off.

Hart glared at him. He could see her suspicions rising. "We're way past the days when being gay will be cause for anything more than a bit of gossip, and maybe a little bullying, but if he's involved with a suicide or murder…" she paused… "so then, what have I missed?"

"Skip a few pages," he nodded at the book.

"It's as if he recently stepped up his surveillance," she said, referring to the book as she flipped through it. "He'd been keeping an odd one here and there and then more recently… James's publicity could have stirred up some feelings." She stopped.

"There." Charlie pointed, drawing her attention to a picture that he'd almost overlooked himself. "Remember I told you that we were not going to have any luck with the twenty-year-old case."

Hart peered at the dog-eared colour photograph. A group of about ten people stood in it in what appeared to be a bar. Some of them were focused facing the camera, others looked left or right causing their faces to be partially obscured. The dead man was in it, he seemed to have been the focus of the photo, he was in the centre and everyone else was moving around him.

"There's James." Charlie pointed at the figure, thinner and lankier than he was now, his clothes probably at the height of fashion when it was taken – his hair was longer than it was now, the curls James so religiously tamed falling loosely over his forehead.

"That's her, isn't it?" Hart pointed to a woman facing the camera in a relaxed yet intentional pose. Her hand was on her hip and she was inches from James.

Charlie nodded. "Lucinda."

Hart looked through the window in the direction of parked police cars where they could see James now standing at his vehicle.

"We've been working on her case for nearly two days now. We share an office; we've discussed the case. Her picture has been on my board for twenty-four hours, and he's shown no indication that he recognises her, no acknowledgement at all." Charlie paced slowly towards Hart and away.

"What do you want to do? You can't officially question James in connection with a murder case, it might get to NBI – an internal investigation. And that lot can be brutal. Can't you just talk to him, as friends?" She used the all-too-familiar acronym of the National Bureau of Investigation who probed suspicions of wrongdoing in the police service.

"That's precisely why I can't talk to him. He'll run me around in circles. The man managed to write an entire novel about a racist, violent officer..." Charlie bent down to the pile of books and handed her James's second novel.

"Well, obviously he'd have read it, if he was in love with him," mused Hart.

"Like this?" He watched her as she flicked through the battered pages. The second book in the series had only been available for two weeks, yet this looked as if it had been read and reread, folded and manipulated. Venter had annotated many of its pages, but the handwriting was tiny and impossible to decipher. On its inside title page it was signed *To Gerry, from James, To the good old days*. And then the date – two weeks ago – and Helsinki.

"So they have met recently, this looks like it's from a book signing – it's not too personal. If he knows anything, we must get it out of him." Hart continued squinting at the handwriting.

"He'll clam up," said Charlie.

"That's James," she said and almost smiled.

"That's why I want *you* to talk to him."

She bit her lower lip. "Do you really want to apply that kind of pressure so early on?"

He stopped in front of her. "This girl's been in an unmarked grave for twenty years, this is not early on. Her family and friends are waiting for an answer." He took a few paces away. "And he has to stay off both cases."

Hart's expression was grave, her brow furrowed and she tapped her upper lip with her index finger. He wondered if this was just hesitation or reluctance.

"I promised him a good case, he's going to be annoyed. He's suggested that I didn't like his portrayal of me in his latest book." She inhaled through gritted teeth. "I'm fine seeing myself as a sex-mad widow bent on having an orgy."

Even in the same house as a mutilated corpse, he had to suppress a smile.

"Right. I'll get back to my office. Send me some notes and the picture," she spoke briskly and authoritatively, "I guess we should be prepared for if he does know the girl. And Charlie," she said, looking him straight in the eye, "you know the need for discretion more than anyone else."

Charlie stopped where he stood.

"There was a lot of waiting when we should have moved, and we gave leeway where there should have been none," she continued. "In the end you proved you were worth us sticking our necks out for."

"Yes, I appreciate..." He drew himself up to full height, but Hart was not a woman who took any notice of attempts at self-assertion. She knew how to make a man feel small even if he was a full head taller than her.

"It's not a question of whether you appreciate it or not, I'm asking you show your colleague the same consideration." The implication was clear in her eyes.

She peered at the picture again, showing she wasn't interested in an answer, then slammed the book shut and handed it to him.

Someone had said to him, when Rachel's case was still fresh in everyone's minds, it'll never go away. It'll always be there seething beneath the surface waiting to be used against you. *Thank you, Rachel, you bitch,* he thought.

"James is my friend..." he began.

"So you shouldn't be on this case, but you are. It won't look good to outsiders." She put her gloved hand on the door handle. Then she tutted. "It's not even a good picture of him, he looks drunk."

Charlie nodded. "But Venter has kept this photo for nearly two decades. It meant something to him."

Charlie was standing outside the flat when he noticed her in the tiny clutch of people that had formed outside the police tape. These were the kind of people who at that time of the morning had little else to do. They could afford to stop to watch the goings-on at a crime scene. He knew that the digital age had accelerated the speed at which news of a murder travelled, all the crowd needed was a hint, to merely overhear a sentence that any one of the officers at the scene let slip and it would be broadcast over every social media app, no matter what appeals the police made for common sense and restraint regarding a case.

He'd seen her before, at a dinner, a Burns Night. Burns Night was one of those occasions when a horde of people with little or no interest in Robert Burns gathered to eat haggis and recite the one poem by him they knew. It was about being foreign, the crowd was predominantly British, a few were actually Scottish, and the rest were made up of people who saw themselves as, or aspired to be anglophile, international being the term that now was used as well as expat in recent years. In this way they hinted that after years in the country they had no real interest in integration.

He hadn't spoken to her – he hadn't even been introduced, but she made herself easy to remember. She'd been hard to miss with her dark bouffant curls and deep red lipstick. He'd noticed her because he'd been regretting having attended the function. In the years he'd been with Rachel, he hadn't bothered with public displays of Englishness other than sport and the monarchy. But it had been his first year after she'd left, he was standing in a room of people most of whom he knew only a little, feeling heavy, old, and abandoned. He hadn't even thought of crossing a throng of people to speak to her, and when a man arrived and kissed her on the lips it was a relief and he felt he could return to his loneliness.

He got to her now just as James did. At that moment she was explaining to a constable that she was leaving but she asked in accented Finnish, "Is it true Gerry's dead?"

The officer responded that she wasn't at liberty to say, tiny rivulets of water ran down the sides of her face, her uniform was not designed to keep her cool and dry, wet weather had been understood as cold – Helsinki was not known for warm and wet days. The constable was brusque and visibly impatient and didn't even look at the woman as she replied.

"Do you know the occupant of...?" Charlie began also in Finnish, but James came to a stop by his shoulder. *Of course she did.* Burns Night had been one of their first nights out together. James had suggested they go because the drink was plentiful and he'd received free tickets from his parents, who had decided to decamp to warmer climes that winter. In such a small circle, it was highly likely that she knew James.

"His neighbour called, he's distraught. He thought I should know immediately, since we're friends." She looked at neither of them as she talked, instead she spoke to the air between him and James in English now, her Irish accent distinct.

"When did you last speak to him?" he asked.

"Yesterday, I called about us going out for drinks," she replied.

"And what did he say?"

"Well, nothing really. Just 'yeah, whatever'," she explained vaguely. "Did he really kill himself?"

"Would you find that hard to believe?" asked Charlie.

A heavy sigh was her answer. It told him whatever they needed to know. To so many friends and family, suicide came as a surprise because they hadn't considered it. They'd assumed their friend would always struggle, that he would always be a little bit down but would inevitably get up again.

"We'd prefer to ensure that there's no doubt at all about the cause of his death," said Charlie. This was true, that even if it were a suicide, it wouldn't be the first time someone had been coerced into killing themselves, gaslighted or tricked.

"Could I have your name?"

"Chloe Foreman," she replied with a touch of reticence. She was dressed to be noticed even when attending the death of a friend. Her raincoat, a luxury Finnish brand, was buttoned up to her neck and she held a wood-handled umbrella over herself. The hem of her dark blue skirt or dress ended at her calves and she wore high platform ankle boots.

"And how did you know him?"

"Gerry," she breathed his name. "I've known him since we were kids, well, almost teenagers. We went to the same school. He's had a tough time this past few years, his marriage broke up. But he was doing OK."

Her posture shaken, she pulled out a cigarette and held it to James. "Light?"

He obliged. James had been silent as she spoke, but his reaction was so swift and natural that it confirmed Charlie's suspicions that they knew each other.

"I can believe he killed himself, I don't want to, but I can. It was his sexuality – he hated himself. He spent all the time trying to fight it – even his parents accepted him, but he couldn't." She looked at James as if he could confirm what she said.

Once he returned his lighter to his pocket, James stood rigidly again. Charlie watched him from the corner of his eye. He couldn't understand the nature of this relationship – he'd swept over to her as if he wanted to say or do something, but whatever that was hadn't happened.

"Could there have been an outside factor that caused it to happen now, at this point, something that pushed him over the edge?"

"Maybe the people around him just weren't there?" A sad smile flickered. "Maybe they just couldn't deal with the misery just then. Maybe if he had waited a few days, they'd have been ready again."

Charlie was sure she was surreptitiously suggesting this about James.

"But you can't be sure?" James enunciated his question carefully and she glanced at him initially with surprise and then with something else – disgust maybe? James met her gaze.

"Look, I have to go. I want to tell my husband. They were friends too. If you need anything more from me, anything about Gerry, please don't hesitate to call." Her smile told Charlie little other than that she was in abject misery.

Charlie turned abruptly at a thud in the direction of the crime scene. He saw some constables congregating near the front door and took a few steps towards them in case the noise was of some significance to the case. When he saw them helping up a fallen colleague he turned back to Chloe to find her encircled in James's arms, her head resting against his chest and his hand on her back.

It was longer than a moment. Then James let her go and Charlie saw her lips move but couldn't make out what she whispered. She waved at him in a brief, abrupt motion as she walked away. James turned his back to her, walking towards Charlie, and he didn't glance back.

When James reached him, Charlie said, "That's not exactly behaviour I expect from DI at a crime scene."

"It's not my case, remember," replied James.

"You two know each other?" he asked. A flicker of James's brows confessed yes.

"And the deceased?"

"Catch up with you at the office." James fumbled through his pockets for a cigarette, lit it and sauntered towards his car, flicking ash along the way.

James

Driving home, he turned the sound up on the radio. A measured sensible female voice spoke to the world, asking *what is it that makes us human?*. He focused on her voice as the air-conditioning blew a pathetic stream of lukewarm air through his car, lowering the temperature just enough that he did not vomit again.

Still, by the time he got home he was trembling in a mix of hunger and misery. He jerked his fridge door open and drained half a plastic bottle of Fanta, feeling the surge of sugar coursing through him, resetting his equilibrium – his physical equilibrium – though his mind remained in turmoil.

He hadn't tried to go back to the office, despite having told Charlie that that was his plan. He couldn't stroll into a building of hundreds of people and pretend that he was all right. The image of Gerry's body, what remained of it, replayed in his head. Flesh and bone splayed across his living room staining its walls and floor.

James had never once been in that flat, he had no idea how long ago Gerry had moved in. Gerry had been flamboyant once. He'd dressed himself in bright prints and, as they played video games in his mother's sitting room, he'd lamented the dull beige armchairs and floral arrangements that were meant to mimic the homes in magazines such as *English Homes and Gardens*.

He wiped his dry eyes.

Even here, he dared not cry. Charlie could reappear at any moment. James had told him that he barely knew Gerry. This was true but it hadn't always been true. He knew he wouldn't be able to explain himself to Charlie and he didn't want to.

He chewed a sandwich made of margarine on white bread without tasting it while fighting back surges of unhappiness. *What happened?* He'd always assumed that he had time, that their friendship, friendships if you counted Chloe, would at some point be repaired. He just hadn't known how to fix what was broken, he wasn't sure how it had broken.

All he knew was that they'd drifted apart over time, each interaction becoming more and more awkward and unsatisfying. Until when crossing Aleksanterinkatu, or in a bar on Iso Roba, neither would approach the other, both of them satisfied with a nod or a wave.

James had been taken by surprise when Gerry had appeared at his book launch two weeks earlier. He'd been signing copies while dressed to his best in trousers and a buttoned shirt by an upcoming Nordic designer – feeling watched by his guests in the room, especially those with connections to the press. The publicist had chosen the location in a newly renovated bar and restaurant, with pale ash and white ceramic panelling. It was the kind of place that had probably given her a discount in the expectation that it would be mentioned in the book's publicity.

The evening was open to invited guests first for cocktails. After an hour the book-buying public had arrived – some having waited outside glancing through the window, umbrellas blocking each other's views. This was bigger than his last book, significantly bigger. The projected sales were high and his advance had been too. Because his market was global he was making money that only the biggest Finnish writers could imagine.

The *lingua franca* of the evening was English, but little groups coalesced speaking Finnish. His conversations in either language were perfunctory. These situations always felt awkward despite his having been in so many. They wanted to ask questions which were either tested and well-worn or were so novel that they could repeat the answers to their friends afterwards. *Are the characters really based on people you work with? How do I get in one of your books? How do you write such a misogynist character if you're not one yourself?*

"Well, obviously they are," declared Hart when the person behind her asked. "I work with him, I recognise half the people in it."

This allowed him to leave that group and wait for the next to call for his attention.

Chloe had swanned through and given him a kiss on the cheek and stepped back immediately. Her husband had a book in his hand and giving him a clap on the back asked him to sign it and to make it count. He nodded in satisfaction with an "Alan, you'd better read this or else…" then his name signed in full instead of his usual signature.

"For when he's proper famous." He grinned at his wife. "I'll flog it."

Chloe had offered vague undefined lines such as "We're so proud of you," and "I can't believe you're probably going to be the biggest thing in Finland." But when Alan moved on, so did she. This is what their friendship had been reduced to.

Charlie and Aija had appeared, Aija looking unusually sophisticated in a mini dress while Charlie could easily have been her partner. He grinned at them and they waved, Aija pointed at the wine and mouthed something that could have been, "Be there in a minute".

Gerry had come up to him, a brand-new copy of his book with a receipt wedged within it.

"Excuse me," the publicist had said to Gerry, "there's a queue."

"No, it's OK," James intervened. "An old friend." He'd taken the book and after a flicker of emotion he'd scribbled *"to Gerry,"* and then hesitating, *"To the good old days."*

"That's so cool," the publicist breathed, having read the missive over his shoulder. He handed the book back to Gerry who'd opened it to the inscription and visibly winced.

"Have you known each other a really long...?" she began, but Gerry's eyes were watery with either drink or emotion or both, he'd muttered a quick "bye" at James, and he turned and stumbled away.

"The star of the show," Aija said as she and Charlie joined him where he stood debating whether he should or shouldn't go after Gerry. The publicist smiled at Aija, looking at her from top to toe, simultaneously radiating disapproval.

"Seems half the office has shown up," said Charlie. "All waiting to see if they're in the book. Aija's betting that I get killed off in this one – far too honest and reasonable, she says."

The doorbell rang and James spun on his stool, his heart thudding. He sat hoping whoever it was would leave. But they rang again. His car was parked in front of the house making it obvious that he was home. He walked towards the door, his shoes not allowing him to be silent. He peered through the glass and saw Aija, looking around with a stack of paper.

He rubbed his eyes and face as if it could erase the emotion from them.

"It's for Charlie," she explained and held the paper out to him. "To sign."

He could have just taken them from her, but he didn't. "Come in." He gestured for her to go inside.

Aija

When Aija had returned to the office earlier that day another plain-clothes officer had waited until she'd sat down and then spun in her chair to face her and informed her that Hart was looking for her. Aija had sighed in irritation and strode across the office and knocked. When summoned in she found Hart holding a folder. She held it out to Aija.

"I want you to go to James's house, say this is for Charlie, and just check what state James is in," said Hart.

"Why not just wait until Charlie or James comes back here?" Aija asked, receiving a glare in return, which she interpreted to mean *just do it*.

"Because the point of it is to see how James is."

Still suspicious of her mission, she continued, "Why does he need someone to see how he is?"

"I have my reasons." Hart crossed her arms.

"How do you know he's at home?" To Aija the idea seemed ludicrous.

For this she received a raised brow.

"You're having him followed?" Aija's jaw dropped. "Is that...?"

Hart dismissed the question. "Try to gauge his mood, is he unhappy, tense..."

"James? Why can't Charlie?"

"So many questions," she replied in a sing-song voice like a teacher. "Anyway, you know him almost as well as Charlie."

Aija felt a flutter in her stomach and opened her mouth to speak.

"You have a husband." Hart leaned in towards her. "Don't throw it away in the hope that James will notice you."

"I wouldn't..." she began but then changed her mind. It had probably never occurred to her that anything could really happen with James.

Hart sat back in her chair, the parcel between them.

"How are things with Matti?"

"Perfect," Aija replied immediately. She meant it, "but he's just so far away." She knew emotional honesty with Hart was always a precarious venture, but somehow she'd become accustomed to the verbal slaps in the face Hart occasionally administered. Never being able to predict her response was where the real tension lay.

"Then go to him." Hart implied that there could be no other conclusion.

"But my job..."

"You're not that good at it anyway. Go and have babies. By the time you come back they'll be old enough for you to come straight back to work." Hart leaned back and folded her arms, radiating pride in her advice.

"I hadn't thought of it that way."

"Do it," Hart said pushed the parcel towards her. "So that in twenty years when he dumps you for a younger model at least you have the kids. Police work will only get you so far, there's a lot of competition and they only allow so much room for women. It's like the army, it's one of those things men aren't ready to give up in the name of equality."

Aija squinted at her leader. "You know," she dared, "I thought that you cared." She picked up the file, waiting for the retort.

"I might," Hart said and gave a mean smile, reminding Aija of a monster in a children's film, "If I did, I wouldn't get cuddly about it. Now go."

Aija accepted her task, knowing she didn't have a choice. She passed people in the corridor, nodding mechanically at their greetings and pulling a smile at the cleaner who always wanted to stop to chat with her, waiting for his opportunity to insert innuendo into even the most mundane discussion.

As she drove she seethed. She was feigning a parcel delivery during working hours just because Hart wouldn't check on her staff herself.

But then who else could do it? She, by virtue of her relationship with Charlie and James, had a far different relationship with Hart than most of the people in the office. There were some officers she was sure Hart wouldn't know their names. They would stand, four of them in either Charlie or Hart's office, and have conversations that had nothing to do with work. She knew for instance that Hart had been through a horrific divorce a year earlier. While she didn't know the details, few others had been privy to statements such as "this is what you get for dedicating yourself to some madman for twenty years". Even through Hart's crisis, the impression Aija received from most of the staff was that they hadn't noticed, that Hart had continued as always, reliably manipulative and perhaps a little cruel.

"This is lovely." She admired the large open-plan room to which James led her. It was bright and modern, strangely like what she imagined he'd live in – completely unlike Charlie's now burned-down house. Its style matched the clothes he wore and the kind of bars and restaurants that he liked to try. It had, in her opinion, been decorated by someone else, with him inserting only hints of his own personality, like the brutal-looking cactus in the corner and the chipped mug that declared he was The World's Best Uncle from which he was drinking his tea.

"No swastikas or mutilated bodies to be seen," he said, but it was superficial humour. His face was expressionless and distant, and his cheeks noticeably hollowed as if he'd aged since that morning when she'd seen him last.

Her lips fluttered in a smile.

"Are you OK?" she asked, knowing he would lie if he answered at all.

Opening the sliding doors seemed to take him a great deal of concentration, he unlocked them and slid them open with a forced precision.

"Did you use a designer? I've always wanted to have a put-together palate, get the whole apartment put together in one go." She slid onto one of the barstools at the kitchen peninsula.

"My sister," he replied, filling a kettle. "Cheaper."

"Hart wants to know if you're all right," she pointed at the file. "This was my disguise – delivery person."

He put her tea in front of her, hot and black, and pushed a sugar bowl beside her as he filled half his cup with hot milk and added boiling water to the rest. He stirred his tea as if he hadn't heard her.

"Why do you write your books?" She was almost never alone with him and since she'd finished his new book, the question had started to nag at her. "Not your publicity reason, your real reason."

He shrugged. "Money."

That wasn't true, she could tell; the answer had come out too quickly and easily.

"You know I'm not going to tell you," he said after she'd fixed her eyes on him as if staring at him would cause him to confess as it did with suspects, but it didn't seem to.

"In your book your hero is a violent, misogynist policeman – an absolutely awful person. Why?"

"It's fiction, Aija," he replied dryly. "The question is why does anyone read it?"

"But you make yourself look like a killer in police uniform. It's you – to us who know you. The way you drink your tea, the food you eat – he's tall and thin. But the violence and the misogyny – is that you too?" She gripped her mug at the question.

"My character's Finnish, it can't be me."

"That's a very convenient cover. A Finn who spent many years abroad – in South Africa."

"Am I that transparent?" He smiled vaguely.

"You probably are, but luckily no one's really looking. At least not from the right angle." She became acutely aware that she was with James alone in his house. One of his character's more questionable acts was to seduce a fellow officer, letting her believe he was a nice man, misunderstood by everyone, but then leaves her after only a few encounters, and she realises she's lucky to have escaped him.

"Do you," she asked, "want to hit people and hurt them?"

"Finland abolished the death penalty eighty years ago. When you catch someone who's drugged a fourteen year-old and repeatedly raped her, don't you wish even just for a moment that you could have it back just for a week so the world would be rid of them?" he asked.

"We all do. Sometimes jail time doesn't feel like justice – but most of the time I'm proud of what we do have."

"I'd never kill someone no matter how I hated what he'd done – but Merimies would."

"An alter ego," she suggested, but he continued to drink his tea as if he was no longer interested.

She knew her questions were the same ones many people asked. But they asked them in public, in front of others. They asked the wrong person – addressing a superstar writer and sometimes policeman, a white superstar writer with an odd accent. There was no way that James could answer, that person didn't exist.

James was an immigrant, unlike her. Though many people called her that. She'd been born here. Her mother had been a student in a Savo town, who'd refused to move to an African country which had been at war. Her father had stayed for a while, a man who strutted underdressed for the brutal winter determined that his clothes be seen. He'd disappeared when she was five, sending the occasional message, never saying where he was or what he was doing.

She'd only travelled to a few holiday destinations, London, Spain. She'd never packed everything she owned and moved to a place she'd never even visited. James would have known another life before arriving here. He'd mentioned, rather than talked of, having lived on a farm and then in a city only briefly before moving to Finland.

It had taken her a while to like him. She'd found him sullen, prone to occasional humour which, since it was unexpected, she found a little frightening. Besides, when she'd confessed to herself, Matti had been in Singapore for not very long when they'd met and she'd still found herself treading lightly among men who she could have considered attractive. After eight years with Matti, she was adrift, still learning what it meant to be a woman away from her man, sleeping and awaking alone again, moving through life without the immediate prospect of sex. Her conversations with Matti were still too cheerful, they acted as if the distance could be disregarded, as if the few months until they saw each other didn't really matter.

When she'd seen James at her first evening at Charlie's former home she'd found herself gravitating towards him feeling, perhaps, overwhelmed by the others who were older, who spoke with confident authentic accents from America, England and Canada, whose speech identified them as being from specific places with a history and culture of which English was a part. Some of them had travelled the world on the sheer strength of "native English". They strutted about in the Finnish world in a way that migrants from other language backgrounds couldn't. Most migrants in the country were Russian and Somali speakers – yet English dominated. She'd come across many English speakers who had lived in the country for years and never learned Finnish – calling themselves expats as opposed to immigrants. That would have been impossible for anyone else.

She could, right now, join Matti in Singapore. She could be an expat too. But she had never seriously considered leaving the country wherein she was raised for something like Matti and James were doing, living abroad without a return in sight.

She took a deep breath, bringing herself back into James's pristine kitchen, and took a copy of his latest book from her bag. Matti had asked her to buy him a copy and get it signed. He called the lead character's violence "an articulation of common unspoken sentiment" and pronounced it "a bloody good book". He couldn't see why she was making such a fuss.

"Who am I?" She'd practised at home, and even outside on the porch as she waited for him to answer the door. She'd tried other variations such as "Where am I?" and "Am I in it somewhere?"

Not even Matti had noticed her absence from the books. Even when they'd discussed the earlier book and Aija had pointed out Charlie; strong and upright, Hart; principled yet devious, and Camilla the pathologist;

efficient and promiscuous, Matti hadn't asked, "What about you?"

She'd read both books twice, the omission glaringly obvious to her. She'd been assigned to work with Charlie for two years, a great deal of that time had meant picking up after the stream of James's adjuncts that came and went, some after as little as a month. How many afterwork drinks had they had, how many microwave pizzas and cups of tea had they consumed in the office as they pored over the details of their work?

How was she so invisible to him when he saw her nearly every day?

It was bad enough that he'd written a ninety-thousand-word book without even mentioning her, but the fact that no one else seemed to notice she was missing hurt even more.

He signed the book, taking a moment to think of something, as her eyes again flitted over the room, looking at his life – books, furniture, looking for clues about the man who wrote those books, who she was discovering how little she knew about him.

He handed her back the book and she slipped it back in her bag.

They talked about a new film, and about Don in IT who was a blatant sexist with a wife and two girlfriends, and that living with Charlie was easy because he was so tidy. He told her that she'd be bored in Singapore after a week, but if she had enough money it might not be too bad after all. He claimed it was a lie, travel didn't broaden the mind, in fact it made you cling to what you believed even more dearly.

"Are you serious?" She laughed, holding out her cup for a refill.

"Maybe?" he replied. "Or maybe I just don't want you to leave."

He turned to the kettle and poured the tea with his back to her. As she watched him she became rigid with worry. If he didn't want her to leave, perhaps he was going to tell her something important – why, though he was trying, he didn't seem like himself.

She realised know she knew none of James's secrets – though she called herself his friend. What if he was about to come on to her? She suppressed her panic as he returned a newly refilled cup of tea and asked if she wanted a biscuit.

Talking to James had been the last task she'd been assigned with for the day. She read a message that Hart had sent her an hour later.

Well?

He's OK, she replied, because she couldn't explain what was wrong.

Chapter 7

Aija

Charlie waved at her as he entered Hart's office. She arrived at her desk feeling surprisingly fresh and cheery. After James's, she'd gone home and sipped alcohol-free wine and listened to music. She'd spoken to her husband just enough to tell him that she'd got him a signed copy and he'd loudly whispered "yes" and punched the air.

"It's just a book," she scolded and then realised that James had written *All the best in Singapore, we'll see you when you get back?* in English. She wondered what he'd meant by using a question mark.

She tapped the pile of paperwork on her desk and, smiling, attacked it.

Among the files she noticed that Charlie had been assigned an additional case – the suicide of a man called Gerald Venter, though he hadn't updated her on it. She'd been looking up The Passion club. She'd spoken to several former employees and had managed to get absolutely nowhere. None of them recognised Lucinda or could recall any incidents of note from that time period.

"There weren't that many black women during that time," said a former bar man named Sampo who now owned a sandwich café in an affluent suburb. "One that young would have had the bouncers on her thinking she was a hooker."

"And you're sure they weren't on her?" Aija had asked.

"I remember the case very well. It had quite a bit of publicity for those of us in night life. The police were in and out asking questions. Half the–" he cleared his throat– "unofficial staff went underground. Most of them were just students or you know, topping up their benefits. I can't recall any significant incidents involving any of them."

She smiled at a colleague as he passed and made a middling comment about it looking as if the sun might finally come out. She then began looking into Venter's history. Venter didn't have a criminal file, so she put his name through Google. LinkedIn gave the outline of a professional in communications and his profile picture showed a blond who looked older than his age, slightly battered as if the photographer had caught him by surprise. His work history only went back to university and under languages it listed that Finnish, English and Afrikaans were of native or professional proficiency. She flinched at the mention of Afrikaans.

He seemed to have been married at some point, she learnt as she scrolled through his intermittently updated Facebook profile. Despite all the new trends in social media, many older people still kept Facebook accounts that now stretched back over a decade. She didn't have access to his friends list, but he had one hundred. She scrolled through the posts. He was tagged in several photos of people in Johannesburg and Durban though there were no pictures of him in those places.

Her eye stopped at a Dolly Grey. She knew James had a sister – a twin sister – called Dolly. Aija's heart began to beat just a little faster as she scrolled. Was James here somewhere, a mere click from a recent suicide? Clicking on the picture, Dolly's resemblance to her brother was unmistakable – she looked like him without being masculine. She was darker than he was. In fact she was almost Aija's complexion. Nonetheless, her hair was so perfectly blonde and straight that it looked as if it cost a great deal to be so brilliant.

The little of her page that Aija could access was interesting, filled with references to her sons, their school, holidays taken once upon a time. A few pictures in Cape Town where she'd posted that she was with their parents and *"having so much fun!"*.

LOOK WHAT I FOUND! someone typed in uppercase letters years ago.

She looked at the picture and a smile erupted on her face. Two children aged about eight. One was Dolly, a head of dark curls, and the other undoubtedly James, his hair a mass of thick blond corkscrew afro curls, bigger and curlier than now. The two had obviously been outdoors playing, their faces were smudged and dirty, they looked as if they had been irritated by the photographer intrusion.

The person who posted was hidden behind algorithms and whatever it was that only allowed a few images of her to come through, encircled by a frame saying *I stand with Ukraine*. Her name was too common to bring back any usable results. Smiling at her find, she took a screenshot in case the image disappeared, and she chuckled when she made a note to tell James about the picture when she saw him next.

Realising she had to get back to work, she went back to Gerry's wife who had remarried and lived in Sodankylä in Lapland. Aija thought it strange that the woman was now married to a bin collector after years with a wealthy urbanite. She looked at her picture, it showed a small, perhaps Asian, woman in very plain clothes – slightly faded black jeans and a floral T-shirt. She made her assumptions about the woman – had she been a holiday bride? She knew she was supposed to be past racial profiling, having known prejudice because of her own appearance should have meant that she wouldn't do the same to anyone else. But she did, she told herself and shook her head, annoyed at herself.

Without any directions from Charlie, she clicked to a file on Lucinda's case. Charlie hadn't added anything new to the case that she had to respond to so she decided to spend a little time updating her other files before returning to Lucinda again.

She was in the more common world of stolen expensive bikes, warring spouses and teens that had absconded with the family silver when Charlie returned with his hands stuffed in his pockets and his brow intensely furrowed. He spoke before he smiled, "Sorry, I didn't file our new case – had a bunch of things to chase up for Hart."

Then he leaned against her desk and seemed to relax. "I hear you came to visit."

She nodded, turning towards him. "Just some stuff I had to clear up with James," she lied. She'd stayed until early evening. Being summer it was easy to forget, to simply stay because darkness didn't mark the evening. She couldn't remember what they'd talked about, but the time had passed just as easily as if they were among a group.

"No sign of him getting his own sergeant?" asked Charlie.

"I've given up dreaming about it," she replied, smiling and glancing at the desk that had been standing empty for the best part of year.

"So, Venter, at first appearance a suicide yesterday. But now we've got fingerprints from the gun. Someone called Declan Linehan."

"What do you think it is, duelling Englishmen?" she asked, looking at where he'd written the name down. She'd never been to England, and most of what she knew about it came from the books and detective series on TV.

"It's an Irish name," he corrected her. "His file says Finnish and UK citizenship. Don't know – maybe they argued over the football."

"Maybe you should be taken off the case," she suggested, though it was clear she was joking, "common ancestry or something?"

"No more than you have an interest in every case that involves a person from Mikkeli. Anyway, you should have seen this Venter's flat. Even the soap was expensive."

"Is there a strong possibility then that it's not a suicide?" She returned to the case at hand.

"Well, it could be that Linehan just helped him get the gun and has nothing to do with the suicide itself. But he'd still have to answer for the gun," said Charlie, grabbing his jacket. "Come on, we'll catch up in the car."

Linehan's file had shown a picture of a man who'd had too much to drink and insufficient sleep before driving into a tree – not fast enough that anyone had been hurt.

He'd slapped a policeman and ended up in court and had to pay a small fine.

They'd called at his office first, that's where he was meant to be according to his office hours, but it was hard to know where someone would be – so many people worked from home, from cafés and libraries. They didn't want to call to make an appointment, it would give him too much time to prepare himself, if not to abscond completely.

The building was a renovated Jugend building in Punavuori, one of the oldest and most elegant parts of the city. It had high ceilings and all its signage was in English. It was the kind of place Aija had interned. But work in an office had bored her and after a month of selling something she could barely remember, she failed her targets and left.

"Can I help you?" The assistant addressed them in English with a distinct Finnish accent. Aija didn't have to ask why.

She immediately replied in Finnish, showing her identification and asking for Linehan.

With a smirk and a perfunctory glance at her screen, the woman said, "It's Thursday, he's working from home. Can I take a message? He wouldn't like us to give out his home address."

"We already have it," said Aija. "We expected to find him here."

"What's he done now?" She was obviously supressing a smile.

"What did he do last time?" Charlie asked.

"A punch-up because he fondled a guy in accounts. His husband was threatening to report him to the police, but I think he was convinced not to with a gift."

"You don't like him?" asked Charlie.

"No." She glanced around as if checking her surroundings for an eavesdropper. "It's a job, you don't get to be choosey in this market." She pulled herself up to sit erect, sucking in her stomach as she explained, "If you find a reason to keep him out of here I'm happy. He'll be at home right now, then he'll meet some stupid friends for brunch – sorry, networking – at..." She glanced at some handwritten notes and gave them the name of the café.

They thanked her and left, and Aija remarked to Charlie how dull it must be to work in an office year upon year.

"It's been so long since I've done anything other than police work, I can't imagine what it must be like – smiling and saying hello to people," he replied. "It's another world – working in the profit-making world."

They arrived at Linehan's address which wasn't far off and also in Punavuori, where he was at the door, mobile in hand as they'd knocked. He was in a bright blue Hawaiian print shirt and linen shorts that came to his knees revealing thick legs. His windblown hair was brown, bordering on red, and he had stubble across his chin.

Aija looked at him and immediately disliked him. She could too easily imagine him molesting a colleague. He scowled at their identification and strutted ahead of them down a short corridor and waved them into a living room.

Don't be so prejudiced, she reminded herself, *give him a chance.*

Charlie

Declan Linehan was without doubt one of the men in the photograph taken from Venter's diary. He was twenty years older, it showed in a face that had filled out and hardened. His hair had thinned and hairline had begun to recede. Glancing back in time, Charlie reckoned when he was Linehan's age, he must have looked older – he'd certainly been heavier, his face would have been red with stress and alcohol.

"Charlie?" he asked as so many did as he squinted at the name and glanced at Aija, who perhaps seemed less interesting. "I hope this doesn't take too long; I'm meeting friends," he proclaimed in English as if challenging Charlie to fulfil what his name promised – to not be Finnish.

"This is in connection with the death of Gerald Venter," explained Aija, as Charlie looked around the room and at the man himself.

"Really?" he asked, his eyebrows raised.

Charlie had noticed that his shirt had two small rips just below the armpit and it was lightly worn down in several places. He glanced around the room.

The flat was in one of the best parts of Helsinki, yet its interior was disappointing. The room was unforgivingly bland. A bookshelf dominated the room and was too neatly organised to be his reading of choice. Large block-like coffee table books in black and white with the names of famous designers were placed where a visitor would be sure to notice them. The sofa he sat on had a large sheep's wool throw. The chair looked uncomfortable, with a back that was too straight and narrow arm rests. They knew his father's business had collapsed years ago. His degree was incomplete, his job blandly described on LinkedIn, but this flat was not cheap. Charlie guessed it could have been a gift or somehow survived the businesses's collapse, perhaps it had already been handed over to him. He'd been taken care of despite his family's financial misfortunes.

"I understand you and Mr Venter were friends?" he asked, repeating the information Aija had given him.

"Yes, Gerry and I have – had – known each other for ages." He looked down and tapped the table with his index finger. "Since we started uni."

"Which university?"

"University of Helsinki. I moved here during high school. And yes, I did it all in Finnish."

His accent was an English, public school accent, upper middle-class yet devoid of any regional identifiers like the accents in the quaint villages in England. He could have been from anywhere. Had they met under different circumstances, in a pub perhaps, he'd have been interested in what brought him here.

"Can you think of anyone with a reason to hurt Mr Venter?"

"So, it is murder." He was suddenly wide-eyed and excited. "I thought it was just another rumour. Do you know who did it?"

"Do you know how to use a gun?"

"Yes." He didn't elaborate. Almost all Finnish males undertook national service, with the majority completing the armed stream, but it was hard to say what path a person with an international background like him would have taken. He could also have taken the civilian route; they'd have to find out what skills he had with guns.

"Could you tell us where you were between five and seven in the morning yesterday?" Charlie asked.

"Who remembers that long ago?" Linehan asked in a cheery voice. Then he looked at them, first at Aija then Charlie, then back at Aija. "What are you suggesting?" With indignation and annoyance in his face, he swung around to the kitchen. He poured from a large rum bottle and took a dramatic gulp.

"Please, could you not have another one of those." Charlie's request came firmly as Linehan raised the bottle to refill the glass. Despite how the films made it appear, it was generally only alcoholics who took large gulps of booze upon being confronted. Linehan must have been a man who was used to alcohol as a coping mechanism. Most guilty people he'd dealt with, no matter how hard they tried, showed some kind of discomfort – they tried too hard to be normal. To shoot a man in the head and then act as if absolutely nothing was wrong would be difficult, but then again hands shaking like Linehan's could be fear of being found out, simply fear or simply alcohol.

"I have nothing to do with Gerry's death." His voice was rising and his face flushing. "Gerry was my friend. How can you accuse me of killing him?" He looked at their complacent faces.

He slammed the glass down on the counter with force. It didn't shatter, but the sound seemed to surprise him. "I was at home, here. I don't have a witness. I woke up. I was at work by nine – I had a meeting. But I don't have an alibi – I don't need one." He shook himself and stood straight.

"When were you last at Gerry's flat?" Aija asked.

"A few weeks ago, first time in months. Chloe had organised a fundraiser and Gerry's apartment is perfect for such stuff. The last few times I've been with him it's been at bars or parties."

"Your fingerprints place you at the crime scene," Charlie said. "Would you mind if Kivinen has a look around?" He gestured at Aija to look through the house as Linehan was too flustered to respond.

He didn't object as Aija asked, "May I?" politely and without waiting for a response went back through the corridor to begin a general sweep of the flat.

"Your fingerprints are on his gun, we are assuming a connection."

"Oh yeah," Linehan exhaled loudly. "The gun. We were just playing around with it. It was new, he only got it a few..." Then he faltered. "Oh god." He stopped.

Once Aija was out of sight, Charlie took out a copy of the photo from Venter's flat. Aija hadn't seen it yet. The file was now in his lowest desk drawer out of her or anyone else's sight, and he hadn't typed in all the case's details on his computer, he knew she'd look.

"When was this taken?"

He showed Linehan the photo. In the photo he was younger of course but still clearly identifiable.

Linehan squinted at it. "What's this got to do with...?"

"Please." Charlie clenched his jaw, aware that Aija might walk back in. "Just answer the question."

"At a bar, I guess. Yes, a bar." He shrugged. "Just a bunch of people I hung out with after uni, for a few years. Must be more than twenty years ago. I don't know. Oh yes, Mac's been in Australia for seventeen years, I saw him celebrate on Facebook." He pointed at the shortest man in the picture.

"What about this woman?" Charlie pointed at Lucinda.

Linehan shook his head.

"She disappeared and her body was recently retrieved," said Charlie.

Linehan looked blank.

"It was in the news." Charlie tried to nudge his memory. "She was American."

"I don't usually follow the news," Linehan replied, slowly enunciating each word.

"Although the case was twenty years ago, there was quite a fuss then. What do you know about her disappearance? Or didn't you follow the news then either?"

"I remember a woman disappearing at the time. But nothing really special," he replied. His fingertips had gone to his mouth, and he'd begun to chew his nails. "I remember the fuss. A little. If you hadn't shown me that picture, I'd never have thought of her at all. When she disappeared, for us it was 'oh, that's sad' and we continued our lives... well, not as normal... but we continued."

"You weren't affected by her disappearance then?"

"No." He wrinkled his nose as if the very idea was distasteful. "No, we had other things going on in our lives. It was like I was in a perpetual state of not knowing where I was. My dad had lost all our money, my mum was running off with some Swedish prince, and I... at least I had my friends. We partied, drank, not as much as we could have, but we weren't saints." He began to get agitated. "Oh god, those were crazy times." He stood still, staring at his feet.

"What about the others in the picture? Venter?"

"Gerry? Like I said, we were all having our issues. Nothing specific that I can remember. He'd just come back, he'd gone to work in London after uni – claimed it wasn't his thing. He just wasn't tough enough for London. He'd tried to get us to all go with him. His dad had found him a job with some contacts. Well, I didn't know what I'd do in London... Chloe–" he pointed at her in the image– "said she wouldn't live in a cubicle, and JJ went to Argentina to live on a ranch – he'd just come back from some cheese course."

"Chloe Foreman?" Charlie asked, glancing back at a noise, but Aija was still out of sight. The woman in the photo was unrecognisable as the woman he'd met the previous day; this girl was slight with straight blonde hair whereas now she was larger, buxom and dark-haired.

"Do you remember who took the photo?" he asked.

"Just someone. It was Gerry's camera. I remember, he'd just got a new digital camera. We asked someone near us. We had been drinking, but we weren't fall-down drunk. I don't remember the rest of them – if I ever even knew them. Crazy days." He smiled unsteadily again.

He made no specific reference to James, but Charlie didn't want to push it – he didn't want to show any particular interest in him, he'd prefer it if Linehan showed recognition himself.

"So just to recap, you didn't know the missing girl and you were not recently at Venter's flat?"

He stumbled over the words, "Not exactly, I've been to Venter's, you know, for a chat and cup of tea, maybe a few times in the last, erm, couple of weeks. Look, to be honest, we're always in and out of there – Chloe always finds some reason." He stopped.

"Disagreements, arguments?"

"Well. No..." His hesitation made his lie obvious.

"Mr Linehan," Charlie said as Aija returned, "I'd like you to come down to the station for an interview," he began. "Your testimony has been inconsistent. I believe it would be useful if we got it recorded."

"You can't arrest me," his voice began to rise, "I've got enough... Please don't. If people see me being driven away in a cop car, it'll be the end of me."

"I'm not arresting you, I'm asking you to answer a few questions," Charlie assured him in a soothing voice. "Perhaps you could pop in this afternoon, you can take your own transport so there would be no issue with being seen. Just so we can clear up questions about your whereabouts. It'll give you some time to think first. Maybe you'll remember something you'd forgotten."

He flicked a smile. Linehan remained tense.

When they returned to the station, Charlie went straight to the office he shared with James, if for nothing more than to seek moving air from the fan James had carried in that morning. Fans were like gold in this weather, with the shops selling out an instrument that not many years ago had been impossible to find in ordinary shops – it was never hot enough to need one.

He glanced over at James who'd muttered something that could have been read as hello, his face obscured by his screen. They'd seen each other the previous night. It had been impossible to tell then what James was thinking or feeling. He'd been smoking more cigarettes than usual and he'd opened a book and put it down again repeatedly and he'd eaten his dinner slowly – so he wasn't his usual self but didn't appear to be particularly distressed or annoyed.

This morning things seemed the same as always, James asked for advice, updated him on the minor cases he was dealing with, and offered him a biscuit from a packet. But he didn't offer any insight into the suicide of someone he had known for at least twenty years and who had clear links with people he knew. And that too was unlike him: he showed no interest in the case. He didn't saunter past Aija's desk to look at case files over her shoulder, he didn't put his feet up on his desk and quiz Charlie on where he thought the case was going and what new information he'd found.

Charlie saw Hart entering her office and he went after her, knowing he couldn't discuss the case with James in the room.

"There you are," she said as if she'd been looking for him. "Fill me in."

He sat down in a guest chair as she made herself comfortable in her large leather executive chair. He gave her a brief outline of his encounter with Linehan that morning.

"Linehan knows something," he tapped his foot as he explained. "But he's not telling. Insists they were all party people and couldn't remember anything of note."

"There are plenty of young killers," she said, waving a hand at the obvious. "Does he have a good alibi? Says here in an old case file he said he was at a party and then left the next morning for home. Since we can't pin the girl's death down to a particular time or place it makes it even more difficult. All we know is she was alive around about that time. She could have been held somewhere and killed days after. We're already ahead of the original investigation. At that time all they knew was Lucinda's whereabouts were accounted for until Friday night, when she was supposed to meet someone – we now know that might have been wishful thinking. We have the ticket for the club, a body, and this photo taken at about the right time and she's in it. Venter and Linehan have given us the first clues about who was around her near the time of her disappearance."

Hart began tapping her fingers against her armrests.

"Linehan listed the group members he remembers but claims he's either forgotten or never knew James. He looked straight at his picture and refused to acknowledge him. Hard to believe considering that he's stayed in Helsinki all these years. There weren't as many foreigners twenty years ago and James is famous now, the least he would have done is show surprise at being in a same picture as him. Anyway, he's coming in for an interview today."

"What about Venter's death?" asked Hart.

"Venter kept that photo for a reason. Guilt? Evidence? His involvement could have driven him to his eventual suicide."

"There is DNA all over the flat, but only Venter's and Linehan's fingerprints on the gun. He says they were playing with it. He's admitted to being in Venter's flat numerous times but there was only so much I had time to get out of him. I had to take Aija in consideration."

"I don't know," Hart spoke to the air, tugging at an earlobe. Her facade was only barely cracking in the humidity; her lipstick had smudged outside the lip line and a thin bead of sweat sat atop her upper lip. "It just seems so," she paused, "easy."

"Easy?" Charlie crossed his legs and for a moment felt offended. "What do you mean?"

"Linehan tried to pretend it was a suicide but left his prints on the gun. Why not clean the gun? Anyone who's watched any half-decent TV show will know that."

"Maybe it is simple. Most killings are," suggested Charlie. "Money, jealousy..."

"But if Linehan has anything to do with James, then it isn't simple," said Hart. "Twenty years is a long time for at least three people to keep a secret."

"Look." Charlie's eyes were fixed on her. "I've known James for years. He may have shown an odd side of himself with this book, but that's just..."

"Just what?" Hart spoke in a deliberate, measured tone, a teacher challenging her student to clarify his assertion.

"Mid-life crisis, I don't know," he replied. "What I do know is that he is a decent guy. This crime took place twenty years ago and I know for sure that James would not have anything to do with this."

"When I read his book, the first thing I realised was how little I know him after these years," explained Hart. "There's a lot of violence packed into there. I'm trusting that he's the man I know now. But what if he hasn't always been this man, what if he was once the kind of person who'd kill a woman?"

"Then I will find him out," declared Charlie, vexed by her calm. "I know you want to insinuate that my judgement will be affected by our friendship, but I am not about to throw my career away now. I've given up a lot to be here." He faltered on the last few words, stopping himself from continuing.

A slow blink from her showed she understood.

He leaned back in the chair.

"About Rachel," she said after a moment, "you did the right thing."

"Of course I did."

"And everybody knows it," she continued. "We're not clapping or patting you on the back every morning, but we all know that you chose to be on the side of what was right... and all of us are aware that we might not have done the same thing in your situation."

Charlie watched her through narrowed eyes waiting for manipulation, some kind of backhandedness.

"And that's why you're still on this case," she continued, her gaze still focused on him, "because you've proven that you put the law above your relationships, and I know that if James is crooked you will not be compromised. Otherwise, I *would* have called in NBI."

Charlie bit his lower lip, embarrassed at what he was about to confess, "The problem is if I lose James, who do I have left? It'll also mean I'm an incredibly poor judge of character."

"Half the trouble we get into is because we want to band together, brotherhood and watching out for each other and all that shit, which is just another way of saying, we look the other way while our colleagues beat their wives and stalk women on Facebook. It takes a fair amount of courage to challenge your friends," said Hart. "If James's a bad egg then he has to go."

She turned to her computer and squinted at the screen. "I really should get glasses." Her tone hinted at a dismissal.

Charlie left her office and looked over to where James sat. Instead of returning, he sauntered to the kitchen to make a cup of tea.

Charlie checked his notebook as Linehan was brought in and taken to the interview room. He gave a terse smile as the man came in. He could see the fear and disbelief in the stiff manner in which he walked.

Back at the station Charlie felt unusually aware of its noise and activity. A few portable air conditioners seemed to blare in every other room but to him the air in the building felt thick with humidity. He noticed rain jackets hanging from chairs and a seemingly endless number of bottles of water and soft drinks littered on desks.

In the corridor going towards the room assigned for Linehan's interview, Charlie wiped his brow and dried his hand on his trouser leg. Here, in rooms designed to be private and insulated from the outside world, no air circulated. A technician stood on a stepladder at an open vent nodding his head at music in his headphones.

Linehan was in the corridor, picking at his cuticles. He theatrically pressed himself back against the wall as a larger policeman opened the door closest to him. Charlie was beginning to think that this was the time for someone with a bit more distance to James to come in. It scared him to think what this Linehan could reveal and what the implications could be for James. But, he steeled himself, he was not a person who quit when things were hard.

At that moment Hart appeared in the corridor. "Have you seen..." she was saying. "Have you got a minute?"

"Give me a mo', let me get Mr Linehan settled," he said.

He'd touched the door handle to the interview room and nodded at Linehan to enter when James came into the corridor, walking backwards and saying to someone as he turned, "I'm sure it can't be that complicated..."

Charlie watched as James's eyes found Linehan.

Recognition. Not immediate. A second or two's delay.

Charlie took a deep satisfied breath – that James knew this man was obvious. They hadn't been two strangers photographed together on a night out.

He saw the way James's eyes narrowed and both men froze. Linehan's eyes fixed on James as his already pale skin bleached of all colour and his hands curled into fists. Charlie glanced at Hart but, not wanting to miss anything, looked back at James.

"Looking for me?" Aija's voice came from behind him – she remained out of sight.

"Um, yeah," James said as he turned back and walked away.

Charlie opened the door as Linehan, looking up and down the corridor with visible trepidation, entered. The two men had been shocked to see each other. There was no way that Linehan could claim not to know James as he'd insisted he hadn't at his flat.

Immediately Linehan sat and dropped his face into his hands, trembling. When he looked up again his eyes spoke of fear, they were wide and flitted from side to side. "Let's get on with this," he spoke gruffly.

Charlie stepped back, organising his thoughts. He told Linehan to wait and he walked out into the corridor, to where Hart was standing arms crossed, her brow furrowed in annoyance.

"How is it that no one is where they're supposed to be?" she pre-empted him. "I need you to–"

"Did you see that?" he interrupted her. "James's reaction, he knew..."

"What?" she asked. She looked into the interview room at Linehan. He was clearly disturbed; he could barely sit still in his chair.

"Did you speak to James about his involvement in either of these cases?" asked Charlie.

"Of course I did."

"Officially?"

"No," she shrugged, not giving any hint of discomfort. "It's between colleagues. For now," she paused, and her eyes narrowed. "Unless you're suggesting something?"

"I don't know. But I don't want James going around giving contradictory statements."

"Why do you think he's not on record?" She swivelled around to him. "I know to leave room for people to mess up, especially good officers."

Charlie bristled. "Someone he knows has killed himself leaving behind a declaration of love and James doesn't seem sad, unhappy – the emotions that go with the loss of a loved one, or a lover. So he could be telling the truth, he hasn't been in touch with..."

"Helsinki's a large enough city for paths to never cross," said Hart. "You and I were both at the book signing. It was the same date in the book, we didn't see anyone who looked off, maybe he was there and seemed perfectly normal."

"And two weeks later he's dead. It's long enough for something else to have triggered his descent," Charlie proposed, "or maybe meeting James..."

James was an obstacle. He couldn't believe he was seeing a policeman as dedicated as James obscuring an investigation.

"Right, into battle then," he said in an attempt to lighten his own mood. He returned to the interview room where Linehan was sweating and fidgeting – his fingers in his mouth then rubbing his forehead.

"I'll be watching." Hart raised her chin to indicate she'd be in the observation room.

Charlie decided his best approach was to get straight to the point. After ensuring the formalities were in place, he took a deep breath. He wanted Linehan to admit he was tied directly to Gerry's death, and he was sure he definitely knew something about Lucinda's disappearance.

He asked him the standard questions: where he'd been at that crucial time, who he'd been with. He was careful not to accuse him directly, he didn't want him to demand legal representation or to refuse to answer at all.

"Let's get back to our interview, I'd like to clarify your position on Lucinda, this time for the record."

Linehan nodded his head.

"She's in the picture with you and several of your friends. Yet, when we met, you alleged you didn't know her, or anything about her, and you were completely unconcerned when she died."

"Exactly," he started to tap the table lightly with his fingers.

"Mr Linehan, for the record I'd like you to–" he began.

"To what? I haven't done anything." He exhaled noisily. "I don't know if I'm here about Gerry or this woman..."

"We're looking at your involvement in both cases."

"I have no involvement. I was out for drinks with friends." The pitch of his voice was rising, as if hysteria was coming on.

"There were a lot of statements taken around Lucinda's disappearance, so why is there no mention of this bar you were at in our files?"

"Because no one asked us." He realised he was walking right into it. His voice faltered. "When they showed us her photo. I didn't recognise her. No one introduced us. I'd certainly never met her before."

"So, you're telling me that no one in this photo knew her?"

"I've never even seen that photo before. We posed, we smiled, we went back to what we were doing."

He was certain Linehan was lying. His underarms were damp with perspiration and his eyes reddening. The fact that he was lying meant that he had something to hide. Charlie was sure, given that only so many crimes could have been committed on a Friday night in Helsinki, this man knew something about Lucinda's death.

"I suggest that Venter knew you killed Lucinda, or at least he guessed that you did. Did you silence him? He was threatening to reveal your secret."

Linehan gaped open-mouthed and lowered his face into his hands.

"Mr Linehan, it looks like you're going to be our first arrest." He knew that even without evidence a man in Linehan's state would have to break.

"No!" Linehan shrieked. "I can't be arrested. This will be the end of me. I've lost everything as it is. No one will give me a chance after this. I didn't kill anyone." He jumped to his feet, hitting his stomach against the table and doubling over in pain.

Charlie stood to check that he was all right, but Linehan shoved him away and rushed for the door. "I have an alibi! I have nothing to do with anyone's death."

Charlie and the constable rushed for the door, stopping him before he could open it.

"Please sit down," the constable asked in Finnish.

"The Friday night this Lucinda girl disappeared, I have an alibi," he pleaded, "I have witnesses. Ask them."

"Who?

"Ask Gerry." He screeched, "Oh god, he's dead. Chloe... no, ask James! James knows."

Charlie froze.

The door wrenched open. Hart stood at the door, making desperate cutting motions at her neck, telling him to end the interview immediately.

"The interview is suspended due to Mr Linehan's obvious distress," began Charlie as he reached for the switch to turn off the recording.

Linehan stopped his hysterics, his eyes rolled to look at the ceiling, his body became slack and he collapsed onto the floor.

Chapter 8

Charlie

Charlie seethed as Linehan was taken away in an ambulance. A heart attack while in police custody. This would be fodder for even the most pathetic of lawyers, he imagined. By the time the fuss of calling for assistance, waiting for the ambulance and watching Linehan being driven away was over, Charlie's teeth were clenched so tensely that his jaw hurt.

If the press learnt about a suspect coming so close to death in an interview room, it would be unforgiving to everyone involved and especially him. Hopefully, if Linehan had something to hide, he would prefer that the whole event was kept quiet. Regardless, upon the doctor's advice, their investigation would be delayed by at least a few days in which they couldn't go near him.

Charlie hovered outside Hart's office.

He growled quietly at the prospect of talking to her. Hart must have engineered James walking through the corridor. He knew it. Yes, James might have had business in the interview rooms but it had been too convenient.

He knew he couldn't confront her. She'd wanted to provoke the situation, to throw oil onto the flames. Still, he closed himself in his cubicle trying to calm down before finally going to her office

"You saw what happened too," he asked Hart who was swivelling from side to side in her chair. "He says James is his alibi for Lucinda's death," he added. "Which makes it ever more confusing."

"Him and James being able to verify their movements on the night Lucinda was murdered doesn't eliminate him from killing Lucinda. It only means both of them would have to be involved, probably agreeing to back each other up. And Linehan still touched the gun that killed Venter." She threw herself back in her chair, her annoyance obvious.

"Have you seen a statement from James during the investigation into Lucinda's death?" asked Hart.

"Nothing." Charlie realised. "But also not from the other two men in the photo. No, but it should be of some interest to NBI if James won't cooperate," he suggested. He couldn't see how else they would make progress in either case. If these two cases remained unresolved, for instance if Linehan's heart gave in, both cases would remain open. If that happened, especially if there was even a hint of impropriety, he could lose the tenuous good standing that he had with his colleagues and even with the public. If there was even the suggestion that he'd let James off without a thorough investigation, then his career could be over.

And if he didn't have his career then what did he have?

"I have to officially question James," he declared.

Hart stood. "I'm going to take a walk," she spoke in neither a less nor more abrupt tone than she usually did. "Join me," she indicated to the corridor.

The two of them walked out of the building into the drizzle without speaking. Dread was welling within him.

When finally they were out of reach of smokers, leg stretchers and coffee drinkers taking breaks from the building he turned to her and said, "It's obvious that you have a special interest in James."

"What makes you think that?"

"Your enthusiasm, let's say, for keeping all this quiet. I know you defended me when I was in trouble, but all the relevant people knew what was going on. It wasn't a secret."

"Maybe I learnt my lesson," she replied.

He looked at her faraway expression and felt his heart begin to race. "You and James?" *How did I miss that?*

"Took you a while," she said, nodding slowly.

He opened his mouth and closed it again. "When?" he asked. "How long?"

When she didn't answer he replied in a louder voice, "This isn't something you can tell me to shut up over – this is part of an investigation."

She found a bench and sat down. He thought for a moment that she looked wobbly, uncertain. He sat down beside her. Despite her being his boss, they were friends. She was reliable above all, in her occasional and sometimes inappropriate humour, to provide guidance and intelligence despite her not being that much older than him. She'd earned her position in relative youth, sometimes, it was known, by using her sex as a lever, claiming not enough was done to promote women. But there was no one who could claim she was not capable of her job.

Her and James. He considered it.

"Before or after your divorce?"

"After," she gave him a look that dared him to insist otherwise.

When he spoke next, his voice was softer, his shoulders relaxed, affecting the pose of a confidant.

"I should have guessed earlier when you let him off so lightly. Trust? Not a chance, the potential fallout from an officer obstructing an investigation is too large." He scoffed, "Between colleagues? When did it start?"

"Not that it's any of your business, but after that accident at the office."

"Accident?"

"Spring, when that guy lashed out in the station and I was knocked over and had a massive bruise on my face." She indicated with her hands where the large red-and-blue mark had temporarily marred her face. "It lasted a month or so." She paused. "What now?"

Charlie shrugged. If this came to the notice of superiors, it wouldn't be considered a significant issue, but if it came to the notice of someone with a grudge against her? There would be many who might want to claim that it had been exploitative. It could be suggested that the best thing would be to get rid of her, distance themselves from her. There would be intrusive questions asked and a great deal of laughter behind partly ajar doors.

"You both did a good job at keeping it quiet."

"No one would ever take me seriously again if it got out." She was calm though, as if assured he wouldn't tell anyone. "He showed up exactly when I needed him. I was building myself up from my divorce, clawing my way into a new life, he was just what I needed to make myself feel more… something more than efficient or effective. I felt sexy." She smiled to herself. "I know you know what that feels like. It's not like I'm blind to your transformation: the stylish shirts and shoes, the new haircut." She smiled at him now, looking him up and down. "My husband's departure wasn't as dramatic as Rachel's, but it left an awful hole in me."

"You hide it well," muttered Charlie.

"You do too, about Rachel I mean. You look like you've got a great life; friends, a roommate, you've lost weight. Who'd know that your entire house was reduced to ash? We're all hiding things."

"But I can't hide forever, you can."

"Of course you can." She was goading him. "What else can you do, walk down the streets crying? It's not like you have a choice."

"Look, I'm only interested in this, this relationship, as it applies to James and the case or the cases. Though, I have to say, it's been an eyeopener." He smiled too, his posture relaxing.

"Of course you're interested, Charlie." She winked. "And not just you, everyone would die to know what goes on between his sheets. You're his best friend and you missed him having an affair with his boss."

"Lovisa." His voice was firm, he used her first name though they were meant to be at work.

"Well, I can't help you. Lucinda and most likely this Venter fella are from the past. James and I talked, nothing intense, but I did realise that he has built a wall firmly around himself. I think the only reason anything happened was I didn't really give him a chance to think it through. He didn't have a chance to say no. I think he just hadn't had sex in a really long time." She shrugged.

"Well, at least that's one thing that fits with what I know about him," agreed Charlie, knowing that feeling and knowing what it felt like to look at your colleagues and assess them, to wonder if they would be worthwhile sexual partners. "There's been absolute silence on that front since I've known him. It's a bit of a relief hearing about you two."

They paused again, watching youth clustered in a group around a mobile phone, watching something as they walked.

"Shall we?" She pointed back to the building. "I'm dying for a coffee."

They started back slowly.

"If it rescues me from your derision," she offered, "can I state unequivocally that I would not, ever, block your investigation in any way. I might still get a thrill from James bending over but I would never compromise my integrity for him. If need be, I'll toss him to the wolves that are NBI. But he, like you, is a bloody good police officer and I stuck out my neck for you and I'm doing the same for him."

James

His heart was pounding fast and loud after seeing Linehan. But he caught up with Aija in the corridor. She was chatting and he took discreet deep breaths to calm himself and to force the encounter from his mind.

"You all right?" she asked, as if she'd noticed something.

"Is that the guy from the Venter case?" he asked.

"That's him," she said. "If you ask me, he's as guilty as sin. I've been doing a background check on him, and I was in his apartment and he's a complete disaster."

"What do you mean?" He tried to look casual as he glanced down at the files in his hands, he couldn't even remember what they were for.

"He's had to pay at least three unofficial settlements, let's just call them what they are – bribes – to people about unwanted sexual advances. He lost his last job because he was completely inefficient."

"Where did you find all this out from?" he asked. He hadn't seen Linehan in years and had never been particularly close to him. But he'd been close to Gerry, he knew of Linehan's exploits through the grapevine, from third parties, people who counted themselves as mutual friends.

"His assistant hates him and was pretty happy to talk about him. We paid her a return visit," she continued, "and your librarian woman left a note for you, she actually brought it to the front desk. Announced to the world that she couldn't trust our e-services to deliver it personally."

He grunted in return. The air had suddenly become heavier, denser than before. He felt as if he was suffocating.

"Thanks," he replied, as he turned a corner, leaving her to continue elsewhere.

Chloe was waiting for him outside his house. James saw her as he walked up to the front steps. He'd been looking forward to losing himself in silence with a cigarette, maybe even going to bed early.

She was huddled against the wall, taking shelter from the rain under a small overhang. She now wore trainers in place of the boots she'd had on yesterday. She watched him as he approached her and he felt a growing dread. He didn't know what he was supposed to say to her at a time like this – that he should have been a better friend, that he should have known that Gerry was emotionally delicate and tried to establish their friendship once again, but it was now too late.

He knew that she'd stayed close to Gerry. Seeing her yesterday morning had made him realise just how close that must have been. He had seen pictures of them on social media and once in a daily edition of a print newspaper. They were the kind of people who went to parties with those who liked to appear sophisticated, who liked to be talked about. She'd often invited Dolly, his twin, to events, but mostly because her husband was a wealthy businessman and a well-known artist, and she couldn't invite him without acknowledging that Dolly too had been a childhood friend. From this, James had always got the impression that they were on the periphery, that they were not in the inner circle. That Dolly and JJ were necessary for Chloe to keep her profile newsworthy. Gerry's connection, though deep, had not been his own. Gerry had been from a wealthy family from Johannesburg that had successfully brought their business to Finland decades ago. They'd lived with a foot in each country until Gerry was of school-going age and they'd opted to move here rather than stay in the turmoil of the then-disintegrating Apartheid state. Their lives in Finland had been a continuation of their lives in South Africa – pool, household help that worked long, probably illegal, hours, and name dropping.

Chloe looked hopeless at his door. Her lipstick had faded and her brows smudged. When she gave a wan smile, he felt a wave of something akin to revulsion.

"Can I come in?" He could see she was trembling despite the warmth of the day.

They entered his house, walking silently through the corridor until they came out to the open living area.

"It's not a good time," he began, because it wasn't. He'd spent his day on a queue of seemingly petty cases, his head pounding after seeing Linehan, which aggravated his thought of Gerry.

"You know I've never stopped being crazy about you," she spoke almost immediately when they stopped at a sofa.

She had to know her feelings had never been reciprocated. To him, she had been a childhood friend. He'd assumed that she'd grown out of what seemed to him a bit juvenile.

"I'll never forget our–" she continued.

"We're not going to talk about that," he said flatly. He had no desire to dredge up memories of kisses in her room, knowing that he didn't want her but that she was a girl and she had been there. To him, a teenage boy, the boundaries of friendship had been temporarily overcome, but they'd ended at kissing while she'd been desperate for more.

"It's become, unfortunately, really relevant to the present," she sighed. "With Gerry and everything that's happened."

He stubbed out his cigarette, he'd taken a single puff before remembering that he'd promised Charlie he wouldn't smoke indoors.

"If there was some way that you two could have made up," she spoke in a pleading tone, "it wouldn't have ended like this."

"I'm not responsible for him killing himself. Don't try to make it my fault. I had no idea he was in that kind of state."

"I thought it was against your nature to hate him, I never thought you could be capable of hating someone so much. But now I'm... not sure."

"What's going on?" He cut through her words abruptly. Her countenance was wrong, she sat as if she had been somehow defeated. "Were you and Gerry...?" he began.

"No!" She almost laughed. "He'd have liked to though. If he could have convinced me that he wasn't gay, then I think he'd have been happier."

"Was it that bad?"

"It was awful. He went around pretending to be straight. He had a distorted view of what a straight male thought and looked like. He was cavorting about, marrying that poor woman. And the drinking – you saw him that night." She shook her head. "Even his mum told us she'd rather he came out."

Gerry's parents, traditional Dutch Reformists, had been people who could not have imagined any greater curse than to have a son with such an obvious interest in the same sex. He recalled Mr Venter standing over them, sneering, "Disgusting, sickening – if we weren't in this country I'd show you the right way with a belt – then you'd know what it is to be a man."

James had called Gerry's mother Auntie Amy and he remembered her dabbing her eyes as she asked, "If you could you just talk to him. He has to understand that we are not like these English people, they are perverts, every one of them."

"Finnish," he'd offered but she showed no signs of having heard.

Even as teenagers, young and carefree, constant aggression from Gerry's father and the shows of self-sacrificial tears from his mother were wearing Gerry down. Even as a friend, James took to shows of indifference, encouraging him to "just leave it". Chloe used to laugh, saying, "He's just exaggerating. Anyway, we love you, our little poofter." At which Gerry would wince and James would throw her a glance to say, "Stop it."

"The last couple of weeks have been brutal," she said. "He wanted to contact you, but he couldn't. If only you hadn't…"

"Hadn't what? Got fed up with the constant fawning over me? It was ridiculous, every friendship needs some level of respect and he didn't have it for me. Would you accept a friendship with someone who couldn't keep his hands off you?"

He could tell from her eyes that there was something she wasn't saying. She couldn't hold his gaze, she locked at the floor. There was something more to her presence, but now he wanted her to leave.

"Gerry was planning to make amends," she whispered. "He would have treated you better – he was older." She leaned against the kitchen peninsula. "Remember when we used to have sleepovers and Dolly would spend all evening yelling at us to shut up and go to sleep?"

He said, "If you're not here for anything other than to reminisce then please leave."

She looked around the room. "I'm responsible for Gerry's death," she insisted.

He frowned. "Meaning what?"

"Not like that," she dismissed the idea with a wave. "I didn't kill him. I should have just told him to stop what he was doing, that he wasn't fooling anyone. Some people manage to survive in the closet, but he most definitely wasn't. To be honest, I think even his father would have him give it up to get his son back – he was so miserable, but he just kept trying.

"I don't know if it's enough to convince the police, but Gerry was absolutely miserable. Like I said, I'm sure he killed himself."

Chapter 9

James

James considered not going into work that morning, but he couldn't think of a believable excuse. The incident with Linehan meant Hart would be watching. He knew any change in his behaviour would attract her and Charlie's attention.

He woke up hungover, his neck stiff from having fallen asleep on a chair on the covered patio. He'd found a light blanket covering him and he'd felt embarrassment, imagining that Charlie would have seen him drunk and alone, asleep outside. He'd had most of a bottle of wine until it had run out and then moved to beer that he'd bought for a dinner months ago, before Charlie had arrived. A book had lain open on his lap for most of the evening, he'd read a few words and then go back over them again and again, unable to discern any meaning or pleasure from it.

He heard Charlie snoring as he passed his bedroom door. He dragged himself out for a run and returned exhausted and soaked, his mind spinning with the possibilities that were waiting for him at the station. He had no way of finding out what Linehan had told them.

He wanted to tell Charlie that he was sure he was in trouble. He should have spoken to him right away. He thought of waking him up right then. He could lose everything, his credibility, his standing among his peers. And there he found the list ended, because who else would care, Charlie would, Aija perhaps – Hart would probably be glad to get rid of him, there would be no threat to her position if he was completely discredited.

He was on time, but only just. His spare shirt flapped behind him on its hanger and was spattered with rain. He was at his desk before Charlie, with his heart pounding and the cup of tea in his hands that tasted like nothing, and even an extra teaspoon of sugar failed to give him the lift he needed. He nibbled at the doughnut he'd found in the communal fridge with a note on its box saying, *Syö minut – eat me,* the only reason he'd had to smile, if briefly, that morning. He fought the urge to look through the notes on Charlie's desk, but decided he was in enough trouble.

"What's up?" Aija asked, walking past him, water dripping from the jacket slung over her arm.

He shrugged. "Nothing," he replied. Aija went into a description of what seemed to him an inane conversation that she'd had with her sister the previous evening. What he learnt from it was that she was completely unaware of the complications in the case that involved him.

She was saying, "Sometimes I think that woman's insane," when Charlie came in. Charlie looked grim. His shirt was creased, and his hairline was dotted with perspiration.

"Aija, I would kill for a cuppa," he said. Aija looked mildly surprised but left, he didn't often ask her to get him a cup of tea, their work environment was lean and no one was considered the other's lackey.

The moment she was gone, Charlie turned to James, "Linehan claims that you can vouch for him for the time Lucinda was killed."

"What time was that?" asked James, because if it had been any other time in his life he would.

"We – I'm – hoping that you could tell me?"

"That makes it very difficult for me to vouch for him."

"I knew you were going to be difficult about this." Charlie scratched the furrow of his brow. "But you do know Linehan?"

"Yes," replied James. Charlie glared at him. "We met during uni, hung out a bit after. He was a friend of Gerry's."

Charlie must have had to look for an appropriate term, he scratched his forehead again. "Boyfriend?"

"No."

"So, you haven't thought of mentioning..."

"You haven't thought of asking," replied James. "Yesterday was the first time I've seen him in months, and even then not to talk to. He could have been in there for any number of reasons – Lucinda isn't your only case."

"No, she isn't. But she is my second case to which you are very firmly tied."

James was confused. "How?"

"Gerry and Linehan both appear in a photo with Lucinda, taken about the time she went missing."

"What photo?" For certain he couldn't recall Lucinda from the days that he was friends with Gerry and Linehan. He'd seen the photo of Lucinda that Charlie had pinned to the board, her face did not elicit any memories. "How does that firmly tie me to them?"

"Gerry's house was filled with stuff about you, pictures, interviews, articles," Charlie replied. "That's why we didn't let you in."

James pondered for a moment. "Returning to my question, how does that firmly tie me in?"

Charlie leaned forward. "Look, James, can you just tell us now if what Linehan says is true?"

"Like I said, I can't give an alibi if I don't know when she was killed."

Charlie's body language was extreme, tense, his hands gripping the desk, his eyes boring holes into him.

"We can't talk to him. He's in hospital." Charlie explained that Linehan had been taken to hospital and the doctors made it clear he would not be questioned any further for a few days at least. Years of drugs, alcohol and unchecked hubris had worn his body down. He had an old heart and an old liver in the body of a relatively young man.

James tried to maintain eye contact and he forced his breathing to remain steady.

They were both startled when the door to the office clicked. Hart entered and closed it behind herself. "Judging by the tense atmosphere, you've started without me. Now," she said. "What the hell's going on with Linehan?" Her eyes fixed on James, and he took as inconspicuous a deep breath as he could.

James could not reply.

"No one is accusing..." Charlie broke the silence.

"Yes, you are."

"We just..." he started again.

"I've been in the police for fifteen years. I'd have thought I was trusted enough to be believed."

"James," began Hart, "we'd like you to–"

"I am cooperating."

James was a policeman, he knew their stock phrases, their tactics. He was also incredibly stubborn when he wanted to be.

"Now," Charlie began.

"Now what?"

He realised there was too little inflection in his voice, an absence of a healthy fear of the situation. It must have seemed as if he wasn't frightened. Something made Charlie glance at Hart, whose face was reddening in anger.

"Now you listen to me." In an instant, she was inches away beside him, seething almost comically. "If you are involved in some murder, you're going to bring us all down with you. All of us, who've trusted you, who've worked with you – for god's sakes, we'd even have liked to think we were friends."

He felt his own facade crack.

"So far, none of this has been on record, but Linehan's accusation is on tape. Lucky for you, he's in hospital." She paced across the room and back, her body was unarguably authoritative, her shoulders thrust back. "Don't try to tell me you don't know what he's talking about, don't tell me you don't know about Venter because you do, and it's bloody obvious that you do. I did not get to where I am by being fooled by kids like you."

She stopped in front of him at a distance where he could feel her breath and the angry energy radiating from her. He didn't know what to say.

"Now I want you to go home. Not the pub, not a restaurant, not to a friend's. I want you to think very carefully about what you're going to say to us tomorrow morning at exactly eight o'clock, because every second of that conversation is not just going on record but is also going to influence what we are going to think and feel about you from now on."

James opened his mouth to protest.

"Go home, James. Now," she said.

He stood. Now uncertain. He ignored the clean shirt hanging from the shelf behind him, he picked up his phone and was leaving the moment Aija opened the door, tea in hand.

Aija said nothing, looking him up and down and then surveying the situation in the office.

He glanced back at them. Charlie was thanking Aija for the tea and Hart asking Charlie about a trivial case of abusive texts.

He was still holding himself together when Eva asked when he'd be back, he flinched when he heard her voice beside him.

"Tomorrow," he said. "Hart has me on community stuff." 'Stuff' being the best word he could come up with.

"Oh no," she said. "I was hoping if you had time, you could help me with some cases."

"Huomiseen," he said, *until tomorrow,* as he sailed away from her.

His face began to burn as soon as he left the office. He moved quickly, he didn't want to be seen blushing as he escaped, and on the verge of tears. His eyes began to sting as he fondled his pockets, praying that his keys were with him and he didn't need to go back indoors.

The tears started when he was in the car and its electric engine purred quietly as he joined the traffic. A slow single trail from each eye that burned a path down each cheek to his chin. He wiped his face with the palm of his hand, sniffed several times and turned the radio on. He realised his car was one of the few places where he could be assured of any privacy. He hoped Charlie wouldn't try to follow him, to ask more questions.

He arrived home to the feeling that he couldn't be alone, because at any moment Charlie or even Aija might appear.

Hart would side with him, not because they'd once been sleeping together, but because she knew the secrets and histories that police officers carried. She knew of their errors and failings while Charlie tended to focus on the best of people – he saw their successes; he patted them on their back – he reminisced about joys, not sorrows. Which is what he liked about him. He liked to hang out with a man who liked to see the best in people despite being in a job in which every day presented him with humanity's worst.

There was a message from his sister on his phone, but he ignored it. He could tell her what was happening. *Remember all that fuss, years ago? About the missing girl, remember that night?*

His mother had been shaken. His family had been in Helsinki for over ten years. His father said it was a lesson in how being too comfortable can make you complacent. There had been drink taken and his father had grown annoyed with him.

He'd been at home, swaddled in pyjamas. Moving between hiding in his room and acting in front of an audience that were unaware that he was in a play.

"We came to get away from this shit," said his dad and his mother sighed with annoyance because she'd been forced to insist over and over that they were safer here than they were in Zambia. Here they slept at night without fear of the frenzied barking of dogs trained to be on alert for intruders. They slept without fear that it would happen again, that a young man paid peanuts would die defending their family from what was never said aloud. The sound of bullets piercing the night, not knowing how many people were coming for you.

His family had followed a strange path to Finland, the only thing he and Dolly were sure of was that they were not entirely sure why they were here. Their farm had been attacked, part of a trend of growing violence in the country as the economy pushed more and more people to desperate measures.

First they'd moved to the city, as he'd learnt later, while they waited for their farm to be sold. Then they came to Finland, at a time when it was still relatively easy to gain entry into what they found to be an odd place. Their parents said that, not being white, without the proof of British or Dutch ethnicity that many fellow coloureds in the region were using to relocate to England, Australia and New Zealand, then Finland was the next best place. They said not to worry, they'd move soon to an English-speaking destination, but they'd settled into Finland and forgotten the feeling of being strangely unmoored. They found themselves financially comfortable with Europe at their feet with no reason to leave, except perhaps the weather.

"Disappearing, just like that. You might have known her. She was so pretty, you'd have remembered her if you saw her," her mother egged him on, her slippered feet crossed in front of her and the TV remote beside her. "Maybe there's something you could help the police with."

"Leave him alone, will you," his father had said through gritted teeth.

Gerry's death had thrown him at the heart of two cases, the only route out he had was to tell both Hart and Charlie. Yes, he could tell only Hart, he could give her enough to satisfy her curiosity, but Charlie wouldn't accept it. Not as long as Lucinda's killer was out there unchallenged.

He didn't see why this had to come up again now. Helsinki had been another city in those days, a city discovering a relative affluence, Nokia, Finland's home-grown mobile phone company, was still a star on the global stage and a growing diversity was bringing with it a seemingly greater sophistication.

By this time he, Dolly and his friends were Finns of some sort. They'd been through part of the Finnish school system, through university, but still they preferred the company of people like them. No matter how many Finnish people they shared their lives with, they could still be found swigging beer, playing cricket and watching rugby – always in English.

From when he and Dolly had their first lunch break at the biggest school James had ever seen in his life, he found a friend – Gerry. Gerry, who was already long fluent in Finnish, still called South Africa home, but reminded them not to get stuck thinking about the past, because, if they wanted it to be – Finland was amazing. Gerry, who informed the others in their class that they were backward hicks if they didn't know what being coloured was, and who glanced to the sky, eyelashes fluttering when they asked again how come James's parents were black and just how could Dolly be his sister?

It was Gerry who nudged Dolly towards people who could be her friends, because, he said, he wanted James all to himself.

He and Gerry went through puberty together – that vague period when they were not just friends, but best friends, when his mother would be phoning Zambia and casually saying, "his best friend Gerry". From the moment puberty had taken over them and they'd realised that sex existed, that the desire for it was at first unrecognised, disguised, it had been obvious that this was where their paths diverged. While Gerry was quite clearly, at first embarrassed at this realisation, drawn to the same sex, James remained one of those boys who remain boys while those around him become men. While to him, it seemed as if Gerry was always either talking about boys or men, or his eyes with a glazed faraway look that suggested he was thinking of sex, James kept running and swimming, kicking footballs without a thought of if a girl was watching. Gerry begun tugging at his sports shirt to cover his thin arms, to flick through magazines while discussing the whims and worlds of celebrities.

But still their friendship carried on. To him Gerry was not just a friend but kin. Who else in Helsinki could recall playing cricket in the dry October dirt or the smell of meat blackening on a *braai* as the sun set on a clear cloudless night? Who else could trade stories of switch-wielding grandmothers serving them doughnuts and cake in the evenings after a scolding? And who else knew what it was like to leave all this behind; the sun, the fun, the family and friends, and start a new life?

It was a small sacrifice which for a long time he didn't mind making.

They had settled into this imperfect unbalanced friendship. Fun, tenderness, the sharing of secrets. But when James showed any admiration for a girl, something that he came late into, Gerry was quick to show his disregard, to sigh dramatically at the mention of a girl's beauty, of Chloe's persistence, or even of James's late, but not worryingly so, deflowering.

James grew into relative affluence for a young man, and Gerry claimed a little independence from his family. With a Finnish passport, whenever he had cash, James spent a few days in another country, sometimes they travelled together, sometimes alone. He, Dolly and the others were at an age when their parents, married with children, were consumed by the world of parenthood.

But they were free.

Charlie

Morning came but James didn't.

The office seemed as it always was. The usual faces of the police force, the cleaning service, an IT repair man. Cups of tea and coffee were ferried between stations, cheap mayonnaise filled sandwiches in place of real breakfasts.

Charlie had taken time over his clothes that morning, dawdling over his shirt, examining the grey in his hair, then returning to his tie – checking for subtle stains and wear and tear, even though it was nearly new. He'd taken his time leaving his car, instead sitting in the driver's seat checking his messages and email though they could be done at his desk and computer. There had been no evidence to suggest James was still at home.

"Slow morning," said Aija. He started, only a moment later realising she was not in fact talking about the speed at which he was walking, trying to forestall the inevitable meeting.

The clock ticked toward the hour. Charlie had never participated in any significant disciplinary action before. Some of his colleagues over the years had strayed, they'd been caught driving intoxicated, subjecting a suspect to violence, viewing inappropriate social media or accused of sexual harassment. He'd never had to sit in the same room as one and condemn them to losing their job, public humiliation and, on occasion, legal action. His had been a special situation, the transgression had not been his. But he had no desire whatsoever to inflict it upon anyone else.

Now he was in a bind, and he was sure Hart could see it. This meeting was not according to procedure. She was giving a man she'd had sex with an opportunity to vindicate himself when she should have already initiated action against him. If he participated in this, then he too could be seen as complicit – a mark against an otherwise perfect profile.

"Any sign of James?" asked Hart.

He glanced up at the clock, they still had ten minutes.

Aija was at her desk just in front of his and James's shared cubicle. She was deep in paperwork, her fingers tapping the hard metal of her desk. To Aija, and anyone in earshot, Hart could have simply been asking about any meeting or even waiting upon him to deliver a parcel.

"No messages?"

He checked his phone again, though he could clearly see that no messages had come in since he'd last checked only minutes earlier.

"Damn," she said and marched towards her office.

Still, James was a brilliant officer and deserved a chance to explain away his behaviour. Perhaps at the end of the day, they could call it a breakdown, yes, strain due to a large workload.

Soon it was a minute to eight and James's desk was still empty.

"Any sign of James?" He found himself echoing Hart as he passed by Aija's desk.

She shook her head and continued.

A grey cloud descended upon him when he entered Hart's office.

She was in her swivel chair glaring at the window, her phone was beside her just within her reach and her jacket, normally slung on a back seat, lay rumpled on the floor. She looked older, as if her makeup this morning was unable to disguise her real, her emotional age.

"He's not coming, is he?" she said quietly.

"Maybe if we wait a few minutes," suggested Charlie.

"You know as well as I do that if he was coming here he'd be here by now, sipping a cup of sugar and pretending he didn't get completely wasted the night before."

"I know," said Charlie.

"What do you want to do now?"

"We should make sure he hasn't done anything to himself," said Hart, suggesting the worst.

"I could go down there myself," he suggested. "The fewer people that know, the better."

"Well, everyone's going to bloody know soon," snapped Hart. She glanced up at him. "If we don't find him and fast, this is the end of his career."

"I'd say it's the end of his career now." He challenged Hart with eye contact.

She glared back, any hint she'd shown of affection to him or to James was now gone. "I want to know what is going on." She leaned forward, resting her arms on her desk. "If NBI get involved we'll never hear the whole story. They'll try to intimidate and bully him and he'll tell them what he thinks they want to hear."

"There's no going back if we do this," he said to her. She was drumming her fingers on her desk, the rest of her was absolutely rigid.

She stopped tapping and looked down. "For the time being let's keep this between the two of us. I have to know that James is clean."

"Not without you giving me official instructions to investigate him." Charlie stood. "I am not going to get myself in trouble. James may be my friend, but he was also your lover..."

She glanced at the ceiling, a mix of anger and annoyance in a heavy sigh. He had been a policeman for too long to start conducting secret investigations on behalf of senior colleagues. Not only would the onus fall on him if anything went wrong, but it would also invalidate any evidence he found while on the case.

He hated what they were doing. They needed to go to NBI. He was breaking the rules and protocols that made him feel proud to be a policeman. He knew about police forces in other countries where police were corrupt, lawless, they were as much danger to their publics as the criminals they were supposed to be against. Rules, procedures, boxes that were ticked and actions that were authorised – that's what kept him safe as well. There was already a flutter, a twitter in the office: the door might have been ajar, the officer observing could have said, or even someone simply messing about with the tape, but it was clear that someone had said something about Linehan's finger pointing.

"Tie it in to the Venter case somehow. I'll say we have reason to believe that Venter had been trying to harm James and are trying to establish if he had been acting on his own or if someone else was involved. If needed," she replied. He could tell she hadn't thought this through, her response had been slower than it normally would have been. She'd been hoping James would appear that morning.

That was her concession. She wanted to find James and the truth. But Charlie wanted far more than that. He wanted to find James and to tell him that everything was OK and that he, they all, believed he had nothing to do with any murder or conspiracy, but he needed the truth to do that.

Out of reluctance to carry out his assignment, Charlie sat at his desk and considered making himself tea. He glanced at his watch and at the door repeatedly.

He typed James's name into Google, something that had never occurred to him before to do. As policemen, they had to be careful not to attract too much attention, but even before his writing career, James had had a few accolades, some awards and commendations from university and work, and one regarding a charity. He clicked on it. James had walked to France to raise several thousand pounds. There was James looking rather battered on a hill with a large church and rolling hills in the background.

This was James, and he wanted him to have existed in exactly this form twenty years ago. He opened his bottom drawer and retrieved Venter's laptop from it, still in its official protective plastic bag.

He ran his hand along the laptop. Was he letting everything get ahead of him? It should have been one of the first things on their agenda, Aija should have gone through it, but he'd overruled it, instead giving her tasks related to other things.

Hart came through her door. She already seemed exactly her usual self. She breezed in and out of offices, in that seemingly permanent cheery tone of hers. He knew too well what happened when the cheery tone changed. She glanced at him through the glass, and he knew she was prompting him to follow her instructions. A constable came up to her, spoke to her and then the two of them walked towards the corridor out of sight. He wasn't going to let her push him. He'd speak to James when he was ready. This, he told himself, was one last stab at finding some evidence before confronting his friend.

The laptop in front of him, when opened, revealed an organised mind. It had been in use for a few years, and everything was organised first by work or play and then by year. Inside each folder were sub-categories: Projects, Inspiration, Contracts. Documents were clearly labelled working or finished or given version names.

If these two were childhood friends then organisation was something they had in common. There was a file named Photos. In it were pictures, many, many pictures. Snapshots of his life, photographs where he was seemingly happy, others of scenery and other people. It would take hours to properly scroll through them – if he chose to. He found more images of James, but there was no way he could go through all of them in as much detail as he wanted.

He sighed. There was no central file called "James". Or convenient letter called "Why I died".

Only when he'd slowed down did he realise Venter's email had many recent requests and reminders from clients. It seemed as if he'd stopped replying, and when he did it was usually to apologise and to say he'd get right to it. This was consistent with someone who was struggling, but why he was struggling, it didn't say.

He checked the outbox, an email addressed to James had been sent the previous week. There was nothing to say it had been replied to.

Hi! Don't have your number anymore, want to get a drink some time?

Charlie checked the bin – nothing. He started to look back in the history but couldn't focus.

"Just to let you know, Linehan is on his way home. Hart said you were OK with it," Aija said, one foot still outside the room.

"Ah yeah. Wait," he said, thinking quickly. "Aija." He turned back to her. "You know that list of the staff at The Passion you're building? We need to check their publicity or events company. Someone might have given her that ticket. Also, try to look at who supplied her with her hair extensions."

"OK, I guess I'll get that sorted out," she replied hesitantly.

He knew that this would keep her busy for a few hours and suspected both paths would lead nowhere. He needed the time. She was the only outlier. James, Hart and he were the only ones who knew what was happening and he knew he had to keep it like that. Everything else could be put down to rumours. "We'll give Linehan another day and then we'll pay him a visit. We don't want anyone saying we've been heavy-handed."

She opened her mouth, obviously to protest.

"We need to do this right, Aija. If we ruin this, we have two cases that may never be solved."

She seemed to relax, and she smiled weakly and returned to her desk.

He called James wanting him to offer an excuse, even a silly one like, "I overslept". The call went straight to his voicemail.

He had to consider another option. And this was what finally spurred him into action. What if James wasn't OK; suicides had been known to cluster. What if...? He grabbed his rain jacket, though he was already sweating.

As he walked past Aija, he tried to look exasperated and hoped he succeeded as he told her, "I'm on my way to a meeting, standing in for Hart. I think I might pop by the house to clean myself up, I'm sweating like a pig."

Aija had waved in response as her phone had rung immediately after he'd finish speaking.

He drove as fast as he was allowed back to James's house. How was he to know James's mental state? He was a man who spoke enough to convince you that he'd told you something of significance. James had managed to write a ninety-thousand-word book and sleep with his superintendent under his nose, so if he were in real distress there would be no guarantee that Charlie would know.

He stood in front of the front door and said aloud, "This is it then," steeling himself. He knew that once that door opened his relationship with James was forever changed. There would be no going back. He'd have chosen his job over his friendship. The door felt extraordinarily heavy as he pushed it open. James had become a suspect in a murder case.

He called James's name, though his car hadn't been outside. He wandered through the downstairs repeating his name.

He went up the stairs and entered James's room, pulling on standard-issue latex gloves as he went. A room that had remained sacrosanct since he'd moved in. James had done him a favour by allowing him to live with him and he'd never had a reason to intrude on his privacy. The room was neat, barring his laundry basket that was filled to overflowing.

There were more books. Like his collection downstairs, it was mostly in English. The books were visibly read, thumbed, battered and annotated, words underlined.

He returned to the corridor, exhaling, relieved that he hadn't found James bleeding to death in his room. Stopping to listen for another person, he heard none and crossed into the office. There he looked around; he'd seen most of the room from outside when the door was left open. He glanced over the desk, but nothing seemed interesting. He pulled open a metal filing cabinet beside it which was made of three deep drawers. The first one held stationery and loose leaves of paper, charts that looked related to his books. The next he pulled open with difficulty as the books within it jammed the doors.

The two drawers were full of notebooks, pressed so close together it was almost impossible to pull them out. They were standard supermarket-issue notebooks, spiral bound, with blue covers and with math grids rather than lines – the kind he'd seen James writing in almost every time he was on his own. There was no way they could be work related – in his own thirty years on the force, he'd never accumulated so much detail. He ran his gloved hands over them, trying to find a loose one. Then using his fingers he pried one out, carefully noting where it should be returned.

Even from the first line, the notebook troubled him. James's writing was only barely legible.

> *Not another book. When does this end.*
> *Note. Many houses is koteja. Going to be unemployed if you can't figure this out up to now.*

He then went into a long description of a shopping trip. Charlie couldn't discern many of the words but from what he could gather, nothing happened. James had contemplated shoes and not bought them. He tried another page in which James described going for a walk, and another where he was debating the merits of watching football over cricket.

It went on page after page, the absence of any purpose to his writing was strange. Why would he, a writer, write about nothing? Weren't writers supposed to be observers of life and complexities and subtleties? The writing in these books – he pulled out another one with effort – was not clever, observational or intelligent.

He forced the books back in, guessing it would be impossible for James not to tell that he'd taken anything out. He went to the bottom drawer and picked the one at the extreme left, where he assumed the beginning would be.

There was no indicator of the date, and the first few lines were clear but pointless, as if he'd started in the middle of a thought.

> *Third time I've smiled today. See. Feeling better. Be nicer to Aija. Remember to post affirmation.*
> *OK. All the positive things in my life:*
> *Dolly (don't tell her)*
> *Job – no more meltdowns please*
> *Must be something else but I can't think*
> *English (I think) guy seems pretty d. Hart cow. I've made a mistake haven't I?*

That must have been when he'd just moved to the Helsinki station, thought Charlie.

The following few paragraphs contained descriptions of the people in the office and a coffee machine. He described Hart as *odd, feel sorry for her husband*. Aija as *coloured – tell Dolly*. He mentioned some other names, some that had left since, in brief sentences: *He has red hair. She is fat.*

The page ended with an optimistic, *counsellor isn't a complete quack – this might work.*

Is that what this was? When Rachel had left him, Charlie had been ordered to see a counsellor who suggested keeping a diary. He hadn't even bought a notebook.

James had never told Charlie that he'd seen a counsellor.

Why should he? He shouted the words in his own head. Do you tell him everything? Do you tell him how you still wake up in the middle of the night with your heart physically hurting because of what Rachel did? Do you tell him how the weight loss is about the realisation that your wife wanted to hump someone else because you couldn't satisfy her anymore?

Of course Charlie would think differently about James if he knew he was an emotional mess, that for some reason he had to write pages and pages of inane text to keep himself sane. Being friends is just as much about what was not spoken as what was.

He slammed the drawer shut, then looked around himself remembering that this was supposed to be quiet, unofficial.

Unfortunately, he sighed, still on one knee, Charlie was a detective and not knowing what James was hiding would gnaw away at him until his curiosity was satisfied.

Chapter 10

Charlie

The photo of James and his friends irritated Charlie by being taken so casually without thought for posterity. Unfortunately, he thought with a wry smile, no one was standing with a sign or newspaper declaring the date as he'd seen people do on social media. No one had thought to jot down the names of the participants, the date and their location so that they'd always remember that night. As with any youth they were probably so assured that they would always be friends that it wouldn't have occurred to them to take note of the details of that day. He couldn't ask Linehan, he'd proved himself to be too much of a risk – a man who would give up a secret if pushed. If more secrets or new secrets had to be kept then Linehan was too volatile. He decided he had two choices; to ask James or to find someone else associated with them.

So here he stood.

"Dolly," he greeted her and accepted a light embrace as if they were friends meeting for dinner. "It's so nice of you to see me on such short notice." The words came out stiff and formal.

Dolly stepped back after opening her front door and cheerfully asked him to come in. She wore linen shorts and a T-shirt and had on flipflops that gave a quiet thud as she walked. He followed her, disguising his reluctance with a smile that felt plastered on. He'd met James's twin sister once before, a woman whose resemblance to him was tempered with some femininity, James's sharp jaw was softened by rounder and kinder eyes.

She too had blonde hair, but he was sure it was coloured. It was bone-straight with only a flicker of a curl at the ends, most definitely not naturally so, and when she spoke, she frequently touched it – almost as if to check that it was still perfect. Her accent wasn't as pronounced as James's, neither in English nor Finnish. In English, she spoke with a neutral European accent lacking the hard final consonants and precisely enunciated vowels that James had.

She, like her brother, seemed like a relic of a previous age to him, people who'd moved here when being English-speaking was an identity, a mark of holding a tangible link to Britain and its satellites – America, Australia and other former colonies. When Charlie was young growing up here, the only time he spoke it was when in the presence of other people like him – foreign. His bilingualism had been constantly questioned, "Where are you from really?" He'd been teased in playgrounds for speaking English with family because so many children believed that all people were Finnish or, at a push, Russian- or Swedish-speaking.

Dolly and her brother would have arrived later when many adults would have been able to speak with reasonable fluency. These days, the language was on every corner, every newspaper and magazine, and it seemed everyone foreign and local, especially continental Europeans, people from Russia and the Balkans, spoke it alike – diluting the concept of a community.

When the twins arrived in Finland, barely still preteens, Charlie would have already been early in his career as a policeman, constantly being called upon to translate at either minor or major incidents. One minute he could be calming a tourist who'd had her handbag stolen and then next trying to keep his food down at a scene where an international drug dealer had battered his girlfriend to death. When in Finland, he'd pine for the grandeur and sophistication of Britain, and when in his family's heartland outside London, his resented their urban poverty – not the poverty of the rural Finland of berrypicking and huge creaking cottages, of swimming in clear water lakes and dining on fish soup, but the kicking footballs down the street, getting leathered in pubs and whistling at women who walked past them on the pavement.

The first thing Dolly had asked when he called was, "Is he all right?" quickly, the words gushing out. Had she been a suspect, he'd have thought her guilty because of the rush, but he knew the families of policemen lived with the looming reality that one day their brother, sister or child might not be all right.

He'd driven to her home in Westend, on the very edge of Espoo, where a short stretch of ocean and metro line divided it from Helsinki city. Westend was an affluent neighbourhood that withstood price fluctuations, rezoning or any other attempts to interfere with its prestige.

Her house was recently built. Its style was contemporary with wood siding imitating the idealised Nordic cottage. It wasn't by any means the largest, newest or glossiest building in Westend, their house could be considered entry level, it didn't have the provenance of the older buildings and didn't have the glamour of the most expensive new builds.

They entered a room from which enormous black framed windows opened onto a large garden that held what to him seemed an extravagant private playground. The furniture looked new and nearly every inch of it was covered in the paraphernalia of child and parenthood.

He knew that her husband JJ was a friend of James's. He was an entrepreneur that allowed their family an affluence that Dolly seemed born to fulfil. She had a polish to her, her posture and a willowy frame that gave her an air of delicacy.

Though the summer sun had yet to make an appearance she was what he, in his thoughts, would have called deeply tanned. His own daughter would call her brown. He was sure that was new, more accepted terminology, and it still interested him that twins could be so distinct in skin colour, maybe because it was something that James simply didn't discuss.

"If you don't mind me asking," he'd finished the sentence off, this had been over a year ago, after he'd first met Dolly. "So, you are not..."

"White," James was grinning knowing the subject would be making Charlie uncomfortable. "Why would anyone think so?"

"Come on, be serious, you look so..." Somehow the word sounded strangely rude when he tried to use it.

"White?" prompted James.

"Anyway," Charlie deflected James's answer, "it doesn't matter. It's just something you'd think you'd know about someone."

"That's where you're wrong," James had answered, patting his pocket for cigarettes. "It does matter. Imagine if Aija spoke Finnish the way I do – do you think she'd be granted the same leeway?"

"I'll get us some tea." Now, Dolly turned back to speak to him as she headed towards the kitchen, at the same time reiterating, "Whatever it is, as long as he's all right."

"He's fine," called Charlie after her as she disappeared. "Saw him just this morning," he lied.

He noticed she didn't apologise for the mess, instead when the tea was ready she glanced around the room and said, "Let's sit in the sunroom,"

"How's the housesharing going?" she asked.

"Fine, but it's perfectly normal for us to not see each other all day."

"Then you don't actually know if he's OK right now," was her response.

"If he wasn't, well, if something had happened in regards to work I'd definitely know."

She seemed to relax.

"When did you see him last?"

"Spoke to him on the phone the other day," she replied vaguely.

"Do you think he's all right?" asked Charlie. "It's so hard to tell."

"Because of Gerry's death you mean." She frowned. "He insisted he was OK. But he wouldn't have told me if he wasn't, so..." She trailed off. "You're friends. You understand."

"I thought twins would share some special bond..." he said, knowing this was just to fill the conversation, something to get her comfortable talking to him.

"Fraternal twins are no more similar or connected than regular siblings. Even more so since I'm a girl. I don't know if you have a sister but there are some things that boys just don't tell girls."

"How well did you know Gerry?" he asked.

"Very well. He and James must have been about twelve when they became friends. Really soon when we first came out here. Gerry was very much a hint that our lives were still normal – the language – we didn't have to struggle with integrating, because we had Gerry, and Chloe and JJ. Unlike the others, we still have JJ."

He didn't have to ask her this, but to satisfy his own curiosity he asked, "And did it develop into something more than friendship?"

"Nah," she replied. "After a few years, it became obvious Gerry was desperately in love with him and he became very clingy. James was a gorgeous teenager, the kind that girls and boys swoon over. It was OK when they were younger, but I think at some point James decided he wanted his own life, a significant part of which was to hang around with girls. You know, how boys are. They were loyal I'd say until uni, then they sort of rekindled again in our late twenties."

"And is this related to why they are estranged? I have to say, I've known James for two years. He's only told me the barest minimum about his childhood, but he's never mentioned a best friend – the absolute best of friends, I've been told."

She smiled like her brother. One side of her mouth rose in the imitation of a smile, the other remained as it was. For someone so loquacious, it was obvious that there were some things she would not talk about. "You said you wanted my insight into a case."

"Yes. You may have seen the news about the body of a girl who went missing?"

She shrugged. "JJ mentioned it. But I didn't see it on the news."

"Did you hang around with your brother or Gerry at that time? This would have been about twenty years ago."

"Not at first. I got the idea that I wanted to travel more than anything. I'd found a job in Dublin – ah, that was amazing. So when I came to visit I made it count. James had his own place, JJ sublet a room from him when he wasn't in cheese country – so I'd stay with them. Chloe had the smallest studio on the planet, and, well, Gerry had some glorious flat because of his parents."

"Do you know a man named Declan Linehan?"

She nodded. "He showed up in uni. I see him about every now and then. I never liked him."

"What did you make of him at the time?"

"Nothing." She shrugged. "Another guy. Bland. Mediocre. I'd probably have forgotten him if his dad hadn't lost tonnes of money."

He took out a copy of the picture, folded to omit James, and showed it to her.

"What?" she asked, looking at it.

"Do you recognise them?"

"Gerry, Declan and this guy here – he's moved away, maybe to Greece. A complete arsehole, but I can't remember him."

"This back here is Lucinda."

"The girl who went missing?" She suddenly sat upright. "Now that woke us all up." Her eyes lit up.

"You knew her…"

"No. When she disappeared, that's when we started talking about her. She was younger than us, but everyone acted as if we knew her. When I say 'we', I mean everyone I knew – mostly foreigners. Her father had a senior position at the university and spoke at any event to do with America. So, I suppose… well, you know, she wasn't like someone off the street. I'd probably been introduced to her at most, but when she vanished, knowing her was a claim to fame. Everyone had some story."

He asked her what she meant.

She leaned back and crossed her legs. "Slut. Angel. Evil. Pure. Who slept with her, who didn't, who tried. Seen hanging out on her own in bars. The same things repeated the world over about a missing girl, the only difference was that this was so close. It could have happened to any…"

He waited but she didn't continue. "If you knew of her, if she was in the periphery of your circles, then it's not impossible that James might have known her."

"It isn't," she replied.

She lingered on the photo, her eyes at the point of watering. "It's a parent's nightmare, isn't it? That your child should go missing. Poor girl. That's why we left Zambia – there was a surge of violence and it was spilling over to us. Our farm was attacked and… " She stopped. "Anyway, that's irrelevant, it's a lot safer now. Do you know how she died?"

"Not yet, but it was foul play."

"It's when I see stuff like this that I understand why James is a policeman." She sipped her tea and handed him back the photo.

"What was James doing around that time, was he interviewed by the police?"

"I don't think so. He probably would have told me but then again he might not have. But anyway, the police would have needed a reason to interview him, there were so many possible suspects – even if they just considered the men around her. They didn't know exactly when she disappeared, they didn't know if she was missing or dead. How many young men his age can attest to their whereabouts over an undefined period? The police couldn't give a where, when or how."

"Do you know if James and Declan are still in touch?"

"Not to talk to. It's a small city or large town depending on how you see it, so you're bound to bump into each other."

"Was there a particular reason they're not in touch?" he asked.

She shrugged. "Maybe."

"I don't suppose you could be a bit more specific – you sound like your brother."

She smiled at him. "Which isn't a bad thing, by the way. Do you have siblings?"

"Two, one lives in New Zealand."

She sighed and scratched her ear. "Has James ever killed anyone in the line of duty?"

He frowned at her question. "Not that I know of. It would be on record. I've never thought to look."

"That's the part I find difficult to reconcile, that James is in a profession in which he might have to kill someone. That he has to be ready to do it. I thought he'd be something at a university or a full-time writer."

"Did he say why...?"

"If James had killed someone and I knew," she said, louder, as if she were giving the final word on the topic, "I wouldn't tell you or anyone else. If there was even the remotest chance that he was involved with that girl's death, I wouldn't have let you in through that front door."

In the rain, that he thought for a moment had stopped, a Jack Russell ran across the lawn, its mouth filled with a ball of socks. Two kids with masses of dark brown hair in ringlets exactly like James's ran after it in ecstasy, one with a long swimming noodle and the other hurling golf balls at the dog as it ran. Each was stick thin like their uncle. They caught the dog and began rubbing and tickling it while simultaneously slapping at it with the noodle. The dog's barks were definitely not entirely of pleasure.

"That dog's going to bite one of them some day," she sighed.

Charlie was enraptured by the kids, he could see a young James, running across the grass.

He glanced at her.

She was smiling but she wasn't joking. "Then I can get it put down."

The kids kept hitting the dog. Charlie paused, giving her a moment to tell them to stop, but she didn't. Finally the dog shot up and sped away and Charlie relaxed, realising that he'd found the sound upsetting.

Dolly didn't comment.

He continued after clearing his throat. "For your information, I think your brother's a great guy. He's honest and principled. But there are two people dead and it looks like he knows something."

"He might. But if you get frustrated by what he won't tell you, imagine being me, his twin sister." She smiled at him again.

As he got to his feet, he wondered if he had wasted his time here. What he had learnt was that Dolly was exactly like her brother. There was much she knew and wasn't saying. One of the boys caught the dog again, and Charlie, despite himself, grew tense, and then was relieved when the boy started to stroke it and to calm it down.

"You know, whenever all this is over, you should come for dinner. The boys would love to meet James's friends. I wouldn't mind too – Aija and even Hart – maybe I should make more of an effort."

There she led him to the door and they said their goodbyes.

Chloe Ahern Foreman's house was surprisingly cosy; a wool rug ran through the foyer and large landscape paintings of the Finnish countryside hung on the walls. It seemed as if its owners had replicated a country cottage in a modern building. Its décor was calm, a place that one would call a haven from work and the outside world.

Charlie had introduced himself again at the door, though her eyes told him she recognised him. She was in bare feet and invited him in with a faint polite smile and even fainter nod as if looking at his credentials was unnecessary to her. He brushed the rain from his jacket before he entered saying that he hoped he wasn't disturbing her.

"Ach, it's fine," she replied, brushing her hair back with one hand.

The makeup she wore couldn't hide the appearance of exhaustion that he saw in her red-tinged eyes and drooping shoulders. It made her look younger, less sophisticated – more vulnerable. Every picture he'd seen of her online – he'd looked her up before coming here – showed him a woman with various dark tones of hair, from deep browns to black, with a style that could be seen as burlesque – nothing like the slight blonde in the twenty-year-old picture who radiated unworldliness.

They took a few steps into a corridor, the end of which he could see led into a living room. Chloe halted, and turned to speak as if she would not let him trespass any further into her life.

"I don't know what else I can tell you."

"I'm trying to find out more about Mr Venter's mental state, how he was, how he seemed in the time leading up to his death," he began.

"I spent all night thinking about him, I know he killed himself." She shrugged. She believed it. That brief movement told him of her certainty. It was honest, unrehearsed. "It was the culmination of a lot of unhappiness. Like I said, he'd been desperately unhappy for a long time."

"Why would he kill himself now?" he asked. "Did something change?"

"I don't think so. I think maybe his emotional resources were depleted," she said, her Irish accent still unmarked by thirty years in Finland. "He was really depressed. He had this way for a long time of keeping up appearances, show up at parties, if anything was opening, he was really efficient at work. But I knew he was struggling. The last time I saw him I reminded myself to take him out to cheer up, but you can't really cheer someone up when they're depressed."

"Would you," he began, lowering his voice because he knew this was a question that most didn't want to be asked, "know anyone who would have wanted him dead? Perhaps someone with a grudge against him?"

She shook her head, lowering her gaze to the floor.

Charlie's eye travelled over her shoulder into the next room into which the Nordic cottage theme continued in greys and browns. "What about his ex-wife?"

"Marita," she answered as if it took some effort to remember the name. "She's somewhere in Lapland. I'm sure she was glad to get away from him. She won't say it, but she married him to get to Finland, there is no way she could have been convinced that he was interested in her. He did the most pathetic imitation of heterosexuality that you could imagine."

"Could you imagine that it could have led to some anger elsewhere, maybe someone who resented him for pretending to be heterosexual?"

"It wasn't anyone's business. Not anyone that I could imagine," she said. "His parents hated him being gay, but he was their only son and wouldn't dream... They're devastated. I spoke to them. I can't imagine what it must be like to lose your, well, I don't have any kids to lose."

"A jilted lover, someone he's embarrassed?"

"Really, this isn't a cosy mystery. Who murders someone for embarrassing them?" She laughed. "Look, he had friends – no, acquaintances – who went in and out of his life, who came to his parties, ate his food and bathed in the glow of hanging out with the right people. But, aside from me – and maybe Declan – he didn't have anyone who was emotionally invested in him."

"He was lonely," Charlie proposed quietly.

She froze as if his words had stung. After a pause she replied, "Very."

He prepared to ask her about James and about Lucinda. As his hand reached for his pocket, a phone rang in another room.

She apologised briskly and trotted towards the kitchen as if she knew it to be urgent.

He followed.

There was work on a large dining table, a laptop, a few sheets of paper, a notebook and a mug full of pens and markers. Beside this was a large soup cup and two packets, one ripped open and seemingly empty. The other packet declared them to be chicken-flavoured calorie-controlled soup, each one, it promised, held only a hundred calories and would keep you full for hours.

He knew those soups, having tried a few when he began his weight loss. Bland, unsatisfying concoctions that left one desperate for real food. He glanced at an array of books on an open kitchen shelf. The cookbooks on it were mostly hardbacks, the kind of cookbooks that were reviewed in lifestyle magazines. Most of them promised weight loss; the 5:2 diet, several celebrity chefs who claimed to have conquered their weight, and other books that declared veganism, whole foods or ayurvedic solutions to weight gain.

He had more questions – Lucinda, James. Gerry. Chloe could possibly hold clues to the cases, maybe she could exclude James from having had anything to do with it.

Chloe was speaking in a low voice as he continued to look around. Just after the books in a corner was a photo of her and James, smiling.

Of course, there were others in the photo. It appeared to be a large gathering, a wedding, or anniversary – something that brought generations together for an afternoon's celebration.

Peering at the photo he saw Dolly with dark, curly hair. Gerry Venter was beside her and in the back, among older people, he recognised what could've been James and Dolly's parents, he also saw the man he was sure was now Dolly's husband.

Despite there being perhaps twenty people in the photo, the photo was of her and James. His eye had been drawn to them almost immediately. They were happy. She was laughing, her blonde hair thrown back with a smile so joyful that it would have been impossible to mimic – the joy was reciprocated in James, she held his arm and her other hand was on his chest.

Charlie resisted the urge to pick up the frame to examine it better. James was obviously a person of significance to her, he was probably the love of her life, or at least at the time had been. Being married, she couldn't have kept a picture of only her and James – it would have raised questions and caused disagreements. This way she could keep it up in the guise of family memories, she could turn to it any time she wanted, she could see him from the kitchen table as she worked, from the stove as she cooked – she could see his face, as it was, every single day.

Obsession? It was not just as a policeman, but also as a husband that he'd learnt what obsession could do when it went unchecked. It could make you throw everything away – everything, he repeated in his mind, *everything*. Obsession was so powerful it could make you take twenty years of a happy life and toss it away. It could make you make decisions that you knew would incur the wrath of society. It could make you feel so invincible that you felt that this wouldn't matter. You would call it things like love, like a passion, you would say we were meant to be together forever, regardless of everyone else – even a patient husband.

"OK, so, I'll get back to you," Chloe was saying, "soon, I'll have to see."

As she came towards him, her mobile still to her face, he spoke firmly, "I have to go, emergency."

Without checking if she'd heard, he walked with what he hoped was a brisk professional pace back through the corridor and to the front door. By the time he reached it and forced it open he was shaking, by the time he closed it behind him and was out in the unrelenting spatter of rain, he was fighting tears. As he slammed his car shut, he lost the battle.

Aija

"Venter's mother's arrived from the US. They're planning to hold the funeral," Charlie told Aija when they met next in his office. "We should talk to Linehan soon, and, even if we don't get a confession, the evidence points very firmly in his direction. With luck he'll tell us why he did it and we can close the books on it." She was once again standing in his office.

Aija looked at her fingers. "What about Lucinda?"

Charlie took a quick swig of his coffee; she knew it was black and sugarless. "We have to look in new directions. Who can tell us about who was around then? The list of her friends and the people interviewed is so long it's meaningless. No one is pinpointed, no one is of special interest. We have to…" Here Aija noticed that he corrected himself, he reeled his rant back under control.

"One thing about Linehan is he'd have squealed years ago, in my opinion," he said, "it took us no time at all to get names out of him."

"If he knows, maybe something bigger or scarier is keeping him from telling," she speculated. Maybe there hadn't been enough pressure at the time? She'd considered it. The idea had repeated itself in her mind again and again – what if they were dealing with inept or even corrupt police?

"The detective on the case at the time has nothing to offer. He's retired and moved to the south of Spain. He says the same things we are saying, only that they didn't even have a body. He says her disappearance was so complete that he was sure she'd left of her own accord." Charlie started pacing slowly in the tiny cubicle, "Hart has agreed to put out an appeal for information. Forensics says she was hit with a cylindrical object, a bat or something similar. Then she suffocated in the bag. No worthwhile fingerprints or telling evidence. They're looking at the fibres found on the outside of the bag but haven't found anything specific so far."

"And James?" asked Aija. *I'm not that stupid,* she wanted to say, and she fixed her gaze on his moving figure.

"What about James?" he asked, without stopping. She could tell from the subtleties of his tone that this wasn't a casual question, it was something he didn't want to answer.

"James is your best friend and colleague; you'd be partners if you could be. Why isn't he helping you on the case?" she asked firmly, wanting an answer. Why wasn't James hanging around peeking through her files, checking back with them every time they returned from an interview? He'd have loved to be involved in a case like this, even informally.

When he didn't reply, she continued, "There are rumours that Linehan's implicated him in Lucinda's death."

"That's not entirely true..." he began.

She could tell he'd pre-empted this, something was amiss. Someone was bound to ask, the constable had been in the room, the conversation was recorded – but that wasn't where it was coming from, no one would risk the wrath of the upstairs if confidential information was leaked. No, from what she'd heard, Linehan had been babbling in his half consciousness as he was carried away.

"From the case files, all we know is that James couldn't or didn't verify his own movements in the days following Lucinda's disappearance." Charlie paused but then started again, slower. "He has his parents' alibi saying he was at home at least from the Sunday onwards. But the police had their hands tied at that time – they had no idea when she actually disappeared and this didn't make him any more of suspect than anyone else. Even now Camilla and her crew can't tell us exactly when Lucinda died."

"Have you also considered that she may have died even earlier," suggested Aija as if the answer he'd given hadn't satisfied her. "What if her sister only says she spoke to her, what if the ticket was planted..."

"I know, I've thought about it." Charlie stuffed his hands in his pockets. "I've spun it around in my head. The permutations are endless, I know, they've been keeping me up at night just imagining how many scenarios apply." He gazed into the distance. "We need something new to happen on this case," he mumbled and then was silent.

"What's going on?" she asked after a moment of watching him. Something had disturbed him about this case, she'd never seen him like this in the two years they'd worked together.

His back was to her, cutting her off.

This fit. The whispers that were making their way around the station were impossible to ignore. Someone had heard that a constable had seen a shrine to James in Venter's bedroom, there was missing evidence from the scene – a computer, the constable was sure. Was it true James had been seen kissing a woman outside the crime scene? And, of course, they were lovers – no, the whisper came, it wasn't clear if the woman or the dead man was the lover.

When she wanted to, Aija was as tall as Charlie was, when she drew herself to her full posture. Her tone dropped, the abrupt unprecedented change in her tone and demeanour could be intimidating to suspects and it came out now. She cornered him, in the most literal sense, he was wedged into a corner, and she very firmly between him and the door.

"If Linehan's alleged something about James, why isn't it on file? I've been through every word. You know me," she demanded.

"Are you accusing me of something, Aija?" he challenged her, his chest out and chin up.

"I want to know what's going on. Where's James?" She was so close she could feel him breathing.

He took a deep breath. "I think you're forgetting your station," he spoke calmly.

"No, I'm not," she insisted. "Even constables are supposed to use their brains."

They both fell silent as a trio of sergeants walked past without stopping, offering quick greetings and returning to their raucous conversation.

"Everyone's dropping hints when I'm around. Saying he must know something, saying that he's involved, maybe even bent," she continued. "And you vanish after an argument with Hart, and this is all in one day."

"Aija," he started, then his phone beeped.

"You two are supposed to be my friends, not just work mates. Why won't you tell me what's going on?" She was still between him and freedom. "Is James involved in something?"

"Aija. You've got to stay as far away from this as you can. That's all I'm saying."

"Is this a cover up?" Her voice was louder.

With a firm push he made an escape route for himself and walked out of his office without looking back, leaving her standing alone.

What he hadn't revealed was what stirred her. He hadn't demanded, "How can you say that about James?" or "Do you think I'd be involved in a cover up?" Something was wrong or he would have defended his friend.

She didn't watch him walk away, she walked to his desk and blatantly looked over the mess that was on it, but it told her nothing. It was unacceptable, something was happening, if James was involved she had to find out. She was not going to allow a cover up, a conspiracy, if she could prevent it.

Charlie

Charlie got halfway home, or rather, to James's house. He stopped at a shopping centre unable to shake the feeling that he'd wasted the time spent driving to and from Dolly and Chloe's houses and speaking to them. He pondered their conversations and made notes on his phone to find out more about the man who'd left the country, the one Dolly said had moved to Greece. And what of Dolly herself, her alibi had been no more solid than her brother's or Linehan's. In fact, if he thought about it, what would have stopped Maddie from killing her older sister, she wouldn't be the first child murderer. She'd have needed an accomplice. It would have been impossible for a fourteen year-old to dispose of a body in that manner.

There were two other friends, JJ, Dolly's husband, and Chloe. But they too, he sighed, looking at a selection of pullovers, were more hands to the net that was pulling in James.

Here he was pondering orange or blue, yet all he really wanted was for the case to be over, for James to be exonerated and for their friendship to return to what it was.

His phone rang. He dropped the pullover back on its pile and snatched his phone from his jacket pocket.

"Hi, it's me!" chirped Dolly. "I hope you don't feel like you wasted your time with me this morning."

He'd barely opened his mouth to reply when she pre-empted him, "Don't try to be nice about it." She made a sound that could have been a grunt. "I was explaining to the boys that you are a policeman and they were really excited." She continued. "They asked me what you were doing here and I told them you were investigating a case. And then James, he's the sensitive one, said, 'I hope no one got hurt.' And, well," she paused. "I suppose someone did get hurt. It may have been a long time ago... but... well. I know I'd be devastated if something happened to my... Oh hell."

"It's OK, Dolly, take your time," he reassured her, his spirits lifting regardless of the case.

"So, I called JJ, my husband, just so I could talk to someone, and he suggests that you come and talk to him."

"Really, why?" He held back his enthusiasm.

"A bit like why you talked to me. He knew Gerry and Declan. I'm not entirely sure which case you're after," continued Dolly. "To repeat, I was busy travelling and things, I only happened to be here taking a break. JJ was probably Gerry's next best friend. But if you're not interested..."

"All right, I'm interested."

"It will take some doing as he has an exhibition, but he says he can squeeze in a few questions after."

She directed him to the gallery that would exhibit JJ's work.

When he arrived, he was surprised to find that Dolly would be accompanying him. She was at the door in a casually elegant dress, bare arms without even a cardigan, standing under a tiny overhang. He was still in his work clothes, but without his rain jacket, choosing to brave the light rain rather than to have to deal with a wet jacket indoors.

"JJ's probably one of the most applauded Finnish photographers," she started as they paused to let another couple enter. "He can devote himself to it and cheese because he's invested his inheritance really well, which is more than I can say about Gerry and, well, Declan's dad gambled almost everything away. JJ," she said and raised her chin as if with pride, "has known James almost as long as Gerry and Chloe." She paused. "Did you know that?"

"No, I'm finding out that we weren't on those terms," he replied as they came to a stop in the busy gallery.

The exhibition appealed even to his untrained eye. The photos were of people in the city, all in some sort of blurred perspective. He browsed through them. They were simple enough that an unsophisticated eye like his could find them appealing, yet complex enough that they were sellable. It was not art exhibited at a community centre; it was the kind of which the cheapest, smallest image cost several hundred euros.

He paused at a silhouette that could have been James, leaning against a wrought iron railing, his face turned away from the photographer. It was dated the previous year. This, like Venter's photos, was taken without permission, a candid shot, but the details of what he was doing or thinking had been occluded in the shadows.

He was asking himself why so many people were interested in James, someone who described himself as having few friends, when Dolly waved at a man across the room. He nodded back at her as if telling her he'd seen her but that she'd have to wait.

He assumed the man with her was JJ. He was as tall as James, his skin a deep brown and face gently marked by old acne scars. Without being tight, his shirt emphasised that he had lean muscular abdominals. His hair was shaved, neatly tapering at the neck. He was surrounded by people. They reminded him of the guests at James's functions, some fans, others who came because it was a place to be seen. They hung around him like an aura each with one hand holding a drink, listening to him or offering him their opinions and referring conversations back to him for words of approval.

"They entered all this into an AI system, and it was unable to classify people by race, it doesn't have the bias yet." The conversation behind him startled him back to the present.

"But is it value for money, if I buy it, will it still be worth anything two, five, eight years from now? If not, I'll order posters online," he heard as he followed Dolly.

"Is anyone talking about the actual art?" he observed when she returned from having air kissed a couple who he'd heard talking about the state of the traffic.

She smiled at a passer-by while talking. "A lot of the people here can't afford it, but they'll write about it, mention it to the right people or have their clients buy it. He has a name people want because it might get them in a décor magazine." She chuckled. "Once upon a time this was my tribe, I lapped it up, I was at exhibitions, concerts, everything. Now I'm a stay-at-home mum, but I stay connected because of JJ. He tried to get me into international sales for his cheese – but I'm a homebody now."

"Where did you go after Dublin?" he asked, as it was obvious that JJ needed some time.

"I came back here. Everyone wanted English-language editors and teachers, plenty of work," she replied, saying hello to someone who stopped briefly. "And things started with JJ, in between his trips to cheese destinations – oh, and let's not forget the beef."

"It's over," JJ declared as he came to join them. He gave Dolly a noisy kiss on the lips. Charlie looked away, feeling a momentary reminder that he'd once had someone he kissed like that.

"Good night?" She wove her arm through the crook of his and leaned against him.

"Brilliant. Just saw off a reviewer for *Hesari*. She's impressed," replied JJ, mentioning Helsinki's largest paper, and he looked over at Charlie.

"This," Dolly declared with flourish, "is the infamous detective Charlie Yeats – also known as James's housemate."

Charlie and JJ shook hands. "I've heard incredibly little about you," JJ spoke with a smile.

"JJ takes pictures and makes cheese. Yes, you can imagine what we get for our birthdays every year." Dolly rubbed her husband's arm with the cheer in her face unabated.

It always astounded him to find people who made a living selling things such as cheese, handbags or linen hats. He couldn't imagine how many bits of cheese had to be sold to fund the house or their lifestyle, even with an inheritance. JJ's life and the life of the guy at the cheese counter at the supermarket had to be worlds apart. JJ and Dolly's clothes were not ostentatious but they were expensive.

"Can you sneak out now?" Dolly asked in a low voice.

"Yeah, sure." JJ sighed heavily. "I'm not entirely sure what you want from me though, but if I can help in any way, I will. I mean Gerry, we used to be such good friends."

"How about some insight into Gerry's life? It would be a great place to start. And I'm sure Dolly's told you that I'd love some clarity about his relationship with James."

JJ's face became suddenly and brutally serious. "Insight… over the last few years, Gerry became a closed book. We'd hang out, but it was as if he didn't tell me anything tangible, he didn't talk about anything deep or meaningful. He was an automaton, work, party, work. Any time you asked, he said he was fine."

"Gerry didn't want our help," Dolly insisted.

"He needed it," snapped her husband.

Charlie saw that they both looked away from each other during that exchange. It looked to him that their disagreement ran deep.

"His parents are devastated." JJ's voice was flat. "They didn't know the extent of what was going on – they think it's simple, a history of depression and things like that – maybe he should have found himself a nice man and had babies it would all have been OK."

"JJ, *loistavaa*!" A woman accosted him, her voice in an alcohol-fuelled falsetto. She launched into praise and was, after a few minutes, dragged away by an apologetic man who nodded a quick bye and took her in the direction of the door.

A few more waved on their way out.

"Gerry needed our help," JJ started again.

"I don't think..." began Dolly as more people arrived to shake hands and cheer JJ on loudly. The people here wore the same expensive labels he'd seen in Gerry's wardrobe, perhaps he'd have been here, at a friend's gallery opening, if he was still alive.

"If you can get away, let's go down the pub," Charlie cut in. They were emotional and would have spoken to him but the interruptions gave them the opportunity to calm down – he didn't want that.

JJ relaxed. He nodded and soon they were in a bar only a few doors away. They ordered at the till and then found themselves some seats. As they waited, JJ and Charlie made some observations about the city and its style changing – how now everything seemed to be contemporary and international, not like the city they'd known in their youth. JJ spent a few minutes explaining cheese, its varieties, how it was made and the current trends in cheese consumption. Charlie quickly recognised that he was easier to speak to than his wife.

"Is it a hobby or do you make money out of it?" Charlie asked when JJ explained that it would have been unthinkable for him, an immigrant, to be making a living as a photographer and fromager, back then.

"Both," JJ replied. "How did you meet James?"

"Got to my office and found him in it. He'd moved here from Espoo while I was on medical leave. We're supposed to have separate cubicles but the renovations never seem to end."

"What did you think of him?"

"Smart – right away," Charlie replied, sipping his pint. "A decade ago, I'd have thought misplaced, but people like him are far more usual in the service these days – less the traditional concept of a policeman."

"It's funny, it's not something he considered when we were kids. Though when I look back it was a natural choice."

"Good to hear," said Charlie. "It takes guts to join the police force, especially when someone has other options. And James has produced results, he's a real asset to the force. He actually believes in what he does. You can see it in him that he doesn't consider it a step down in life, that he doesn't do it because his real dreams in life were thwarted. Even if he only does it part time you can tell it's something that fulfils him." He stated that with confidence, feeling that he needn't have explained so much.

"You've got him perfectly." JJ chuckled.

"And you," he nodded to JJ. "How did you meet?"

"We were about twelve I guess. I'd just come back from visiting my grandparents and then found this new guy. Gerry, Chloe and I moved here when we were much younger, but we had the same struggles. My parents insisted on me calling all my friends' parents Sir and Mrs or at the least Auntie and Uncle – it was unthinkable for us to call adults by their first names. The locals found us strange, you'll remember that it wasn't the most diverse place then. I found these two fascinating – James climbed trees and went home covered in mud from the beach. They stayed out late, just because they could." Here he smiled at his wife as the three of them sat down, continuing, "We made other friends of course. But they shifted, were nebulous, but we were the core. But, you know when you stop telling each other things, when you stop paying attention because you're–" he glanced at Dolly again– "busy," he finished.

"It's as if we don't live in the same town," JJ continued his story. "When I had my first shows, Gerry and James would both be there. But dealing with Gerry was really hard, I started to sometimes forget, let's say, to invite him, and other times he'd forget to come."

They all fell silent. Charlie knew that they'd be asking themselves what they could have done differently and if they had done that one thing, would Gerry still be alive?

"From what I understand," began Charlie. "They were close and..."

"They were really close," said JJ, and he smirked.

"What was that?" Dolly asked.

"Nothing," chuckled JJ. "Memories."

She glared at him.

"How close?" Charlie leaned forward, the itch to know desperate to be scratched.

"They did everything together, that's why James's acceptance was so important," said Dolly.

"Dolly, that's not what he wants to know," insisted JJ.

"James was the first person that Gerry came out to," explained Dolly. "We all knew he was gay, but it's when he first articulated it."

JJ smiled again. "And James laughed at him?"

"It was the start of everything going wrong," Dolly said and elbowed her husband.

"No, it wasn't. He apologised. They made up," said JJ with finality. "They were friends after."

"That's not what Chloe told me, apparently Gerry held it against him for ages," insisted Dolly.

JJ chortled and Charlie smiled with him, urging him to share what was so funny.

"What?" Dolly asked, her eyes narrowing.

"Dolly," JJ said laughing, leaning ever so slightly away from her. "There are some things boys don't tell girls. Even if you are twins."

Dolly gave a low growl. "What do you mean?" she demanded, she squeezed her husband's arm.

JJ chortled some more and responded only when Dolly gently smacked him on the arm.

"OK. The official version, the one we told you – Gerry comes out to James like 'James, I think I'm gay.' James bursts into laughter: 'ha ha!'." He looked genuinely happy at the memory. "The real version," here he glanced at Charlie, "we've just won at football. We're showered, we're clean, we're happy, we're skipping like rabbits down a lane. Arms linked over shoulders. The coach

– remember him – tells us to keep it down, we're not bloody animals, as he's huffing and puffing off on his bike. Then I shouted something nasty about his fat behind and the coach starts to wobble on his bike obviously too embarrassed to turn back and I start laughing, right. Then I turn back and Gerry and James have their tongues down each other's throats."

Dolly's anger intensified, she sat higher in the seat, threw her shoulders back, and sat rigidly in place with her jaw clenched.

"Seriously," JJ shrugged apologetically and said, "and they looked as if they were enjoying it. And I was like, what, no witnesses! Absolutely no one there to see it but me."

Dolly was squinting at her husband and Charlie hid his amusement in sips of beer. Who'd have thought – James? *Well, everybody had thought, even him.*

"Then, and this is the honest truth. They finish, step away from each other. Gerry looks on top the world. James looks into the sky for half a moment, and then bursts out laughing." JJ ended his anecdote looking into his beer, the laughter replaced with sadness.

The couple were silent. And Charlie watched Dolly digest this information that looked different in the light of Gerry's suicide.

"We didn't tell you because," JJ turned to look at Dolly, "we agreed that it wasn't the kind of thing we wanted getting around."

"We?"

"We were fifteen year-olds in what was probably the safest place in the world to be gay at the time, and even here wasn't that safe. James and I would have been labelled queer too and that would hardly have done our nascent sexuality any good. I mean, even with all my bravado, I had a million questions about my own body. I remember thinking, am I gay by association? Not because I was homophobic, but because I barely knew who I was." He paused, "But enough about me, they made up, and I tell you if Gerry was here today, happy and healthy, I wouldn't have thought twice about that incident. It only matters because everything else went so wrong." JJ looked up at the ceiling. "Later, when Gerry came out for sure, James apologised for hurting his feelings, he claimed he thought he was having a laugh."

"Gerry adored James to a point that it was ridiculous," Dolly added, shifting her weight in the seat as if uncomfortable. "So did Chloe, but at least she was more dignified about it."

"When they'd stopped talking to each other, every time I saw him, Gerry always asked about James, first thing. Each time I met him that's the first thing he'd want to know, 'Have you seen James? I heard he's a policeman, does he look good in uniform?'"

Dolly's eyes were focused on her glass, Charlie watched as she took another sip without raising her head.

"That kiss unfortunately was the apex of Gerry's freedom," JJ continued. "His parents were seriously old country and homophobic as hell. When he was about seventeen, to appease them, he started, you know, acting straight. Started wearing denim shirts and saying he had a girlfriend. At first it was all a joke. Then it became something he did around the parents all the time. But with us he stayed as he was – floral shirts, grinning at guys' backsides. Then years later, after this Lucinda girl went missing, he was suddenly 100 per cent heterosexual. Dating women, and... and whatever he thought straight guys do."

"He just stopped being Gerry," continued Dolly. "No fun clothes, no ruling the dance floor."

"I actually considered that he had something to do with Lucinda's death, but I decided no. It was more complex. I think the whole thing left him feeling emasculated – worried that he couldn't protect his friends if something happened to them. But come on, we all, I, felt like that." With that JJ covered Dolly's hand with his tenderly.

"So if I understand you right, you're saying this change in Gerry took place after Lucinda went missing," asked Charlie.

"We all slinked off into our respective corners so to speak. I went travelling again, Dolly moved back here from Dublin... we lost that bond we used to have," JJ said as he tightened his grip on his glass. "And, no, it wasn't anything, as far as I knew, to do with Lucinda."

"How sure can you be?" asked Charlie.

JJ waved his free hand in the air and Charlie decided not to press it and risk alienating the couple.

"What do you know of Declan now?" He changed direction, since, in his mind, Declan was a possible suspect.

JJ spread his hands open, his palms upward. "Nothing that I can attest to. Rumour has it that he's in deep trouble. He made some deals with very unethical investors – and he's being jettisoned by his employers. They're pre-empting queries by their other clients because they don't want to be soiled by association. He's a bit of a headcase. Years ago, I helped him out – I pointed him out to someone who wanted native English – let's say, an English face for his business. It was simple, basically reading from a script. He messed even that up, I was so embarrassed that I vowed never to involve myself with him again."

Once again the lives of the wealthy struck Charlie as so unlike his own – he couldn't imagine friends who gave you jobs – easy ones at that.

"Could he have had anything to do with Gerry's death?"

JJ gestured again that he didn't know. "Probably as much as any of us. Not taking time for Gerry maybe. But Declan's always been a bit of an arsehole. I wouldn't expect him to be there emotionally for Gerry – for drinks and parties, yes, but not for proper emotional support."

Charlie saw that their drinks were nearly finished and the conversation would end soon. This wasn't an evening that would allow socialising and gentle sustained drunkenness – not when he was investigating their family member.

"I could have paid Gerry more attention. The last time I saw him, he looked wretched. I should have stopped to check up on him. But I had that 'not again' feeling," JJ drew himself up and then sighed.

"When did you see him last?"

"About a week ago maybe? He was reading – no, drowning – himself in a book in a café – he was hunched over and his face buried in it," JJ described the scene, hunching forward in imitation of Gerry. "He looked like he needed sleep, a bath and a shave."

"Could you see what book?" he asked, as he drained the dregs of his glass and was about to suggest they end the evening.

"James's newest." JJ waved a hand in dismissal. "I know, I think it's utter rubbish – it's so unlike James."

Dolly looked away, but not quickly enough that he didn't see her eyes were watery with tears. "I think we should go," her voice trembled.

"Thank you both," he said to them as they rose to leave. "I really appreciate it."

Chapter 11

Aija

Hart had stopped at her desk without a greeting or an attempt to soften the blow. "Find someone to cover James's cases." Had she not been standing beside her, Aija would have thought the words were aimed elsewhere.

"But..." she'd began.

"I don't have time for this, find someone and say I told them so." Hart had vanished upon her words and Aija had watched her march away, her back straight and her chin up, not a hint of softness in her posture.

Aija had examined the small pile of files, knowing she didn't have an option to refuse her task, and went to see Charlie.

"Hart asked me to share James's file among the detectives. Would you like the librarians?" She was smiling, thinking of how they'd teased James about being stuck at the beck and call of the city's flagship library's staff. Charlie had the right temperament; he was patient and gentle.

"No," he echoed when she offered him a suspected drug dealer at the Helsinki University.

He stopped flexing his hands and raised a knuckle to his teeth. "Why don't you do it?" he asked with a wave of his hand as if she was an irritation.

She knew what James had been working on. It was known that James was a brilliant detective, and it was rumoured that he was in line for promotion above Charlie. James should have had either Lucinda's case or something similar. However, somehow the gods of interesting cases had overlooked James for the last month or so. His crimes were middling at best, dull really – and she didn't want even more tedious cases to add to her own caseload.

"Sorry, I'm swamped." She waved a hand towards her own desk. "Hart wants me to finish onboarding Eva."

"A senior officer is supposed to do that."

"Can you see any to spare?" she replied, not meaning to be rude. Still, she didn't see why the things no one else wanted to do ended up on her desk, despite the general agreement that she was a rather inept detective.

It was summer and predictably as many officers as could get away with it had gone on leave. No matter how well it was planned and discussed ahead of time, it always happened that they found themselves just barely within the prescribed numbers. But now with James nowhere to be seen, Eva still a newcomer and Charlie "busy", the inverted commas somehow visible in her mind, she was stuck with seemingly endless forms to fill in and a plethora of trivial cases that someone had to attend to.

"Shouldn't I be helping with Lucinda? It's high priority," she insisted just as Hart walked back past the door, hoping that Hart would hear her and take her side.

"We can't spare you," said Hart, "you're practically holding the detective section together."

"With paperwork," Aija muttered.

"Freeing up much needed manpower to keep us going," replied Hart with a blatantly insincere smile. "Don't be difficult," she sighed angrily. "Not in this rain." She walked away again.

"Then you could onboard Eva?" she asked Charlie, realising that her bid to get Hart on her side hadn't worked. "I can follow up with forensics on DNA or anything else they may have picked up."

"I'm pursuing some leads and I've already spoken to Camilla about DNA."

He was determined to keep her locked out of the case, she thought. At worst he didn't even care about Lucinda, perhaps he was doing nothing at all. Maybe he was lying, and he simply didn't care enough to do anything. But that wasn't Charlie. She thought, being angry at him for not trusting her enough to involve her was shaking her belief in him.

She knew he was better than that. She remembered when she first arrived and there was still a lot of smoke in the air about a wife who was a paedophile. The woman had been carrying on what she called an affair. Aija had seen references in the paper, but due to the laws about reporting cases involving minors, she'd had no indication about the identity of the woman. Charlie had looked like a man who was finding it difficult to get out of bed each morning, he'd still been overweight and sweated even in winter when she arrived.

"Which leads?" she asked.

He'd just firmly turned his chin to the sky and bitten his top lip when a firm knock announced Eva. She looked cheerful, as if she'd just laughed at a joke and was savouring the feeling of joy it had left her with.

"Hi, how's the morning?" She nodded at them both.

"Oh gosh, Eva. Sorry, are we supposed to meet?" She recalled her to-do list which clearly listed, *meeting Eva* and a time that had passed half an hour earlier. "Sorry, I'm absolutely swamped."

In truth, she simply didn't want to sit with Eva and listen to earnest questions or her eagerly told tales of what to her may have seemed simple police-client interactions but to Aija seemed like genius.

"Don't worry about it," she gestured with her hands to emphasise it, "just that Hart told me you might have a surplus of cases."

"Here's something," Aija replied quickly and handed the librarians' case to Eva. "James said this has potential to be a bigger problem. We also have a selection of break-ins for you to choose from." She gave a broad smile that she hoped seemed friendly and not malicious.

Eva flicked her a smile that could have meant anything and replied cheerfully, "Hart was right, you really are her right-hand man."

"Right-hand man?" It escaped her before she had a chance to stop herself.

"Who else knows everything that's going on here?" quipped Eva, and pointed at her neat pile of files with a to-do list pinned on top.

As soon as she was out of sight Charlie snorted. "The duelling librarians – an exciting start to her detective career in Helsinki. Just be really nice to her next time you see her – you don't want to make an enemy of blondes. I'm off to follow those leads."

He stood quickly and was gone. Aija still had a strange feeling from Eva referring to her as Hart's right-hand man. But then she let it lie, it was most certainly part of Hart's eternal machinations. Was Hart telling Eva that she was the person to go to for files but not for detective work?

Aija glanced in both directions and tossed her pencil to her desk. It clattered to the floor. What leads? Charlie hadn't filled in a full report since the first one recording the crime. He hadn't been himself just there, being abrupt and moody weren't qualities she associated with him. That *no* was something more like a response James would give.

After a few more stabs at her paperwork she put her computer to sleep, covering her eyes with her hands. Lucinda's image flashed across the inside of her eyelids. Lucinda – a young woman put to death in a bin bag. Aija decided she had to find out what happened, if Charlie wasn't going to tell her, she'd find out. She wasn't prepared to sit at her desk listing employees that no one was going to interview.

Aija drove back to the crime scene. It had already been cleared up, only police tape remained flapping in an almost indiscernible breeze. The site had been reduced to muddy indentations in the ground. She knew the team would have been as thorough as possible. They'd have combed through the debris of the years looking for anything relevant to the case. She hitched her backpack further up towards her shoulders and walked in a widening spiral around the crime scene. Finding nothing new, she then began walking to the main road.

She tried to imagine what happened. The person who brought the body here was strong, even if he'd – they'd, she corrected herself, *don't limit yourself* – brought the body by car to the edge of the forest, they'd have had to either carry it or at least use a bike or wheelbarrow of some sort. It would have had to be at night when there'd have been almost no chance of being found by dog walkers and runners.

Twenty years ago the forest would have been much larger than it was now. It would have been available for long hikes, not just short family walks and overnight camping. She got to the edge of the forest and looked at the new builds which were probably all constructed in the decades since Lucinda died.

In front of them were older houses, legacies of the seventies – terrace houses and standalones. Large houses, some quite valuable, that's how far she'd have had to go to get help if she'd somehow escaped. But no, Aija shook her head. She'd have been alive but she couldn't have been conscious, she'd have struggled – they hadn't found evidence of binding – a black bin bag would not have kept a reasonably sized woman contained. She'd have ripped through the bag. No, she'd have been unconscious, a dead weight that needed a strong person to carry it.

Two or three people could have shared her weight between them. More than that would have been a struggle, coordinating their journey and their load. Someone might have been on the lookout. carrying the shovel and selecting where the body would be dumped.

There were too many variations. Aija stopped in the woods and looked around herself. In short all that was needed was a group of people who could keep a secret – whatever their motive for doing so could be.

No wonder it seemed as though Charlie was giving up. Someone could even have moved the body over the years, a witness that returned to the scene. She kicked the soil with anger and was leaving when her phone rang.

"Are you busy?" asked James. When he needed her, he usually just assigned her a task, he rarely considered if she had something else to do.

"Yes, very," she answered, then wished she could retract it, because then she stood a better chance of knowing what was going on.

"It's a quick favour," he continued. "Only I can't get back to work, Hart has put me on leave for a few days."

"You're either seriously ill or have really pissed her off," she joked.

"I'm not seriously ill," he replied, his voice unchanging, but she sensed some humour. "But I need something that Charlie has, and I can't ask him for it, or he'll tell."

"I'm listening," she replied. Her heart began to pound in her chest.

"It's a picture." He described it – a photo of Lucinda, Declan and Venter. He couldn't say anything else about it.

She bit her lip, not wanting to reveal that she didn't know about this photo. A picture of Lucinda and Venter, what was Charlie up to? She was in fact grateful to James for telling her about it.

"It will be in his desk somewhere."

"You want me to go rooting around in his desk for evidence?" This sounded like something that would get her fired.

"Yes," he replied. "You can't let him know. Just a picture of it is all I need, and delete it from your phone when you're finished, that would be cleverest thing to do."

"James, are you in some kind of trouble?" she asked, quickly walking to her car. She was practically cheering with excitement. A picture; an important picture! It had to be of some significance or Charlie wouldn't have kept it from her.

"Why should I do this?" she replied to his silence. She was excited to finally have some direction, but she slowed herself down – she shouldn't let James take advantage of it, and despite their friendship, she told herself she wouldn't do anything that would jeopardise her job. "I know I have as much a chance of you explaining to me as Charlie. I know we're friends, but I'm not going to get myself in trouble for you."

"I can't tell you that."

"Then I can't get it for you," she challenged him. "And don't lie – I know you too well for that."

"It's a clue – proof even," he added. "That the people in the picture had something to do with Lucinda's death."

That seemed too obvious to her and she guessed he realised it.

"And Charlie won't act on it," he continued. "He's protecting someone." His response was slow, as if he'd had to consider it. "If you don't send me that photo we might never find out what happened."

"OK," she breathed. She too had to know.

"I knew you would help," he replied.

Eva was hovering around her desk when she got there. Aija was itching to look at this photo.

"The librarians called." She spoke Finnish as everyone else did in the office. "They wanted to talk to James, I insisted I was in charge of the case. They were surprised that there was a case. Even the wife insisted that there was nothing to worry about."

"Thanks for letting me know," replied Aija in Finnish too.

"So, that's fine then?" asked Eva.

"Well, James said they were definitely something to worry about," said Aija. "He said something about surveillance."

"Well, I thought something more interesting?" said Eva dismissively. "Something came in through the wire about drugsdrugs." Her voice hinted that she wanted to be assigned to it.

"I don't really know," Aija replied and stopped. "Look, it's not up to me to hand out assignments. I'm just a sergeant."

A cloud of what could be construed as anger gathered at Eva's forehead. "Look, Hart told me to ask you. She said you knew the appropriate cases for me."

Aija could see why Eva was upset. She'd probably worked hard to earn her promotion and now she was asking someone of a lower level than she was for guidance.

"OK. I have a host of things I can give you but nothing really exciting, so if you're happy with that," Aija clicked on her computer and entered her password. "I'll send you these, OK?" She selected some minor burglaries and the case of smuggling unauthorised baby toys and shared them with Eva. This seemed to placate her and she walked away, her back erect and her hair bouncing.

Aija made a face at her and then glanced around to make sure no one had seen her.

She walked as casually as she could to Charlie and James's office. No one would suspect her as she was always there. But the knowledge that she was "up to no good", as Charlie would have put it, raised a film of sweat on her forehead as she plotted.

She sat at Charlie's desk and, knowing that if something was secret it would be in one of the last two drawers, she pulled out her spare key. She found among the pieces of paper a photo in protective plastic, telling her that this was police evidence.

She took a photo of the image that she would send to James – but not yet.

She was about to shut the drawer when she saw some correspondence, addressed to Charlie and printed out with parts underlined in pen.

She again looked around before taking a quick picture, shutting the drawer and leaving to examine her spoils.

It was still drizzling so she stood in a covered area that attracted smokers but that today was quiet, damp, only a few insects buzzed.

She looked at the letter first, saving the joy of the picture for later.

Action Required, it announced in bold lettering. And then continued. It was a rejection of Charlie's insurance. The company acceded to the fact that the house and its contents had been destroyed, had been fully insured, but that in the absence of the co-owner and majority share owner Rachel Yeats, it could not be paid in full.

"Oh," she heard her own exclamation – she felt as if she'd been slapped in the face. It was dated several days earlier.

Charlie had been silent about it.

No, she reminded herself. He had told her the opposite, that everything was almost sorted out.

He'd have to prove that he was entitled to Rachel's claim in order to collect the money, buy a new flat and move from James's. She had little idea of what his house would have been worth, but to collect only a fraction of the money would mean that he'd be unable to live in the kind of house in which he'd lived for the last fifteen years.

He couldn't escape his wife, could he? It was bad enough that she'd been having sex with a teenager and had lied about it and then vanished. It was awful enough for him that the police were still unable to locate her and that her actions had left a massive imprint on his life. Two years later, the insurance company couldn't allow him to move on.

If this was a conspiracy, what if Hart, or worse, higher management, was using Rachel against him – somehow forcing him to compromise the investigation? What if he felt he couldn't survive more of what had been hurled at him when Rachel disappeared?

He'd confessed, when their friendship was developing, that he didn't look for her – his wife – he was afraid that when he found her he'd take her back. He was afraid that in a woman that had not only compromised the wellbeing of a child, but also his life and his children's lives, he would still be able to see the woman he'd loved for so long.

She paused, not scrolling to the next photo, the one James had requested. Charlie had lied to her, then. She stopped to breathe, knowing she shouldn't be offended because there had to be a reason. Charlie was one of the most decent men she knew, she reminded herself.

Then she sighed, afraid of what the next photo would show.

She'd only glanced at it in the drawer to see that it fit what James had described. It had been the only photo in the drawer, so she'd assumed that was what James was after. What if it compromised Charlie even further? What if she had to choose between Charlie and James, or worse, Charlie and the truth?

So far in her career in Helsinki, Charlie, James and Hart told her what to do. No one other than these three ever asked her to do anything. She'd been insulated against the greater reality of police politics and administration. It was as if she belonged to them, which wasn't a bad thing. But she could see Eva circling, threatening the status quo, and she wouldn't be the last. Without Charlie and James she'd be subject to the realities of being a black woman in the police, the worst cases, the longest hours and the least credit. There would be no more of "the association of make-believe Englishmen", a moniker which with her current contrived advantage she could afford to laugh at. Every other policeman spoke English, sometimes even a third or fourth language like Eva – in the end neither the fluency of her speech or the seeming authenticity of her accent was of real use, only when in the company of two of the department's highest-performing policemen and its superintendent was she someone to be taken any notice of.

Her finger hovered over her phone. *Then I'll quit and go to Singapore,* she assured herself and swiped her fingers across to the next photo.

James and Lucinda in the same photo.

She looked at the photo again and again, a seemingly drunk James, a jolly Linehan, Venter smiling; a group of young people having fun. There was no record of the photo. She hadn't taken an image of the back, so she didn't know if anything had been written on it. But it had to be important, or Charlie wouldn't have hidden it. Could it have been on Lucinda's last known night, the night that she disappeared?

She glanced at the police headquarters building ahead of her, watching people coming and going. It seemed forever ago that she had studied what it meant to be a policeman and a detective. Sometimes it seemed countless detective movies from Agatha Christie to the latest Nordic sensations affected her work far more than actual police training. In this case she would have to think for herself. Imagining what she had to do next, she had to map her situation – the case. What did she have?

The only people she knew were related to the case were Lucinda's sister, Linehan, Venter and James. She couldn't approach James without knowing what the situation was with Hart and Charlie, it could get her into trouble.

"Have you got it?" she asked him on the phone after she'd forwarded him the picture.

"Aija, thank you. When this is over, I don't know, I'll take you for a beer."

"Why are you in the photo with Lucinda?"

"I don't know," he replied and ended the call.

She didn't know what he meant by that. She pondered it for a while, but then, leaving a cryptic message at the office, she drove to Maddie's, Lucinda's sister's, house. She did this with reluctance because she knew she had no authority to be there. She had to trust that Maddie would think it was a routine follow-up.

Charlie would find out soon enough what she was doing and he'd be angry, but he too was acting outside their remit.

Maddie was almost excited to see her. "I thought you'd have forgotten about us, again."

"Things are different now," Aija reassured her. "We're not going to let this lie. I just need more help from you." She showed her the photo on her phone.

There was a silence as she looked at the image. Aija gave her a moment. Maddie stroked the screen and then looked up at Aija.

"It was taken around the time she went missing," Aija said gently. "It's only just come to light. Do you know anything about these people, or where it was taken?"

"I know him," she said after squinting at the photo. "The Merimies writer. I've read his books. Can't wait for the next one. Is he really still a policeman? Hasn't he made enough money to just run off?"

"He's really passionate about his work," Aija said. One of the lines she'd adopted to deal with his fans.

"Do you know him outside that context, have you seen him before?"

"No. And I don't recognise where it was taken. I was too young to go out at night." She paused again. "But this guy," she pointed at the picture, "he could have been one of Lucinda's boyfriend's friends. He was loud, in a loud shirt." She was pointing at Linehan. "And at a stretch, this guy could be the one she was interested in, but at a real stretch." Now she was pointing at Gerry.

Aija repressed her smile. She thanked her after a few questions that felt inane; would they have been seen together, what was her favourite place to meet him? She knew Maddie didn't know the answers, but at least she was asking the questions, which was more than Charlie was doing.

Why hadn't Charlie got to this? These were basic investigation tactics – perhaps he was waiting for Linehan to be cleared from hospital. But no, this was wasting time. He had to be protecting James.

It was natural that he would. His ex-wife had nearly ruined his career by carrying on with an underage boy. If James, someone everyone knew he had a strong relationship with, was involved in a killing, it would reverberate through the department. The police were determined to keep the image of the police force clean. The fact that James had become its poster boy with his books made it even more important, she surmised. She could see Hart convincing Charlie to make sure James's involvement would never become common knowledge. But she couldn't let the truth be buried, even if it meant her friends lost everything.

James

"Things must be pretty dismal if you've come to see us during the day." Dolly offered him tea without asking how he took it. She knew exactly how he took it. And that was the problem with her, his twin. She was a constant between the past and the present, she was also the reason why even when he'd tried to escape this city he came back.

That she was married to JJ made the connection to the city even stronger. JJ was a reminder of the good times. He was a witness to the days when he, Gerry and JJ were young and no more or less inhibited than any other teenage boy. It was a time before rifts could be dragged on for years. If they had known that one of them could be snuffed out in an instant, that one of their lives could end one humid summer morning, maybe he or JJ would have tried harder to get the two of them to mend their relationship.

"It's tragic, I know. You guys keep it down!" JJ called at the twins who'd started a mysterious banging noise outdoors. "Have you thought of talking to someone about it?"

"He's talking to us," Dolly said, picking up the teapot and putting it down again, the tea had already been poured.

He could tell Dolly didn't want this conversation. She, like he, preferred to hold everything close to her chest. The idea of going to a therapist wasn't repugnant to her, but she'd never be able to let go enough to another person about her true feelings.

"It's hard to imagine young Gerry ending up killing himself. But old Gerry, yes." JJ and Dolly nodded in agreement.

"The last time I saw him, I should have guessed." Dolly shook her head and paused before continuing, "That he was on edge. But to be honest I just wanted to get away from him. He looked so pathetic. He was telling me how much he liked your books. He was holding one. It looked like it had taken a thorough beating."

She, as always, had a pack of Tennis biscuits on the table, though these days it was probably just habit. A long-held craving, a memento of life on a different continent in a different universe. They could just as easily have been replaced by *korvapuusti* or new vegan nut biscuits.

"He wanted your number, I reminded him that he had it," she continued. "I told him you'd be glad to catch up with him."

"Would you?" asked JJ. He was the one who of the three of them had gone on to what could be called a normal life. He was prosperous, happy. He was a family man who had strong enough standing in the community that the normal inconveniences, the racism and the anti-immigrant sentiment were insufficient to knock him down from where he was stood.

"I would like to think I would," stated James. "What he said, it was the worst time to say it."

Dolly placed her hand over his and he let the warmth flow through.

"He didn't mean..." began JJ.

"Yes, he did," disagreed Dolly through gritted teeth. "He was always jealous of you – I know he thought it was love. But he hated that you were happy, normal, he resented the fact that you had a life without him."

JJ looked away at the ceiling. "We'll never know because none of us had that conversation with him. I told Charlie about the time I saw him with your book. It was only a couple of weeks ago. He looked wretched, holding on to the thing for his life. He didn't see me, and I just turned a corner. Got away as quickly as I could."

They all fell silent, drinking tea in the wet heat. That morning the thick clouds had begun to move across the sky, laced with foreboding, as if they were to leave only after a dramatic storm. But the forecaster had dismissed their promise of an exodus with the predication that the rain and heat would continue unabated.

James took out his phone and showed them the photo. Dolly gasped and took the phone from him. "That's the picture Charlie showed me. I didn't know you were in it." With her fingers she scrolled across and zoomed in and out at the faces.

"That's that night," JJ hissed. "Who the hell kept that picture?"

"Gerry."

The two of them froze.

"Who took it?" That was the only thing James could ask. He'd spent the best part of an hour scrolling, enlarging, staring at, examining every clue that Aija's picture would give up.

"That girl took it, the runner, on Gerry's new camera. I don't remember this guy – he left the country, hasn't he? And Chloe," JJ paused. "She looked like someone else. When did she change so completely?"

JJ put a hand up to his face and rubbed his forehead. "What a night."

"Put it away!" Dolly abruptly handed it back.

He put the phone back in his pocket.

"So, you guys were the last to see her, is that why you're interested?" JJ said. "How come no one's ever mentioned this photo?"

"Let's not talk about it." Dolly's voice was raised to almost a shriek. The boys hurtled into the kitchen and attacked the biscuits, disregarding their parents' remonstrations.

"I'm going now." James stood battling the emotions that were rising again.

"No, James, stay," said Dolly. "We won't talk about it. Just stay, we'll sit outside and have a drink."

"What does this photo mean?" asked JJ. "Did Gerry know what happened to Lucinda?" He matched James's height. "Could what happened to her have anything to do with you?"

"I don't know." He was standing now.

"James, stay here," insisted Dolly.

"It's OK, James. You come back any time you need us, we're here." JJ knew him well enough to know that he wouldn't stay.

Charlie

James finally answered his phone. He'd let it ring too many times. Charlie knew James, a good policeman would have had his phone with him all the time.

Charlie was in his car, furiously eating an apple and sipping Vichy – an old Finnish brand of aerated water. From where he was parked, he could see the station but wasn't ready to go in.

"Where are you?" he asked, pausing to wipe away a scrap of apple from his shirt. He'd chewed it so quickly and forcefully that he'd barely tasted it and now was left with what felt like a lump in his stomach.

"I've just been to see Dolly," James replied. "I know I missed the meeting, but I had to talk to her first."

"Hart is livid," began Charlie, then he paused. "I want to apologise." He hadn't planned what to say.

"For what?"

"For treating you like I did. You're not just a suspect or a possible bent policeman. You're my friend." He felt his chest tighten, waiting for James to reject him.

"I didn't give you much of a choice, did I?"

Charlie thought he heard a car door slam as James answered.

"I could have handled it better. Sat down with you or something. Not accuse you to your face," said Charlie. "I want you to know that no matter how this pans out..."

"Don't make that promise," insisted James. "If Rachel reappeared right now, you wouldn't take her back, would you?"

He had to take a breath before he answered. "Of course I wouldn't."

"So, if I turn out to be..." James fell silent.

"What is it?" A sense of dread rose within him.

"I can't explain..."

"Please try. Would it be easier if we met up?"

"No, it would be a hell of a lot harder."

He heard a strange sound from James's line. Was he crying? "James, whatever this is, you have to tell me."

"OK." He heard him take a deep heavy breath. "It's just that, the photo..."

What? What? What? Charlie clenched his mobile.

"I think I might have something to do with Lucinda. I just don't know what."

All he could say was, "What the hell?"

"I don't remember anything, it's just too many things happening in one night for it to all be coincidence," James explained in a low voice.

"Listen, don't you dare talk to Linehan. He's already under suspicion. Don't speak to anyone until you've talked to me. Where are you? I'll meet you there." Charlie put his hand on his keys that were still in the ignition.

"I've got to talk to someone first," James said after a pause, seeming to regain some composure, "I'll catch you afterwards," he said and hung up before Charlie could speak.

James

"Gerry read my book?" James demanded of Chloe, who looked afraid when she saw him at her door. She opened it wider and let him in.

He'd driven around in circles, debating if he really wanted to know more about the photo or about Gerry. He'd come to the conclusion that if he didn't know more, not knowing would gnaw away at him, or rather, he rephrased the notion, chew him to pieces, shredding his sanity from limb to limb.

Once resolved, he found her address and trivialities about her, when she married and where she was born, then he drove to her house.

She shrugged. "Maybe," only when he'd repeated the question.

"Why was he going about carrying it?" he said. "Why?"

"Come in," she said. They were standing at the threshold, her arm resting on the door jamb. It was raining just enough for James to feel it coalescing at his neck and dripping through his neckline, down the back of his jacket. It didn't occur to him to put the hood up.

If Chloe had looked tired and bereft before, today she looked on the edge of sanity. Even in the few moments at the door, her eyes never ceased darting around as if she was being pursued. She looked up, behind him, at him, at the floor, at her arm, then suddenly she shut them tightly.

In his years on the force he'd learnt about people on the edge, and Gerry was already dead. James tried again in a gentler voice. "That night, you told me you and Gerry left me there, at the bar. With whom?"

"No one. I don't know. We weren't paying attention," she said, beckoning him to follow but only as far as an interior corridor, from which he could see a room but paid no attention to it.

"With Lucinda, the missing girl?"

"She has nothing to do with this, I didn't even know her," she snapped in reply.

"I saw a photo of that night. It's like a black hole in my life. It's like I wasn't there. There are no hints, no snatches of memory. I'm begging you, what happened to Lucinda?"

"Why can't you just leave it alone? You pretended you were OK and now Gerry's killed himself," Chloe carried on as if he hadn't spoken. "When Gerry read your new book, it was like everything he'd done to stay afloat was just pulled out from under him. It was as if he'd crashed. It made me terrified to even try to talk to him."

"Why would talking to him scare you?" he demanded. "You were friends."

"I've tried to run away from here so many times. But if I'd left Gerry, he definitely would have cracked and told someone. I always had to be here, or else he would tell or worse still, Linehan would kill him. We've had to be friends. I've had to constantly pull him up. I've had to be the person who creates his social calendar, making up all sorts of parties, suggesting that we meet friends, calling, organising. I've had to dance when I haven't wanted to, karaoke when I'd rather be at home in bed. And then since the book, I just haven't been able to..." She took a few steps to the left and then returned along the same path, stopping and looking at the floor before looking back at him, "...pretend."

James leaned against the wall, small snatches of sense coming through what she was saying. With one hand, he straightened the frame that he'd bumped into.

"Gerry has, had, never stopped being in love with you. It got worse after. When you throw guilt in on top of everything... He was convinced that your memory loss was all a charade. That you were determined to torture him with it. He just couldn't take it anymore. He just couldn't stand the idea of what he'd – we'd – done."

"It wasn't a charade, I can't remember." He stammered and squeezed his eyes shut at the absence of memory – at waking up with a hole in his life. Chloe's voice cut through the darkness.

"I believe you." Chloe sounded exasperated. "But Gerry thought you were needling him with it. The last time I saw him, he talked about a confrontation, you'd have a massive argument and there'd be confessions and, he wanted, he could finally start healing from what he'd done."

"And what..." asked James, afraid of the answer, "had he done?"

"I could lie," she faltered. "But he's dead and I've had enough too."

Aija

"Don't tell me you're on an errand for Hart. She hasn't got a clue where you are," Charlie's voice was almost a shout when Aija answered his call. She didn't dare not to pick up.

"No, I'm just heading home to change." She left it there. It was a muddy day. She'd just lied to her friend and superior.

"Right, I'm supposed to be on my way to meet James, but he's delayed. I'm going back to the office to get some work done."

"I'll see you soon, an hour or so." She ended the call and pressed Linehan's doorbell.

He opened the door with a drink in his hand. He didn't look inebriated. He looked unconvincingly cheerful when speaking, "Aija, please come in," with a little bow as if she were a guest.

"I just have a few more questions for you." She didn't. "It shouldn't take long."

They stood in the corridor, him eyeing her for a moment too long and then gesturing towards the living room. She didn't like being here. This was a man whose underwear she'd sifted through, books she'd pored over and bed she'd looked under and found nothing but dust.

"If you give me any trouble," he began, putting a hand over where his heart was as if to remind her of his condition.

"Just some questions, and I'm gone." She punctuated her promise with a smile.

He nodded.

"You know James?" Again he nodded. "Can you tell me anything at all about his association to Lucinda Barnaby?"

"The girl that went missing? He didn't have one," replied Linehan.

"Look at them here." She showed him the photo. "They're practically holding each other, was it a one–?"

"No, *you* look at the photo," he insisted, glancing at it only for a moment and then seizing her wrist and pointing the image at her face. "Can't you see, he's not there?"

Aija looked at the snapshot of a man's life at a moment twenty years earlier. Linehan's hand had gripped her wrist. If he'd known how to overcome a powerful woman, he could have pulled her down or hit her.

James was facing the camera, but he wasn't looking at it.

"Drunk, so what?"

"His drink had been spiked – well, that's what we realised had happened. I have no idea who did it. He was there, but not there. He started saying weird things, not mad, just off, next thing we had to hold him upright. We only found out later that he had no idea where he was – absolutely no memory of that night." Linehan covered his face with his hands over his eyes and his fingers spread out.

"What about Lucinda?"

But Linehan didn't look as if he'd heard. "The rest of us were drunk. Not fall-down drunk, we knew what we were doing," he continued. "I don't know what we were thinking… Gerry said, Gerry said he – James – looked so beautiful just lying there. We'd got him to my flat. Then Chloe kissed him and everything just went wrong." Linehan gave a hiccough and then after a moment began to cry. "I wasn't a bad person. How could I have done that? Everything just went so wrong."

Aija's heart was thumping. Her hold on the photo tightened as his grasp on her wrist loosened. "What went wrong?" Though she wasn't sure she wanted to know. Not like this, from a snivelling mess.

"I became the kind of person who'd do that… who'd take advantage of a friend, someone completely defenceless, we were the ones who were supposed to take care of him."

Aija's face froze, understanding what he'd just said.

"There was so much blood. I didn't know there would be blood." He choked, coughed. "And we laughed. It was Gerry who ordered us to, we had to get rid of him – we were sure he was going to die and we tossed him in a ditch like complete fools. If he'd died… I sometimes imagine that he died. Maybe I could have got my life back together." He took a few strong breaths and his voice rose. "If he was dead then I wouldn't have to see him… all the time… then I could… smiling, holding that book seeming so fucking happy – while I'm just so fucking miserable every single moment of every single day. When I see him, I know he still doesn't know that it was us."

"And Lucinda?"

"What about her?" he demanded.

Aija didn't reply. He, like Chloe and Gerry, had a clear motive – if Lucinda had known what they'd done they had a good reason to kill her.

She watched him cry in complete disgust. Her stomach churned with suggestions of what his cryptic confession entailed.

He took another hard sniff. "In the book he described Merimies torturing some guy to death and Gerry was convinced it was aimed at him. How would you like the love of your life dreaming of torturing you to death? Gerry read the whole passage aloud for us. Saying, 'That's what the man I love wants to do to me.' But I swear, if I'd known he was going to kill himself, I wouldn't have left him with a gun. I am not a bad person."

He'd managed to keep this a secret for twenty years. Lucinda had been killed that same night. The two crimes were linked somehow. Aija was sure of it. If she wanted to keep investigating, to prove what they'd done, she'd have to tell Charlie that she suspected she knew the motive behind Lucinda's death. He would demand to know why she was interviewing a suspect without authorisation and would remind her that she had, in fact, jeopardised the case.

She shook Linehan's hand from her wrist. Neither needed to say that what had happened here would remain between them unless either of them took a risk that could ruin them both.

James

He had killed Gerry. That realisation was coming to him as he stood in silence pondering what Chloe had just finished telling him.

"Now you know." She'd ended a brief, matter-of-fact retelling of that night with a nod – perfunctory for a moment and then dissolving into a trembling chin and watering eyes.

The clock had ticked after that, a long pause in which he searched his mind for emotion, a tangible response. Instead, he'd poured himself a glass of water while she sat there rooted in place at her kitchen table. He glanced around, his gaze falling on a picture taken at a wedding, he couldn't remember whose.

"James, you're torturing me," she said. "Say something. Do something."

"Like what, report you to the police?"

"How about cry? Scream, shout?" she pleaded. "Living with this has been a millstone around my neck."

"You've done pretty well for yourself. You have a husband and a career," he replied. "Doesn't look like you're suffering to me."

"Trying to appear sane is hard work." Her voice cracked. "Every single day is a struggle." She took a deep breath. "I have never, ever done anything like that again in my life, I've tried so hard to make up…"

"Make up for it?" he shouted. Now a rage began to boil in him. It bubbled furiously. "How? By lying to my face, by telling me you didn't know what happened? That I was some drunk incapable of finding my way home? You made me believe what happened to me was my fault."

Chloe took a step back and looked down at the floor.

Then the bubble of anger burst and an enormous gaping ditch opened where his anger was supposed to be. He couldn't identify the emotion. Perhaps it was even an absence of emotion.

He picked up his jacket, and, after a long hard look at her, he made for the door.

"What are you going to do?" She followed him.

"What can I do? Drag a man from his grave to answer a crime – you and Declan are hardly going to gently acquiesce to what you've done." He knew she wouldn't.

He walked as if in a thick mist to the door. He could hear his heart beating and feel a pulsating at his temples. He was aware of each step he took on what he now realised was a hardwood floor. He stopped just as he realised that he'd taken his shoes off as he entered – as if he wasn't a policeman – as if he had just been a guest.

"Lucinda?" he asked. There was nothing left to ask about himself. Motivation, details, what they'd told each other – had they laughed or been embarrassed? Had they taken their, or his, clothes off? Questions, that had on some nights kept him awake for hours, he knew he would never formulate.

In his books, James, cloaked as Merimies, dreamt of retribution. Merimies was in pursuit the man who'd raped and killed his wife and had pledged to torture the perpetrator to death. Now here was his Merimies moment - his reckoning. His assailant was in front of him.

But he felt useless. Chloe stood fidgeting and looking at her feet. Declan was probably still within reach. James could report the crime and it would be taken seriously by the system. But it wouldn't get him back twenty years of his life.

So he asked again, "Lucinda?" He was a policeman and a good one. Someone, if not him, would get justice.

"What can I say? She was there that night. We were probably the last to see her." Chloe waved a hand. "She's got nothing to do with us."

"She has a family who are desperate to know."

"And how does knowing help?" she hissed. Then she tapped a loosely curled fist to her mouth. "It's nothing to do with me or Declan or Gerry, and if it comes to that I will go, swear to it."

He stumbled briefly on the steps leaving the house that he seemed to have forgotten were there. They didn't kill Lucinda.

And neither did he. He knew now that those missing hours of his life had nothing to do with Lucinda's disappearance. He also now knew the whole truth of that night, of time, innocence and happiness that had been stolen from him and he could never get back.

Aija

"I think I may have fucked up," she declared. She'd left Declan Linehan, her car directed at the station, with emotions vacillating violently between pride and shame.

She tried visualising herself reporting her findings in a calm, astute manner to Charlie.

He was James's best friend. Maybe this was why he didn't want her on the case. He might have known. One of the women detectives had been raped as a young teenager. It came out. Helsinki is small for a capital, there were people who worked on her case still in the department – people with memories of the case being brought before a court, sworn to secrecy, yes, but they remembered her nonetheless.

Aija only found out when it came up at an office *pikkujoulu* early the previous December. The officer was completely drunk and in between her turns on the dance floor, leaned against a wall and yelled loudly enough for those in the immediate vicinity to hear. "Three years! He raped me and he got three years! I got a life sentence," she crowed before she passed out.

Her life sentence, as she called it, was HIV. Her rapist had frequented brothels over the border in Russia and had infected his wife and her. It was muttered around the office, repeated. But it was not gossip, not something that someone told with a tingle of excitement. It was an explanation, the arrival at an understanding of her idiosyncrasies. They now knew why she pursued crime with such vehemence, why the authorities were perhaps a bit relaxed when chastising her for aggression towards suspects and why she drank so fast and so forcefully the moment she left the station after each shift.

Aija's second option was to tell James what she'd done. And that's what she was here for. Keeping silent was not an option. For someone who'd done so well keeping a secret for twenty years, Declan had been ready to explode. As the investigation progressed, it was going to come out that she coerced Declan into confessing.

This was why she wasn't a good police officer. She sat for a moment in the car with her hands in her lap. She could see James in his car parked in front of his house. This was why she was mediocre, suited to paperwork – because she hadn't thought her actions through. She was someone Hart could see retiring from the police to become an expat wife.

Finally, after watching his car in the driveway with its unmoving driver, she dragged herself from her car.

"Hi!" She tapped on the window, he glanced at her. The window rolled down a few centimetres.

"Not a good time." He turned down to stare at his fingernails.

"There's never going to be a good time." When he didn't respond she stepped back. "I've really fucked up," she reiterated. "I'm sorry." She felt like a child confessing to breaking a family heirloom – it's broken and can never be fixed. It had been his life for twenty years, now she'd smashed into it like the crazed villain in a children's cartoon.

The window rolled down a little more.

"I spoke to Declan. I shouldn't have. Charlie told me to stay away from the case. I thought that you killed Lucinda."

"Hmm," was what he gave her in reply to her tirade.

"I was wrong. I want to apologise for…"

"Can you get to the point?" he said, glaring at her. He was daring her to say what she'd found out. Because this was what people who came in and out of their office every day feared – not being believed, being challenged, asking to verify, asking for proof.

Her mouth fell open and she couldn't speak.

"I quite fancy a drink, join me," he offered.

"I've got to get back to Charlie."

"Really?" He got out of his car without a jacket or umbrella and slammed the car door shut, window still open behind him.

She couldn't speak.

"Are you trying to get away from me? You were always up for a drink before."

"Knowing hasn't changed..." she began, the look on his face told her she was going the wrong way. "Actually... it's changed everything, hasn't it?"

She saw the flicker of a smile and he strolled to his front door, and she followed him out of the rain.

"I don't know what I'm supposed to say," she said as he rinsed two glasses that stood beside the sink. She sat on the same stool as she had on the previous visit.

"What made you talk to Declan if you were off the case?"

"It's not really time to talk about me..." she started. But they were not going to talk about him either. "Hart made me onboard Eva and she's just so clever and knows everything and... She's so easy to notice. I'm so forgettable." Her confession tumbled out of her.

"That's pathetic." he replied, his face devoid of kindness.

"That's not very nice," she snapped, before reminding herself what she'd just found out.

"Sorry," he replied and that surprised her.

"Have you always been you or were you someone else before?" she dared ask. Because she liked him, she didn't want to imagine that her James had once been different, any more than she wanted to recall Charlie when she first met him – unhappy.

He shrugged and then sipped his wine. "I was the same. Maybe just a little less scared of the world, and maybe I slept better."

"You don't seem scared."

"And you don't seem like you mind that everyone considers you mediocre. I thought you were satisfied with your life," he said.

"Well, I was OK, then Eva comes in…"

"Taking over your kingdom… Your usurper. Are you worried she'll take me and Charlie away from you?"

She didn't want to answer that. "I was using my initiative as Hart always told me to. And look at how my pettiness has affected you."

"You didn't fuck up, you found out something that has completely eluded Charlie – I didn't kill Lucinda."

She smiled into her wine. They were silent for a little while.

"But I killed Gerry – I drove him to it," he said without emotion and drained his glass. "He read my book and thought I would really do those things to him – that I hated him that much. Strange, because it was a fantasy, a way of dispersing my anger. It would never occur to me to hurt someone like that."

"You didn't even put me in your bloody book," she whispered, but still he looked up.

"Would you want to be in it? Charlie is a pedantic plodder, Hart a sexual predator and I'm a racist homophobe. What did you want to be?"

"Noticed," she replied as her phone rang.

"You'd better answer your phone, Charlie will be wondering where you got to," he told her and turned to the fridge.

Chapter 12

Charlie

Charlie arrived at his desk. Livid. He still hadn't heard back from James. He told himself that he was angry because of the prospect of his friendship ending. He thought of calling Aija but couldn't bring himself to.

He opened his drawer and found some of the evidence removed from Gerry's home. Without Aija to delegate to, he'd fallen behind in registering it. He looked at the book, James's book. He'd noticed it earlier but hadn't thought much of it. That book could only be a couple of weeks old, he knew because he'd been at the launch. At a stretch he could have received it as an early copy or as a friend, but Charlie knew it would have been with a dummy cover.

It was battered from almost every angle. Its spine was damaged, and it was dog-eared and the pages brown. As he took it out with a pair of gloves on, he saw how even with that damage, some areas were worse than others. He flicked to the section where the pages were most badly mutilated.

He flinched. It was one of those sections of extreme violence, tastefully rendered according to some reviewers, but still violent.

> *The cold steel cut through his pale flesh straight and true. His skin split open as easily as the hide of pig, a slab upon a plate, only this pig was still breathing. He screeched into the fabric that plugged his mouth…*

The section was violently underscored in blue biro, the pressure of the pen pressing the line onto the pages that followed.

> *"You know what you've done," Merimies spoke as the man bled. Beside him were the medical supplies he needed to ensure that the man did not die. He was going to know how long a man could live in this amount of pain.*

Charlie skipped a few sentences. But he could see that Gerry hadn't, the underlining and occasional minute lettering continued.

> *"There's nothing you could say to justify doing that to a twenty-five year-old, a beautiful person with the whole world at her feet." Merimies stood over the dying man. "No court can give you the punishment you deserve." He could feel a light returning to his heart, a light he'd pursued for years.*

Charlie looked at the frenzy of writing beside the passage. Even with a magnifying glass he couldn't make out the words written beside it.

> *He would give him an hour more. Merimies had to be at work in a couple of days. This man was tenacious, resistant to death. He had to die. Not just because he couldn't leave a witness, but because when Aino had been avenged – when this man's soul was extinguished, then Merimies would be free.*

There in the margin was the one word Charlie could discern – *me?*

He leaned back in his chair and stared at the door, a blankness descended where his thoughts should have been.

Gerry had killed Lucinda. This was as much a confession as any. It would be laughed out of court but, then he took a deep breath, had James known?

No.

He skimmed through the book in its litany of rapes and murders. It had triggered Venter to kill himself. Not in some vague possible response to reading violence, but in a personal way. That question mark said it all. He was asking if James would do that to him as the killer.

There was a short sharp rap on his door and Eva opened it without waiting for a response. "Long time no see," she said in English, and he forced himself to give as genuine a smile as possible.

"*Kuinka voin auttaa*?" he responded with a *how can I help you*, trying not to sound like a shop assistant.

"I was looking for your roommate," she switched to Finnish after a flash of annoyance. "Something in his files I need some clarification on, something about a domestic stabbing."

"He's not well. Ordered him to go home. I should remind him to see a doctor."

"James still ill?" asked Hart. Eva jumped at her appearance. "Tell him to file for sick leave and I don't want to see him till he's all sorted."

She flashed a large smile at Eva as she left, and Charlie answered, "Will do."

"I hope you don't mind me saying," Eva said in a barely audible voice and looked around as if to check that Hart was gone, "she's a bit creepy."

"You wouldn't be the first to say so." He couldn't deny that working with Hart was like working with a person you suspected of being a vampire. "As long as you do your job, you're fine with her. You'll get used to the manipulation and browbeating."

This time her smile was nervous. She hesitated and then closed the door behind her and still she spoke in a low voice. "I feel as if I got off on the wrong foot with Aija, she doesn't seem to like me."

"What makes you say that?" he asked, thinking how he didn't have time for this.

"She's a bit cold to me."

He wanted to say something bland like, "She'll get used to you", or "Take her for a coffee".

"As long as she does her job and you do yours, you don't need to be friends." He thought he sounded like James or Hart.

"Yes, but it would be nice to be friends." She replied reddening slightly. "You four seem pretty tight, I've never had that… at work."

"Give it time, friendships start from somewhere," he said and then, a stab of meanness running through him, he continued, "you might ease off the crush on James, it makes him uncomfortable."

She turned scarlet. "Was it that obvious?"

"Yes."

"That's my fault, I suppose." She took a deep breath. "You know when you meet someone and you think he's noticed you and hopefully that there's something special… But this isn't a very professional discussion." She pulled herself up. "Anyway, I've been following up on his cases."

"You're supposed to report to Hart. I'm not your supervisor."

"She says to tell Aija, she's below me."

"Are you pouting?" he demanded. "This is a police station, not a kindergarten."

"But Aija is a sergeant and not a very good one I've heard."

"Aija can," he stated, "however, follow instructions. And that is going to get her further up the ladder than cherry lipstick and smiling at James."

Eva bristled.

"Now I suggest you make your reports, get Aija to go over them – because you don't seem to have figured out that Hart wants you to get some tips off Aija so that you don't waste her time. She'll show you how to file them right and to make sure James can pick up where he left off. None of us gets to start at the top."

For a moment she seemed stunned, frozen, then blinking rapidly she turned away.

He felt a sting of regret. "Eva," he called and when she turned back with a forced smile on her face, he said, "Sorry for being so harsh. There's a lot of stuff going on right now. Just ride the wave for a few days, then we'll have a chance to see what you can do."

"How about this, I'll hang on to them until James gets back and I'll report directly to him." She stuck her chin out, defiant.

"Have it your way." He shrugged off her arrogance. "Maybe James will buy you a beer to thank you."

She gave a perfunctory smile in lieu of swearing, he thought, as she left.

Knowing that James had not killed Lucinda nor intentionally harmed Venter, he felt a certain levity. The case was nearly over. The question of whether James knew or not was the only thing remaining and quite frankly, with Venter dead, he could write his final reports and return to mending his own life.

Within moments Hart knocked on his door and looked in surreptitiously when he told her to come in.

"Are you hiding from our new detective?" he checked with a genuine feeling of warmth that he hadn't felt since the day Venter's body had been found with the insides of his skull emptied across his living room.

She sighed theatrically. "Tiresome woman. I think she's been reading some sort of manual..." She stopped.

"Charlie, sort this James mess out. Please. It's getting hard to keep being me." She sat in James's chair. "Tell me something good."

"Well," he waved the book at her. If James and Aija had been here it would have given the moment more drama. "This is solved."

"James's book."

Charlie let her quip slide. "Linehan claimed he'd seen Venter recently. He reported having played with or examined the gun recently enough that his fingerprints were still on it. Venter had seen himself in the book and had killed himself." He summarised the events as he saw them.

He leaned back with a feeling of achievement, linking his fingers behind his head.

"That sounds plausible," she agreed with the complete lack of enthusiasm that he expected. "But you can't prove any of it."

"But at least it's solved," he said.

"Especially where James is concerned, you mean."

He nodded.

"With my NBI cap on, I'd say that James, at best, has admitted to knowing more about Lucinda's death than he should." She continued her direct piercing gaze.

"Maybe. But that can't be proven."

"No. I won't accept that," Hart brushed him off. As he watched she folded her arms and leaned back into the swivel chair, her body reiterating her words – she would not accept it. "You're looking for the explanation that gets James off the hook, not for the truth."

"This is the truth," he insisted, though he knew exactly what she meant.

"Lucinda and Venter are linked and so is James. To remain silent, for whatever reason they might have, has enabled a killer to get away. And if James knows, he might as well have pulled the trigger according to me."

Feeling deflated, he knew she was right, and it hurt him to think he could be so obviously biased.

He thought about Rachel as he went to see Linehan. That morning he'd called the insurance company again about her standing in the way of the settlement. They were still adamant, waiting for further clarification and, no, there was no way of escalating the situation. He had to wait. But not to worry, it was just a few more days, the claims officer told him.

He didn't have much of a plan other than appealing to Linehan's desire to stay out of trouble. He was going to emphasise, or rather, play up Venter's role in Lucinda's death – to make it look as if Linehan had a lot to lose. He wanted Linehan to give evidence of his or Venter's guilt, exonerate James, then this whole mess could be over.

Perhaps it was time to be less polite and to be more heavy-handed, he decided.

It was with the prospect of verbal violence, posturing and intimidation that he arrived at Linehan's. It wasn't new to him, as a young constable being frightening was often the antidote to being frightened. Now it was more a tool in the arsenal of being a policeman, being used judiciously not just because of the wisdom that came with age but with the public's lower tolerance to forceful police officers.

The door opened after a few knocks that turned into thumps. He could hear music inside and guessed that

Linehan would be inside cutting himself off from the world. He was rewarded with a wild-haired, red-faced Linehan, a corkscrew in one hand, who opened the door only a few centimetres, not letting him over the threshold.

"Will you people leave me alone?" he growled, "You'd better have a good reason."

"I have a very good..." he began.

"I'm going to make a complaint. You people are harassing me, twice in one day?" he squealed, stumbling though there had been nothing to trip over. "When you know it could kill me."

"What do you mean twice?" he asked. He kept the door open with his foot, but he imagined the heavy wooden door if pushed with enough force would crush it.

Linehan tried to push the door shut, but not with enough force to cause Charlie any pain. He looked from side to side as if he was checking if someone was beside him.

"Your... sidekick was here," he croaked. looking back inside, visibly shaking. Then his eyes widened and he threw his head back. "And I've told her everything I'm telling anyone, so fuck off."

He couldn't simply turn away at the man's demand, so he shoved the door open. Neither could he ask him to repeat what he'd told Aija; it would make him look disorganised and inefficient and possibly get Aija into trouble.

"The evidence is piling up, Linehan." The accused man's eyes widened. "I'm going to get you."

"Go away, will you?" he shouted, burst into tears, and fled into another room.

He didn't bother following him. He left, and, as he closed the door behind himself, he called Aija. He had to know what she had found out.

"Hello." After several rings, she answered, her voice cautious.

"Where are you?"

"Your house..." she began quietly.

"At James's," he said sharply. "Did he get you to go around to Linehan's and harass him?"

"James didn't know anything. I thought I'd speed up the case."

"By seeing a suspect without my permission!" He fought to keep his voice down. "What did you find out?"

Though it was over their mobiles, he heard a distinct hesitation.

"Nothing that made sense," she said, as if she'd not been able to come up with anything cleverer.

"You stay at James's. I'm coming over." He scowled as he spoke to her. "In the meantime, I suggest you think about your future with the force. And by the way, you are not to tell James anything about your visit. This is my case, and if I say you don't talk to anyone about it, you don't. You will not ruin this case for me."

"What did Aija tell you?" He'd arrived to find them at the kitchen bar, neither were talking. Both had glasses of wine and James was slicing onions. The aroma of chicken escaped the oven and filled the room with a welcoming smell. For a moment, Charlie had a window into what was once normal life, but his anger took over again.

Neither had passed a greeting when he barged in. His face felt warm and throat constricted. He felt as if he could easily cry.

"I want to talk to James alone," he said to Aija, not looking at her.

Aija mumbled something about going to the Ladies and sloped away.

"Again, what did Aija tell you?" he repeated. "She's been to see Linehan and somehow thinks it's your business, not mine."

"She didn't tell me anything," James began only after a heavy laden breath.

"She's here instead of the office. I'm not an idiot."

James looked away and took out a packet of cigarettes from a kitchen drawer and looked about himself in search of matches. He reached towards a packet that stood on the counter.

Infuriated, Charlie seized the cigarettes and tossed them away. They hit the wall and James looked back at him, his expression of surprise and perhaps confusion.

"Look, I won't let her investigate because this could be dangerous for her career," he explained. "If this all falls apart, it could take her down too."

"So what, I'll be sacrificed so that everyone else can live?" James asked. Charlie knew his fear was justified.

"It's not that, I'm doing everything I can to unlink you from this case."

"But there's no link, Aija..." he stopped. Then he returned to looking from side to side, avoiding eye contact. Then it was obvious that he didn't want to tell him something.

"Look, don't tell me. All right? Whatever it is – you hold on to it. Because it's obviously important to you, but I can't just stop looking for the truth."

"Why not?" demanded James, saying exactly what Charlie had thought many times over the course of the last few hours. "Gerry's dead and there's no evidence."

"You can't imagine that I would just walk away from this," he spoke with that rising inflection in his voice that he fought whenever the thought of his wife came up during a conversation. "That girl is someone's Rachel. Her family were waiting or at least hoping she'd come home. How am I any different?"

James lifted a blond brow. "Rachel?"

"You don't think I imagine she's still alive, do you? Yes, she could be voluntarily hiding – if that's possible these days. But what if something happened, what if she tripped and fell in some forest somewhere and her body's decomposing unnoticed – like Lucinda?" He thought James nodded, or perhaps he just dipped his head at the idea. "Or she's been held somewhere." He couldn't stop there. The events of the day, finding a possible solution and then losing it, still being on the case, he strode over and picked up James's cigarettes and tossed them gently back at him.

"My whole world is stuck in a holding pattern around her; I can't claim insurance on my house, a guy from the sex crimes department still drops by to 'say hi', he says." Charlie sat down, his heart pounding. "When I meet her parents, we still don't know what to say to each other. I can't even get a divorce. You – yes, you, as well as Hart and Aija, but mostly you," he continued, "have helped me hold myself together these last two years, and I don't want to lose that, but it's as if you're determined that I should."

James slid a glass of wine in front of him and he felt some semblance of relaxation, James was still there, they were still friends.

He wanted to stop rambling and get back to the case, but the weight of his situation had been pushing down on him, from being frightened that he couldn't solve the case, to the lacklustre explanation he gave Hart. He took a large sip of wine and sat down. "I never planned to find myself alone and an object of ridicule and suspicion. It's like everything I worked for, my family and my job, were secondary to her getting a fourteen year-old in bed." He still had to steel himself at the suggestion, to close his eyes when the thought emerged. "And I didn't even notice – some policeman I make."

He could tell James was listening, though he remained silent.

"At least at work, I can repair things. I can be taken seriously again," he whispered. "I can't do anything with the rest of my life."

"You can," James replied finally. "Or, you have to. We don't get a choice in what other people do to us."

Now would have been a good time to ask him what he meant, but he didn't.

"I need to solve this case, James," he articulated his quest slowly, "and if that means the end of our friendship and ending up on my sister's sofa, then so be it."

"Ask Aija," he said after fidgeting, quickly rubbing his face with his empty hand and briefly pinching the bridge of his nose. "Tell her I told you it was OK."

James

As he finished the words, the doorbell rang. James left Charlie at the kitchen counter and answered the door to find Hart. She was seething.

"Your phone's off, you're a policeman – you're supposed to keep it on!" she demanded as she barged into the doorway forcing him to move out of her way. She marched into his house – she knew the way, the house hadn't changed since the one night she'd spent there.

"What have you done?" she hissed as the water slicked off her jacket and she tossed her umbrella carelessly into the corner.

"Hmm?" he asked, not in the mood for words, nor for any more questions from women who seemed angry, confused or concerned.

"Someone's walked into YLE and declared they are responsible for Lucinda's death." Hart glanced around the kitchen. "She demanded to be interviewed. And none of you are there."

At the mention of the national news channel his jaw fell open. Charlie sat up on his perch, his expression also one of shock. Aija returned and stopped beside Charlie.

"I've sent officers to the TV station to make sure she doesn't leave. Dispatch called me when they couldn't reach you." Hart brushed her back with her hand and upon straightening her jacket seemed to calm down.

"Surely they can't air her confession on TV," said Charlie, picking up his rain jacket and reaching for his keys simultaneously.

"Not live, but they are interviewing her. And if she says anything juicy, you can guarantee it will be broadcast a moment later and we'll probably look like fools. They'll label it a supposed confession until we've confirmed she's not a complete liar, they don't want to give weirdos the stage, but they also don't want to be accused of a cover up."

James leaned against his fridge, his stomach began to churn and he began to feel hot. "I want to be there when she comes in."

"No chance, James." Hart stopped him with a raised palm. "She already told us you were there that night – probably what got YLE interested. NBI is sending a detective. I've done all I can to protect you and I'm beginning to think that was a big mistake."

The pain in his stomach turned to nausea and he turned back. He looked back and Hart was watching him, her eyes afire.

"I want to know what the hell is going on with you." She stood in front of him, her arms crossed and her handbag slumped on the floor beside her telling him that he was trapped.

"I was sexually assaulted that night." He replied without blinking or a quaver in his voice. He'd never before articulated it. Charlie drew a breath. Aija looked away.

Hart, he saw in her eyes, was not going to let that explanation lie. "What do you mean? And what has that got to do with anything?"

"I mean," he began, strangely grateful that she'd forced him to continue. He had to tell. Since Chloe had told him details that he had never known, he'd felt as if his mind was a tornado, hurtling about at high speed. Only Aija's arrival had made it possible for him to still be standing. Listening to her and Charlie had delayed thoughts of his own misery and delaying the decision he knew he had to take – to tell or not.

"I mean, I woke up in a hospital the morning after with absolutely no memory of what had happened. All I knew was that I'd been raped," he threw his hands up, "which was blindingly obvious, and the doctors told me that I'd been drugged."

The doctors had asked him what had happened, but no memory would return. A woman with tired eyes and a baggy sweater had spoken to him – had she been a police officer or a counsellor? He'd refused to cooperate. When the analgesics wore off, the pain was so intense that all he could do was cry. "The last thing I remember was having fun with friends. Then I was in a hospital bed.

"Then today Chloe finally told me what happened. Her, Declan and Gerry – my so-called friends. She says they weren't even that drunk." Chloe, horrified, had thrown in details he'd never wanted to know – that she'd had to find something to penetrate him with, that they'd all had their turns, that they had laughed. She'd shrugged, powerless to change the past. Now her words formed images that kept flashing through his mind and brought bile to his throat. He wasn't going to cry and wail. No, he'd done enough of that.

"Oh, god." said Charlie. "You found out it was them today?"

He nodded.

That was enough. He wasn't going to tell them about having to go home to his parents because he was unable to care for himself day after day. He'd been drugged – some fools out there with their pranks, he'd told his father, and woke up in hospital. He just needed some time for the drugs to work their way out of his system. It was an easier story, one that retained some dignity. Dolly and his mother had glowered at him, resenting making his favourite food and seeing it uneaten. The pain of the food passing through his system still unbearable. *No, I still can't remember anything. No, I still don't want to go out for a drink.*

"She says Gerry was convinced that I wrote the books about him, that it sent him over the edge. She has absolutely no doubt he killed himself."

Then he was suddenly irritated by their meaningful stares, the ones you cultivate in the police force to let people know that you're listening and that you do care.

"So, I have an alibi," he took a deep breath and held it. "I'm sure there'll be medical records if you want them."

He turned around and turned off the gently burning chicken. He turned back to where the three still stood uncomfortably.

"We should get going," he said.

Aija

James hadn't killed Lucinda.

James hadn't been detailed in his tale. It had been straight to the point, leaving them to fill in the spaces if they chose to.

She heard enough survivor's stories and seen enough medical reports to know what it could have entailed for a young man. A few years ago she'd had to sit through a training course designed to shatter the long-held belief that men could not be raped. Prior to that, people only spoke about other things happening – sexual assault, molestation, euphemisms – but not rape. She'd emerged from it feeling slightly ill, but she had learnt something. Though it didn't prepare her for this – she still had no idea how to respond to hearing the story from James himself.

In these last two years she'd realised James was odd – but not in the way that suggested trauma. Only now, after having listened to him, did the notebooks and the novels make sense. She wondered how much it took for him to hold himself together through cases of almost exactly what had happened to him. He'd told them that all he knew was that he'd been picked up from a ditch in the middle of a construction site near the Natural History Museum, an event described to him by police.

If shame was a physical object, it would have been a black stone obelisk in the room. Her heart was thudding with anxiety even though she'd learnt part of the story from Linehan.

"Well," pronounced Hart, even though Aija could tell she'd had to think of a suitable response. "Don't we all feel like right dickheads. Let's go." She shook off her raincoat and put it back on.

Charlie remained rigid, facing James, their eyes locked. Of course, he knew James couldn't have told him. They dealt with the silence of traumatised people all the time, people with experiences so horrific that they could never utter a word about them even under the duress of police investigations.

Say something, Charlie, she wished as she followed Hart's lead.

They were almost at the door when Charlie spoke. "You let me stand there ranting about my life when you'd just found out your best friends did this to you."

Aija couldn't tell if that was a question or a statement. She didn't turn back, pretending she wasn't in the room with them.

James selected an umbrella from the coatrack and handed it to him.

"Are we supposed to believe this confession?" James said, which meant that he had told them all he was going to about the matter.

"We'll see," said Charlie, showing that he understood. "She won't be the first to see murder as the opportunity for attention."

An NBI investigator named Nieminen was waiting for them outside YLE's main station. The confession to Lucinda's murder would be on the news, there was nothing that could be done to keep it secret. A little group of police officers gathered outside the studio around mobile phones and tablets waiting for the interview to be pre-recorded, such a confession would be too dangerous to show live, the potential for the station to be humiliated was too great.

Eva fell in step beside them with a terse expression on her face. No one said anything as they stood just inside the room beside the open door. The presenter, slender and elegant in an ankle length skirt, said a few words to the crew and the signal went on that recording was in progress.

As it began, Aija felt a stab of validation. She'd been right, the killer was strong. She was as tall as Charlie. Her afro hair was shaved close, almost disappearing at the back of her neck. She wore no makeup or jewellery but somehow looked majestic. She spoke in clear calm Finnish with her hands perfectly still, as she sat in a bouffant, ultra-modern spin chair on a stage set up for the morning show. She'd given her name as Julia, and pronounced it Yulia, the Finnicised version.

"Tell us your story," the interviewer said.

"I was the last person to see Lucinda alive. And I've waited for twenty years for someone to ask me. No one had ever come," she began. "We were friends, she used to work across the street from me. It wasn't hard for us to notice each other."

Aija knew she meant that there would have been few if any other young black women in proximity in those days.

"The two of you were friends?"

"Yes, I was doing an internship in an advertising agency. She really liked the idea and thought it was something she might do. We'd go shopping together, we wanted to be more ladylike – more sophisticated. Whatever that meant to us at the time."

The interviewer leaned forward, the earnest look in her face contrived to convince the audience. "Please tell us what happened to Lucinda."

Julia took a deep breath. "It wasn't that late in the pub – Solar, it was called – but things were getting rowdy. It had been raining and all the floors were..." she trailed off. "Some guy pushed a camera into my hands. He practically yelled at me, 'Take a picture!' I'll never forget, his eyes were bright and face red and his hair was wild and all over the place. Lucinda looked amazing, she pushed her way into the photo, uninvited, but no one seemed to mind. She was trying to talk to him, the man she liked. But he was all over the other guy – that writer – the one who's famous now," she gave a quiet grunt and then smiled apologetically. "The men were all sweaty and it made me feel ill. How was it that the girls were so beautiful, like Lucy, so put together, still oozing sensuality at that time of night? When the men – or were they boys, overgrown boys – had sweat stains and were splashed with beer and wine.

"Or maybe that's what I focused on. I remember, when I force myself, that I could see that Lucy's lipstick was smudged, that her foundation had rubbed a faint brown line on her collar. But, at the time when I looked, all those tiny imperfections disappeared and Lucy was perfect. She was wearing jeans and a tight-fitting black top, you could see her silhouette perfectly."

She paused as if waiting for another prompt from the interviewer. When none came she continued, "Lucy couldn't get into the group. They wouldn't let her in. I think she was confused – she knew him, the guy she wanted. He'd shown some interest in her. She said they'd met for coffee many times. But that night he didn't want to know – well, it was obvious to me he was interested in someone else. When she came back to me, she was disgusted – disgusted at everything, the evening, the bar. She said, 'I can't believe that he's behaving as if he doesn't know me,' but I could believe it."

"How did this lead to Lucy's death?" The anchor looked expectantly at her.

"I didn't know what these feelings I had for her were before. But that night I realised it was love," Julia continued.

Aija could see that this was not a confession, this woman had desperately wanted someone to listen to her and now she had a significant portion of the nation doing so.

Julia regained her composure. "I said I'd cheer her up. I took her to a hot dog stand at Rautatientori. It was cold but I couldn't feel it, neither of us could. Then we found another bar, that was so full that there was no way anyone would have remembered seeing her. But we found a corner where we could talk. She told me about her family, that she loved living in Finland – that she was so glad they'd moved here."

"When did you last see her?"

"About five in the morning!" Her face lit up as she said this. "An amazing night. I've never–" She looked confused. "I tried to kiss her, at the corner of Kamppi metro station. She pushed me away and walked away from me, towards Temppeliaukio."

Aija, James and Charlie reacted at the same time. The church, a landmark construction, was within easy walking distance of the museum where James said he was found. Aija bit her lip to stop herself from saying anything aloud.

"Why didn't you tell the police all this?" asked the anchor.

"I couldn't," she choked, and the silence that followed, Aija guessed, was filled with guilt, shame, fear. It could have been one or all three. "If I hadn't kissed her, if she hadn't walked away from me… I waited for her to return, then later, I waited for the police to come."

"And the police never asked you, they never…"

"I saw them around asking questions. I was at the university doing my degree at the time. They harassed the boys, especially the few black men they could find. I guess in some way that night I was hiding – I was being discreet. I didn't want anyone to see us – that's why it's my fault. Maybe if someone had seen us…" She began to rummage with her microphone. "I have to get out of here."

"The police," began the anchor.

"Oh no, please," she begged, as if suddenly thinking better of the interview. "Not the police. I can't do this." She dissolved back into the chair. "What have I done? Everyone will know. My family, oh no, they'll be so upset."

As Julia was weeping, the presenter wrapped up. She had a slight look of disappointment. She had obviously wanted more, though this in itself was significant. The studio lights dimmed.

Hart thanked the presenter, who immediately started asking questions. She was escorted out. She had nothing extra to add herself but explained how Julia came to speak to them.

"We'll give her some time to calm down," said Hart. A constable was beside Julia speaking quietly. "She does at least offer a few extra hours of Lucinda's life."

Aija would have imagined they'd talk about it alone, but she realised why Hart hadn't shut the door. Everyone was there watching them, the NBI investigator, the uniformed constables, Eva, no one could claim that information was being hidden.

"What about James as a possible witness?" inquired Eva. Her eyes had been overtaken by a childish excitement and she was standing in the inner circle between NBI and Hart.

"According to him it was a boozy night that he remembers only because he ended up in hospital after slipping on ice," Hart said. "I'm sure he'll provide medical records if needed."

Aija exhaled. Just like that James was exonerated. Only a court or NBI would ask to see those records and right now they had no credible evidence to suggest James was involved.

"Still..." insisted Eva.

"Are we sure gawking is in our job description?" Aija said loudly, glancing at the other police officers who were watching captivated. Perhaps because she was standing right beside Hart, they accepted her authority and dispersed. But Nieminen the NBI investigator remained with them. Aija knew not to mention anything she might be thinking in front of him.

Nieminen watched James, who seemed to be impervious to the man's stares.

"So, what about James as a possible witness?" he reiterated.

James opened his mouth, but Hart spoke above him. "Nothing, I am satisfied with James's alibi. If required we can subpoena his medical records, but unless we have any tangible evidence, I'd rather we kept my officers out of this."

Nieminen took a deep noisy breath through his nose.

"Fair enough," he said, sitting up rather jovially, Aija thought. "Believe me, unless we have good reason to think he killed her, I want police kept as far out of this as possible." He slammed his folder shut. "Still, he stays away from the case, as does the rest of Team English." He cleared his throat. "We have to make sure everything is above board. The footage is still in the hands of YLE. Every conspiracy theorist will be ready to pounce, not to mention every homophobic, anti-immigrant... James Grey fan."

Aija almost laughed with relief. She had a sense that things were getting back to normal. James ran his hands down his face, took a deep breath and there he was, the same as he'd always been.

The small group began to disperse. Hart leaned over to James and hissed, "Go home." After she stood, she turned to Charlie giving an order, "Follow me, you too," nodding at Aija.

Hart stopped in a recess in the corridor. It formed a nook with a coffee maker and a few brightly covered benches. There was no one else within hearing range.

"You do realise that there will be some bits of this story that are best left out." Hart closed the door herself behind them and directed her sentence to Aija.

"It's not my story to tell. But what now? We can be certain Venter committed suicide and..."

"It's them. The two survivors have basically admitted to being at Temppeliaukio – that's where they dumped

James," said Hart. "Which means they had to have been there."

"We have not a shred of evidence that Linehan, Venter, Foreman or any of them killed Lucinda. Our case is circumstantial," said Charlie. He was tense. She could see it from the way he was kneading his knuckles, looking around the room slowly yet not focusing on either of them.

"The police files should say where James was found. There would have been a call out. That's independent of his medical case," insisted Hart. "Surely Foreman or Linehan would crack under that kind of pressure. They were at the scene."

"No," said Charlie. Low and loud, he sat up in his chair. "We are not dragging James into Lucinda's case."

"That's not your decision."

"It wouldn't make a difference to the case. We know he was found there, so we know they were there too. But it doesn't give us any more evidence." He leaned forward to her. "And I know what it's like to be trampled on in an investigation. I know what it's like to have people sifting through your underwear, reading your emails, asking horrible humiliating questions when all you thought you were doing was living a life. *Where were you when, how did you not know?* And I just sat there, head down, hoping everyone would remember that I was decent person. Now don't get me wrong, if Lucinda was a living breathing young woman, I would drag it all back up – but Lucinda's dead and James is alive."

Aija opened her mouth to say, "but what about her family," but she closed it. Finding Lucinda's killers would not bring her back.

"Look at all these lives wrecked, people who could have been things, people leading lives that they hadn't planned." He stopped, stuttered for a moment and then was quiet.

"So we close the case. We're sure Venter or Linehan did it, but we can't prove it," said Hart, much too easily. She looked at Aija. All Aija could do was breathe.

There was a kerfuffle and the sound of someone running in the corridor.

"*Ylikomisario*. We have an incident," panted a constable, bright-eyed and excited, "and it's a big one. A response team had already been dispatched, she explained as they all began to run for the door.

The response team had done its job – it had stopped the crime and hopefully limited the damage. The detectives' job would be to find out why a woman walked into Oodi and fired a gun at her husband and tourists and readers, children and staff at peak afternoon hours.

Aija, her heart thumping in anticipation, jogged to her car with Charlie and James.

James

By the time he arrived, the action was over.

At least four people were dead. Four was a significant portion of the yearly average murders in Helsinki. He'd, without seeking permission, climbed in the back seat of Charlie's car with Aija driving and Charlie in the passenger's seat.

Oodi, a building with a constant stream of visitors, was still under siege, but now by a team of police officers who'd barricaded the building. Some tried to calm onlookers and those who had been evacuated from the building. Ambulances whirred coming and going, and small tents were being set up to hide details that the public need not see.

James knew he shouldn't be there, nonetheless wearing his flak jacket that identified him as police, but he stood with his colleagues at the ready for any complications. Aija, Charlie, and Eva all milled around on the periphery like him. It was not to be their case – another detective on duty was at the front of things talking to the responders and witnesses.

"She's been taken into custody?" asked Hart, a deep blue bulletproof vest over her clothes. "Who is she?"

"Senni Saunela," the officer in charge read from his notes.

"That's the librarian." James spoke for the first time since he arrived.

"This was your case?" Hart asked, and the officer in charge's frown burrowed even deeper. They spoke as low as they could with the noise that surrounded them.

"It was, I was on leave, remember." He realised immediately that he had to be on his guard, he couldn't afford to be drawn into something else. He had already attracted too much attention. "I left a recommendation that she and her husband should be on surveillance. There was a history of firearms, but that was the husband, not the wife. I was sure she was going to crack. I didn't envision this though."

"Who took this over?" James watched as Hart glanced at Aija who raised her chin.

"Eva," Aija responded after a moment.

"Why her?" the officer in charge demanded. "She's new, isn't she?"

"You said to share out James's cases," Aija spoke to Hart, as if emphasising that Hart was the superintendent and she answered to her. "There was no additional complexity, their involvement with weapons was clear and their behaviour made them suspicious. The couple were to be watched."

"So she purchased a gun while under surveillance?" Hart stepped forward, her expression one of incredulity.

Aija shrugged. "I'll get on to Eva," she said and took her phone from her jeans. But Eva was already moving towards her.

Hart watched her approach. "Am I needed for something?" Eva arrived, her face flushed.

"The two of them were nuts and they were a credible threat to public safety," James continued. "They kept coming back here, with a history of firearms. Is he one of the dead?"

"No. She was apparently a really bad shot," responded the officer in charge. "Managed to kill four and injure nine while the husband has a bruised elbow."

"Hart wants a word," Aija said to Eva, nodding towards their superior. She stood beside Hart as the chief barked at Eva.

"This was your case? Four people are dead – explain it." Her arms were crossed, back straight and her face said she was extremely angry.

Eva seemed baffled. "The librarians – but there was nothing to worry about, I spoke to him, and he said everything was fine. She asked about James and didn't seem interested in talking to me."

"And what about the surveillance?" asked Hart.

"I left it," Eva stammered. "I decided it was an exaggeration."

James groaned and put his hand to his forehead, which was growing warmer. Four people dead, he'd never experienced this before. Oodi would have been full of children, teenagers, remote workers. There would have been people drinking coffees and eating Finnish pastries at the café. It was a social place, that was its ethos. Firing a gun in the library, he took a sharp breath but it didn't help.

The crowd was thickening as passers-by realised that something significant had happened. They were on mobile phones, texting, whispering and shouting to one another and pointing.

"James had said how he wasn't getting any good cases," Eva continued, her voice shrill, school playground defence tactics – pass the blame to someone else. "I thought he was trying to play it up – make it important."

He could have hit her. He felt the boil of anger in his stomach. Linehan, Gerry, Chloe and now four bodies – families that would be grieving because Eva – no – because he wasn't there.

Eva too crossed her arms. She and Hart could have been mistaken for two teachers bickering outside the library. But Hart asserted herself.

"Virkman, back to the office," said Hart. "James, you're not even supposed to be here."

Aija, Hart, Charlie, and the officer in charge walked towards the crime scene. Their voices low, keeping in mind that people were watching.

He found himself alone. He wanted to call Charlie back, or even Aija, even just for a moment. His mouth was dry, his stomach once again was in knots, and he was frozen right there in front of the library as police stood to the front of him and the crowd grew thicker behind him.

A tear ran down his cheek. He felt no compulsion to wipe it away. His limbs were devoid of all strength. This tear was, to his horror, immediately followed by another, and then by a stream that paralysed him, rendering him unable to run or hide.

By the time his hand moved to his eyes, it was too late, he was weeping – the team of policemen and the crowd he could barely see through his tears, but he could feel their derision – he could sense their shame and disgust at such a pathetic figure.

Somewhere in his periphery, he was sure he heard the snapping of a camera. And there was no doubt in his mind that every second was being recorded.

His legs were giving in, he willed himself to stand, but he could feel himself falling.

A strong grip seized his upper arm and led, no, it dragged, him away towards the shelter of the police cars. Once there, Eva handed him several pieces of tissue fished from her bag and guided him to sit on the steps of a police van. He was crying now, uncontrollably, he could hear her speaking in a brisk, efficient tone, "He's behind the furthest van, you'd better get over here," when he felt himself sink back and the world went black.

When the others arrived, Eva had revived him and his head was limp in her lap, a medic had appeared – a woman who was probably thinking that she had far more important things to attend to than a policeman who'd fainted.

They approached in what to James seemed like a haze. Their outlines were smudged, their forms indefinite. He saw Charlie pull off his rain jacket as he approached, and he felt himself smile and for a moment thought he saw a patch of blue in the sky.

"What's happened?" He could hear Hart rather than see her. Aija appeared a moment later at his shoulder and he could feel them all, the medic included, watching him, a blubbering mess of a man only metres away from where dozens of people were standing.

"I'm OK," he tried to say, but his chest tightened, he could neither breathe, talk or stop the cascade of tears.

"Panic attack," said the medic, in a tone that suggested she saw this often. She held his hand in hers, the plastic glove a barrier between them.

"Gerry and now this, I can't..." His tears were those of a man who couldn't regain control, his shoulders shook. "Everyone's watching," he hiccoughed through his hands. With the spasm that followed, he vomited, the liquid landing on the medic who was closest, but who seemed unphased. The spasm came again and again until there was nothing left to expel.

"James, try to breathe," the medic instructed, her English accented with a gentle, almost musical tone. "We could do with less of an audience," she said to the others.

He shook his head. "No, don't go, please," he begged before another rush of tears overtook him.

"It's OK, we're here." He felt Charlie's hand on his shoulder, a familiar presence for a moment, but even that turned upon him, a lecherous pawing coming for him. The terror seized him and once more he fell into blackness.

Charlie

Charlie knew that James would be embarrassed. Embarrassed at his collapse, humiliated at the ambulance driving him away from a crime scene. Charlie sat in the back without asking and watched him as they drove. It was quiet inside, insulated, the responder tapped her fingers in time as if to music only she could hear as they drove through the city to the hospital.

He had time to think, but he didn't. Instead, he watched every bit of the scenery that he could catch through the small high windows. He let the sound of voices coming over the radio be left incomprehensible – he refused to find meaning in the short cryptic sentences the responder shared with the driver. His friend, unconscious in front of him, a case left open, bodies in the library. He fought back even the slightest intrusion of thought, instead matching the rhythm of the responder's tapping with a gentle drumbeat in his head that blocked everything else out.

He knew that when the doors would open, the noise of the world would start again.

James wouldn't be able to recall the trip to the hospital. As they slowed down in the unloading zone, he thrashed frailly as if in a nightmare. The responder leaned over him, watched for a few moments and said with a smile, "He's asleep. Nothing quite like a nap when things are getting too much."

"It just got too much for him." He repeated her words to Dolly who, subdued, was filling a plastic cup with water from a dispenser as she walked slowly along the corridor reading signs and glancing into wards as she waited for James to be released. He'd only told her that James had had a panic attack, he'd left out the details of what that looked like, he hadn't checked but he was sure the footage would already be online – James was enough of a celebrity to attract attention, he was sure of that.

He'd called Dolly himself. She'd arrived out of breath in sneakers with crumbs clinging to her T-shirt, JJ beside her speaking to her in a low voice. She sailed past him, but JJ gently pulled her back towards Charlie.

"He's all right, they gave him something to sleep," he assured them both. "He had a panic attack. It was a particularly awful crime scene – we don't see that sort of thing every day."

Dolly and JJ had gone into the ward to see him, Dolly walking at a speed that told him that he hadn't calmed her at all. When they'd returned, she'd been brushing at the crumbs on her top, she'd straightened her top and smiled at JJ when he mentioned he needed to get something to eat and that he'd be back soon.

Now she didn't answer. She sipped slowly and looked up and down the corridor.

"There will be awful insinuations over the next few days, people will want someone to blame, but James is absolutely in the clear," Charlie said and was glad she continued her silence. "There will be a lot of pain and anger."

This time she nodded as she sipped.

"All these lives, thrown in new trajectories, living new lives that they didn't ask to have," he continued and leaned against the door.

"Gerry, Declan – even Chloe, such different lives from where they were meant to go. Misery, alcohol..."

"I suppose so."

"And you, has killing Gerry set your life on a new trajectory?" Charlie asked.

Dolly's eyes flicked towards him, but she made no other sign that she'd heard.

"You told me you were determined to travel – to make the most of your EU passport, but you married and stayed here – you knew what happened to James, so you stayed."

She leaned forward to refill her cup. When she straightened, he continued.

"Did the police call you when they found him? You must have gone to the hospital; it wouldn't have been impossible to tell he'd been sexually assaulted." He pressed.

Her voice was measured, calm. "So what now?" She was so like her brother, able to don a facade of normality. But her brother's mask had shattered. He could imagine, under the right circumstances, hers would too.

He didn't have enough evidence, but he didn't tell her that. It had dawned on him in the time since Julia's TV confession. A woman whose ambitions had been shattered.

He'd overlooked Dolly. She'd also had dreams once. She'd told him about wanting to be a world traveller. She'd been living in Dublin, already building a life abroad. But that night she too had pivoted away from the path she was already on. He knew it couldn't have been about Lucinda's murder, Lucinda had been too far outside her environs, she didn't care for Lucinda any more than for any other female murder victim.

Since James had told him what had happened, he knew he had felt only a fraction of the rage and sadness she must have felt over the last two decades.

"There are some things boys don't tell girls," he quoted her words back to her. "He doesn't know you know."

"Gerry wanted to tell James he was sorry," she said in a strong whisper. "He leapt out at me after the book signing. He was going to confess, go to the police as soon as he got the balls. He wanted me to help him do it. He thought he could redeem himself in James's eyes. James wouldn't have been able to cope." She turned towards a sound. "Of all people, I never imagined that it could have been Gerry."

She took a long sip, finishing the water in her cup. "He adored James."

"You went to his house that night or morning..."

"Gerry's house?" she asked. The look of surprise was almost convincing, but for the slight curl to her lips, a suppressed smile maybe. "Why would I do that?"

"We're going through the DNA and fingerprints now," he was lying. If he was going to put James through more hell, he had to have as much evidence as he could first. "We will get evidence."

"It's been a week since Gerry died, your evidence hasn't done much so far," she explained, her tone unchanging, calm. "You have no evidence and you're hoping I'll confess. Like you said, many lives changed that night, why should it be me who killed Gerry?" she said and he knew she would not be swayed.

Her husband returned with a paper bag of sausage rolls and a bottle of Jaffa orange. "Any news of sleeping beauty?" he asked. "You OK, Doll?" He caressed the small of her back with his free hand.

"Charlie was just telling me they've had no progress on Gerry's case. No DNA, nothing," she said to her husband.

JJ nodded and offered his spoils to Charlie, who replied, "No, I'm fine. Think there's a half-cooked chicken stew waiting at home. Nothing like a bit of salmonella to end my day." He felt his smile was too broad to look natural, but he couldn't help it.

There were still questions he was dying to ask, but he bit them back.

"Anyway, I've got to get going." The sensation of having failed completely washed over him.

Chapter 13

Charlie

When Charlie arrived home after the incident and James was still in hospital, he'd locked himself in the bathroom and cried in a relentless deluge. Each time he tried to rise from the closed toilet seat, it forced him back again. He cried until his chest hurt and the toilet roll was spent.

When he emerged, he asked himself why he'd had to hide in an empty house but knew it was because his shame was so complete.

But back at the office, everything seemed to compound this feeling.

"Obviously, I feel you're obstructing these investigations," Nieminen declared, standing above him with a mouth full of *korvapuusti*. "Your notes and reports are all thorough, too thorough maybe. I have to wonder what they're not telling me."

"You have the facts there," Charlie replied. "There's no point filling it with conjecture. I have a thousand ideas, but I guarantee you, if I had even a shred of evidence to support them, it would be in there."

He could feel the letter from the insurance agency folded in his trouser pocket.

After everything, Rachel, the fire, and now James, he desperately wanted a resolution to the crimes that took place that night. But he didn't have enough in him to keep investigating and to keep finding nothing. According to the files, Venter died by suicide and a few more hours of Lucinda's disappearance were accounted for. He couldn't prove anything else.

"I'll be reporting that I'm satisfied that all matters relating to Grey were satisfactorily handled, that he has a validated alibi for Barnaby's disappearance and that he was immediately removed from the case involving his friend," said Nieminen. "And that your reasons for closing the cases were valid."

Short of bullying, torturing, or manipulating Dolly to tell the truth – none of which were options – he had nothing more than conjecture.

Charlie knew it was selfish to be glad he'd survived all this with his career intact. So far as he knew, James and Aija's jobs were also safe, while Eva's survival was in doubt. He knew Nieminen had yet to speak to James – the department responsible for their wellbeing would not allow it. But even Nieminen seemed to lack enthusiasm for any hint of impropriety, especially in the light of the shooting.

James would be questioned about the Oodi case – when he was able. But even without an interrogation, his notes on the case had been detailed and clear – that this woman had to be monitored. While he'd been vague about what he thought she might do – he'd clearly suggested her husband's safety might be compromised. But it hadn't been followed up. Eva had thought herself much too interesting, much too important to deal with a case. She'd spent her time instead in pursuit of a drug dealer and that case had come to nothing.

However, he'd called her and told her that if she needed to talk to anyone, he had plenty of experience being the office pariah.

"Thank you," she'd whispered, he could tell she was on the point of tears. She'd been suspended pending investigation.

Yes, Eva had been arrogant, but those four people could still have been alive if he'd agreed to follow up James's cases. Why shouldn't he have? Had he too considered himself above a domestic violence case simply because there had been a case of significance, one that would prove to everyone that he was still a great detective?

He had thanked Eva for what she did for James. Because of her swift action, James got to keep some measure of dignity. The full scale of his panic attack had been hidden from the press and onlookers on phones and cameras and broadcast. Regardless, that snippet of time had been repeated on every form of social media and mentioned in the large Finnish newspapers.

In the days that followed, the rain stopped. James emerged from his room only to sit sullenly in the living room, and then to stand looking into his garden before returning to do nothing more than to make a cup of tea or eat slices of buttered bread.

Almost every morning since the shooting, Dolly had arrived with her boys, who, oblivious to their uncle's suffering, screeched with delight through the garden, climbing its wall and attacking its trees and garden and digging up mud in its still sodden earth. What she came to do, Charlie wasn't sure. While he was upstairs, she read in the kitchen, occasionally looking up to give instructions to the boys.

"I thought we were going to somewhere hot for the holidays," one of them, he still wasn't sure which, whined as he came down the stairs, the two parties both out of view of each other.

"I told you not for a while yet," she said. "We have to wait for Big James to get a little better first."

"How long's that going to take?"

"A while, but don't worry – we won't wait forever," she replied.

On that he heard the boys' footsteps as they broke into a run. Avoiding her as he'd been doing, he picked up a copy of the *Guardian Weekly* from where it lay, which gave a short but telling article about the Nordic English-speaking literary sensation. It was ready to be cut out, dated and preserved somewhere. Their website had followed it up with mention of his collapse, but this seemed to have cemented his position as a hero – "the writer so dedicated to his true calling that he collapses with emotion at a killing." The comments had applauded him. Charlie had been relieved and happy.

Now he turned from the newspaper to a website listing hundreds of houses and apartments. The insurance company had acceded to only granting his share of the insurance – he was too tired and too unhappy to fight their decision. He wanted to look ahead, but now his dreams of a new life were more modest. Every time he scrolled through the ads now, he realised he didn't need a family home, a garden and, as they referred to it on home renovation shows, "tonnes of storage".

All he needed was space to invite people for pizza and somewhere to store his bikes. Somewhere that when the urge to cry over came him, he'd have the privacy to do it.

Aija

She hadn't told Matti what had happened. When he asked if James was all right, she'd brushed it off as best she could, saying, "We all get overwhelmed sooner or later."

She'd taken to arriving at James's in the evenings just to check on him, as long as he'd let her. She knew that soon he'd want the distance between them reinstated. He wouldn't want the constant reminder of everything that had changed.

She had been lucky – very, very lucky – to get out of the shooting at the library with her career unblemished. That morning Aija had suggested that Eva merely be placed under supervision, she had no way of knowing what her disinterest could have led to.

"What kind of place are you going to be after?" she asked to make conversation with Charlie, who she could tell wasn't quite himself yet. "Maybe something ultramodern hip, close to town?"

"I got insurance, I didn't win the lottery," said Charlie, taking a very large sip of tea and leaning back into his chair. "Definitely something smaller, made for one. It's not like the kids are ever coming back."

"What happens when my house burns down and I need somewhere to stay?" called James from where he was staring at the cactus, his back towards them.

"I'll get a place with a large closet," Charlie replied.

They were trying to get back to normal, no matter how tenuous that normal had been.

Hart had arrived. She claimed she had nothing better to do and wanted to make sure she wasn't losing any more detectives. She poured herself a glass of wine, selecting a glass without asking where to find them.

"I've suggested you get a promotion," Hart told her as soon as Charlie had excused himself for a call. "It wouldn't happen right away," she'd glanced at James who was smoking in the garden, "NBI want to be sure you're clean. I said I'd stake my life on it, so don't disappoint me."

Aija had stood back and offered a wan smile in thanks.

"Even with James down for the count we can't keep Eva, despite your request. If the public found out, we would be buried."

"What do you mean down for the count?" she'd asked.

"Psycho services want him off work for three months, no less."

"He won't agree to that."

"He doesn't have a choice," Hart had replied. "This has hurt his chances for a promotion, breaking down in tears in public is still not seen as what a police officer should do. And besides, to be honest, it's a hint that he can't cope."

"Oh," had been all she could say.

Then Hart had leaned against the door jamb. "And what about you?"

"I've told Matti that I'm not going to Singapore." She'd told him finally. She was needed here and with just a little effort she could get better at her job, perhaps one day she'd have a job like Hart's.

"And?"

"We'll just keep on as we've been doing."

Hart smiled. "Good, I need you here." She took a large swig of wine and went out to where James was standing.

James

His nephew Alexander informed him that "if Bigfoot was real then he would no longer be a monster". He spoke with bright eyes from having been outdoors running about with his twin. "That's because monsters by definition are not real," he declared proudly and then was gone, his attention focused elsewhere with the immediacy and lack of context that only a child could muster.

It sounded like something James had heard in an online video.

He could become a full-time writer, he thought. He contemplated James and Alexander, who were still bent on defeating his cactus. Maybe, he thought, he could call Saana. He could tell her he'd ghosted her due to stress and ask her if she would consider dinner with him. The proof was splattered across the internet: #mensmentalhealthcrisis. Someone had shared a brief clip captured just before Eva had obscured him. However, like all internet sensations it had worn off with little effect on his life.

Now what? he asked himself. He'd been told to stay away from work for three months. During that time he could flee, he decided, and simply never return.

He'd woken in the hospital feeling disoriented. It was as if he had in that singular collapse reached a crescendo – where all the noise in his life had been building, gathering, stewing and then finally erupting.

He had stayed at the hospital for only been a few hours. It had been too warm and the bed was uncomfortable. The staff spoke in low concerned voices on the few occasions they'd spoken to him. Then Dolly had appeared, breathless, with JJ on her heels. She'd burst into tears over him and clutched him crying.

JJ held his arm for a moment and then looked away. "What the hell happened?"

"Things just got on top of me. You know Gerry, this Lucinda woman, and everything."

Dolly had hushed him, "Gerry is gone, don't even think about him anymore."

As he had dozed, a woman in a bright orange printed smock, sneakers and a skirt appeared saying that she'd been sent to follow up his case. She said, in a gentle yet firm voice, that he'd obviously had a bad experience, it was nothing to be ashamed about, the shock of dealing with four people dead in an instant would shake any officer. He was lucky, he hadn't seen the bodies. He closed his eyes as she talked and had fallen into a brief and peaceful nap.

Then what? He would be stupid to think everything would suddenly be all right. The others who knew, Charlie, Aija and Hart, he was sure had changed in their interactions with him. He couldn't say how. He couldn't pinpoint a difference in how they behaved towards him, but he knew something had changed. Was it something in the way they kept asking how he was, or if he wanted a cup of tea?

His experience was omitted from the case files. There was no mention of an assault having taken place that night. Any speculation that he would have any knowledge of the events that led to Lucinda or Gerry's deaths had been kept out. He hadn't spoken about that night since they'd rushed out of his house to see the interview with Julia.

After a week, he realised he wasn't getting rid of them. They – Aija and Charlie especially – had entrenched themselves in his living room. Hart's visits were sometimes brief or sometimes required her to have a taxi called after too much wine.

He picked up a notebook and a pen, thought for a moment and began a description of the sensation of doughnuts on a warm day. After only a few minutes, he stood and began to roam the house. He knew that any attempt to leave it would be met with questions. James and Alexander were needling Aija in an attempt to get her to play with a football that had already tracked mud into his sitting room.

He watched Aija with two children that to a casual onlooker could have been hers. There was something about that scene that made him consider Merimies, the protagonist in his books, awaiting a new adventure. What does a man like Merimies do when the monsters are no longer monsters? What would Merimies do upon finding the people responsible for his pain were ordinary, yes broken and unhappy, but ordinary people? The corrupt, violent detective was after all, according to the many people who attempted to analyse his character, a piece of his writer.

"Singapore!" screeched Alexander from outside. "Where's that?"

Merimies would do something. That's where the two of them were different. He'd allowed life to lead him through it, while Merimies acted, he seized life. He pummelled it into submission.

James would not become a vigilante – he didn't have the stomach to realise Merimies's violence.

Perhaps he would go somewhere – Estonia, Zambia? But the two seemed too familiar.

Or perhaps he would do something, download a dating app.

Charlie

Charlie smelled burning. "What the hell is that?" he demanded of no one. The smell triggered memories of the fire that destroyed his home that flashed through his mind.

Charlie could see black smoke and ash rising into the sky through the patio window. A breeze was directing much of the debris into the living room. He looked up to see that the smoke detector had been disabled.

He jogged out through the doors to where Aija stood splattered in mud watching the twins.

On a large barbecue stand a fire burned as one twin poked at it with a stick and his twin fed it with notebook after notebook.

On the ground beside them was a pile of James's jotters dumped in an uneven pyramid. There had to be a few hundred of them. Charlie's mouth dropped open in surprise as James arrived with more.

"This is fun," said Alexander, rushing to his uncle to grab them from him. "Want to try it?" he asked and handed Charlie a notebook to burn.